ETURN TO PRIOR'S FORD

The Prior's Ford Series from Evelyn Hood

* *available from Severn House*

RETURN TO PRIOR'S FORD

Evelyn Hood

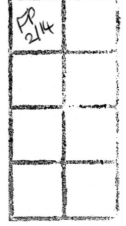

This first world edition published 2012
in Great Britain and 2013 in the USA by
SEVERN HOUSE PUBLISHERS LTD of
19 Cedar Road, Sutton, Surrey, England, SM2 5DA.
Trade paperback edition first published
in Great Britain and the USA 2013 by
SEVERN HOUSE PUBLISHERS LTD.

British Library Cataloguing in Publication Data

Hood, Evelyn.
  Return to Prior's Ford.
  1. Prior's Ford (Scotland: Imaginary place)–Fiction.
  2. Villages–Scotland–Dumfries and Galloway–Fiction.
  I. Title
  823.9'14–dc23

ISBN-13: 978-0-7278-8219-6 (cased)
ISBN-13: 978-1-84751-459-2 (trade paper)

All Severn House titles are printed on acid-free paper.

Severn House Publishers support The Forest Stewardship Council [FSC], the
leading international forest certification organisation. All our titles that are printed
on Greenpeace-approved FSC-certified paper carry the FSC logo.

Typeset by Palimpsest Book Production Ltd.,
Falkirk, Stirlingshire, Scotland.
Printed and bound in Great Britain by
TJ International Ltd, Padstow, Cornwall

This book is dedicated to
Alison MacLeod
with love and gratitude

Acknowledgements

My thanks and my gratitude to the following people for their generous assistance during the writing of this book.

The Reverend Alison Burnside, who throughout the series has patiently answered my questions regarding the work of one of my favourite characters, the Reverend Naomi Hennessey.

Charlotte Peck, landscape architect, who has given me so much good advice on the restoration of the Linn Hall estate.

Stephen O'Brien, for providing valuable insight into life in the police force.

Pat Elliott of The Borders Design House, Auchencrow, Berwickshire, for advice on the restoration of Linn Hall.

I am indebted to you all.

Main Characters in 'Return to Prior's Ford'

The Ralston-Kerrs − **Hector Ralston-Kerr** is the Laird of Prior's Ford and lives with his wife **Fliss** and their son **Lewis** in ramshackle **Linn Hall**.

Ginny (Genevieve) Whitelaw − is helping Lewis Ralston-Kerr to restore the Linn Hall estate, which, like the Hall itself, has suffered years of neglect as the family fortunes dwindled.

The Fishers − **Joe** and **Gracie Fisher** are the landlord and landlady of the local pub, the Neurotic Cuckoo. They live on the premises with their widowed daughter **Alison Greenlees** and her young son **Jamie**.

Clarissa Ramsay − lives in Willow Cottage. A retired teacher and a widow who has found new love with **Alastair Marshall**, an artist some twenty years her junior.

Sam Brennan and Marcy Copleton − live in Rowan Cottage and run the local village store together.

The Reverend Naomi Hennessey − the local Church of Scotland minister, part Jamaican, part English. Lives in the manse with her godson, **Ethan Baptiste**, Jamaican.

The McNairs of Tarbethill Farm − **Jess McNair** and her younger son **Ewan** are struggling to keep the family farm going, following the suicide of Jess's husband. **Victor**, her elder son, has deserted the farm for married life in the nearby town of Kirkcudbright. **Ewan** is in love with the local publican's daughter, **Alison Greenlees**, but since his father's death, he has decided that the farm's future must come first from now on and he will never be able to afford a wife. Alison and her son think that he's wrong.

Jinty and **Tom McDonald** − live with their large family on the village's council housing estate. **Jinty** is a willing helper at Linn Hall and also cleans the village hall and primary school, while **Tom** is keen on gambling and frequenting the Neurotic Cuckoo.

Helen Campbell – lives in the local council housing estate with her husband **Duncan**, a gloomy man who is a gardener on the Linn Hall Estate, and their four children. **Helen** hopes one day to be a published writer, and until then she earns much-needed money by 'taking in' typing.

Meredith Whitelaw – is a professional actress and Ginny's mother. She is a flamboyant woman who considers her garden-loving daughter to be an ugly duckling and longs to turn her into a glamorous, fashionable and well-married young woman. She is the bane of Ginny's life and has the knack of disrupting the lives of everyone she meets.

One

Helen Campbell erupted from her house in Slaemuir Estate, rushing down the path and out through the front gate without bothering to latch it.

Along the road she raced, leaving the council house estate behind her as she crossed River Lane and plunged into Mill Walk, the private housing estate. When she arrived at Ingrid MacKenzie's house she ignored the front door, continuing instead to hurry round to the neat conservatory overlooking the immaculate rear garden.

It being a pleasant June morning, the conservatory door was open so that Ingrid and her guests could enjoy the warm breeze as they sipped at their coffee. Jenny Forsyth and Marcy Copleton had already arrived, and Ingrid was pouring coffee as Helen appeared in the doorway, by now reduced to gasping for air.

'Helen, it's lovely to see you, and yes, you are a little later than usual, but you had no need to hurry.' Ingrid was, as always, immaculate; her long blonde hair wound in a plait around her head, her outfit perfect. Although it had been many years since she had given up her career as one of Norway's top models to marry a Scottish university lecturer and present him with two blonde daughters, now in their teens, she had not lost her looks, her svelte figure or her poise.

'Oh yes I *did* have to hurry – look what the post brought this morning!' Helen flourished a folded sheet of paper at her friends.

Jenny's reaction was faster than the others. 'It's not . . .?' she asked, and then as Helen nodded: 'You haven't . . .?'

'Haven't what?' Marcy wanted to know.

'I've only gone and won the *Women's Lives* magazine competition!' A wide grin almost split Helen's flushed face in two. 'Their letter –' she waved it at them – 'arrived just as I was about to come here. I've *won* – and that means I've been commissioned to write a serial for them!'

'Using the outline and first part of the story that you wrote for the competition?'

Helen nodded. 'The fiction editor phoned this morning to find out if the letter had arrived. She said that I was a clear winner, and she was quite surprised to hear that I've only published one short story before.'

'Does she know that you're too busy typing stuff for other people, and being Lucinda Keen, Agony Aunt, for the local paper to get on with your own writing?' Marcy asked while Jenny hugged her friend.

'I said that I took in typing, so to speak, but not about doing the Lucinda Keen page.'

A few years earlier, Helen had started writing a village column for the local newspaper, and had then been offered the job of doing the Lucinda Keen, Agony Aunt page as well. Her best friends knew about it, but nobody else – not even her husband.

'Quite right,' Ingrid said firmly. 'The fewer people who know about that, the better. Nobody would send letters in to the newspaper if they knew the person who was going to answer them. Have you told Duncan about winning the serial competition? What did he say?'

'He doesn't know yet, because the letter's only just arrived. I had to read it three times before I believed it. I'll tell him tonight, but you know Duncan – I don't expect to get much of a reaction.'

Helen's husband, a taciturn man, was the gardener at Linn Hall, on the hill above the village.

'He'll be pleased about you getting paid for it,' Jenny said.

'That,' said Helen, collapsing into a chair, the letter clutched to her heart, 'will delight him. Imagine – one thousand pounds! I can't believe it myself!'

'If you take my advice you won't tell him exactly what you'll be paid,' Ingrid said. 'You deserve to keep some of it back for yourself.'

'Oh, I couldn't do that!'

'I think you could – and should. What do you two think?'

'She's right, Helen,' Jenny said. 'You're entitled to keep something for yourself.'

'A hundred pounds, perhaps?' Marcy put in. 'After all, you're the one who's going to have to earn the money. Doesn't Duncan keep something back from his wages? He enjoys going to the Neurotic Cuckoo for a pint a couple of evenings every week, doesn't he?'

'Yes, but he's entitled – he works hard for his money.'

'And aren't you going to have to work hard for yours?' Jenny asked.

Helen shot upright in her chair and stared at her friends for a moment with startled eyes. Then she said, 'Oh, golly – I'm going to have to work my socks off if I want to get this serial right. What have I let myself in for?'

'I think you should give her a strong coffee, Ingrid,' Marcy advised.

'This news,' Ingrid said decisively, 'calls for something stronger than coffee.'

'What if I can't do it?'

'Do what, Helen?' Ingrid asked as she arrived back in the conservatory with a fresh pot of coffee and a bottle of whisky.

'Write the serial.'

'What exactly did you have to do to win the prize?'

'They supplied the first sentence of a story and asked for a further three thousand words.'

'Which you wrote, otherwise you wouldn't have won,' Ingrid pointed out. 'Marcy, I'll pour the coffee, and you add a shot of whisky and hand it round.'

'It was all a bit of fun at the time, but now that they want another four episodes I'm not so sure. They already want me to make changes to the first bit, to fit in with the magazine's style. I don't know if I'm going to be able to do an entire serial,' Helen panicked.

'Put a double shot of whisky in her coffee,' Jenny advised. 'She needs bolstering up.'

'I don't want to be tipsy when the kids come home for their lunch!'

'Another spoonful of whisky won't make you tipsy.'

'Our Helen doesn't need more whisky, Marcy, when she's got talent. Listen to me, Helen,' Ingrid commanded. 'You've won that competition on merit, and clearly you've proved to the magazine editor that you can do it. She wouldn't have given you first place if she didn't think that you deserved it. You said yourself that you were a clear winner. You *can* do it, and you *will* do it!'

'Ingrid's right, Helen,' Marcy cut in. 'You have no idea how much we've missed your common sense, Ingrid; it's so good to have you back in Prior's Ford.'

'It's lovely to be back.' Ingrid bathed her friends in a warm smile. 'I've missed you so much. There was a time when Peter and I thought that we were going to have to stay in Norway permanently to help my mother to run the hotel once my father died, but Freya took to the work like a duck to water and saved the day.'

'Don't you miss her, though?'

'Of course, but she's eighteen now, old enough to take control of her own life. The way things are going she'll end up taking complete charge of the hotel. It's strange,' Ingrid said thoughtfully, 'that since marrying Peter I've found my home here, in his country, while my oldest child, born and raised here, feels more at home in Norway.'

'Ella seems glad to be back,' Marcy commented, and Ingrid smiled.

'For that, I'm pleased. She's too much of a tomboy for my mother to cope with on her own. And in a way I've still got two daughters here; Anja's not much older than my Freya, and so like her in many ways.'

'What are you going to do about the shop now?' Jenny asked. Before returning to Norway to help her mother and her then ailing father with their hotel, Ingrid had owned and, with Jenny's help, managed The Gift Horse, a craft shop, in the village. During her absence it had been taken over by her niece, an interior designer, and was now called Colour Carousel.

'Anja loves being here and she's done well with Colour Carousel,' Ingrid said now. 'I'm happy to leave it in her hands. As I said, I feel as though I still have two daughters here.'

'She's caused quite a stir – every young man in the place fancies her like mad,' Marcy said dryly.

'She talks a lot about a young policeman who's moved into

the new estate across from the farm. Who knows?' Ingrid said. 'She might marry him and settle down, as I did when I met Peter.'

'Ow.' Jenny twisted round in her chair. 'Something's just poked me in the back.' She felt behind a cushion and produced a paperback book. '*The Men in her Life* by Lilias Drew.' She turned the book over and studied the reviews on the back. '*Both bold and funny . . . Being a mature woman needn't get in the way of enjoying life to the full . . . Chick-lit for older women . . .* Don't tell me you're reading this sort of stuff, Ingrid?'

'Why not? It's fun, but I have to keep it out of sight because it would probably shock Peter.'

'Let me see.' Helen took the book. 'Lilias Drew – I've heard people asking for her books in the library.'

Ingrid nodded. 'I buy the books because there's always a waiting list in the library. She writes chick-lit for older women, and she does it very well.'

'Can I borrow it when you've finished?' Marcy wanted to know.

'Of course. I have another one of hers upstairs that you can have now. Remind me about it before you go.'

'Can I have it when Marcy's finished with it?' Helen asked.

'Best not, Helen,' Marcy advised. 'Not while you're working on your serial. Lilias Drew's books are quite sexy – they might give you ideas that wouldn't suit your serial.'

'So you've read them as well?'

'Only one – I have very little time to read.' Marcy ran the village store with her partner, Sam Brennan. 'I think I'm right, Helen, in saying that *Women's Lives* isn't what one would describe as a sexy magazine?'

'No, it's not. Perhaps I'd better wait until I finish writing the serial before I borrow the books!'

On such a perfect morning the very best place to be, in Ginny Whitelaw's view, was perched atop the grotto on the hill behind Linn Hall.

The first time she had set eyes on the small grotto, built of large dark-red stones apparently piled haphazardly on top of each other to form a round cave with a flat roof, it had been hidden

by ivy and surrounded by overgrown trees and bushes. Once
used as a playhouse by Lewis Ralston-Kerr, born and raised
in Linn Hall, it had been left alone and forgotten when he
grew up.

But now that Ginny was working in the estate surrounding
the Hall, things were different. She had fallen in love with the
place after being fortunate enough to land a temporary summer
job renovating the overgrown kitchen garden; now, four years
later, she was still working at Linn Hall, and almost part of
the Ralston-Kerr family.

In the previous year she had turned her attention to clearing
the choked stream that had once tumbled downhill via a series
of waterfalls to feed both the pond in the centre of the old
rose-garden and the small lake near the estate's border. While
releasing the stream, which had been blocked up, turning the
hillside behind the old house into a swamp, she had discovered
not only the grotto but also a forgotten treasure trove – a
collection of rare and exotic plants brought from abroad by a
member of the Ralston-Kerr family at a time when their stately
home and extensive grounds had been cared for by a staff of
domestic servants and gardeners.

Through the years since then the family fortune had melted
away, taking with it the indoor and outdoor servants.
Realizing that the rare plants would attract more visitors to
the estate's open days, she had spent the winter carefully
freeing them from weeds and bushes, and nourishing those
that had managed to survive years of neglect. In the spring,
Lewis Ralston-Kerr, at her urging, had brought in experts
to identify the rescued plants, and the resulting interest and
publicity boded well for the forthcoming summer opening,
now only weeks away, to the public.

The undergrowth around the grotto had been cleared and
most of the ivy cut back, leaving the little building with only
a light covering. The swamp caused by the choked stream had
been planted with moisture-loving trees and shrubs, while
wooden walkways made it possible for visitors to admire the
foreign plants, now carefully labelled, without disturbing them.
There were picnic tables near the grotto, and rustic garden
seats had been placed at careful intervals on the hill to enable

visitors to rest and admire the view Ginny was at that moment surveying.

It was like being at the top of the world. From where she sat cross-legged she was able to look down the hill to the roof of Linn Hall, now wind-and-water-tight, then across the entire estate – the refurbished kitchen garden behind the old house; the three neat, terraced lawns descending like gradual steps from the side of the house to the rest of the estate; the rose garden and lake glimpsed through trees; then beyond the estate to the village of Prior's Ford, tucked into a curve of the River Dee like a child safe in the crook of its mother's arm. A breeze rustled through the trees around her, and the sky above was a wonderful shade of blue, with just a cotton-wool fragment of cloud here and there.

It was because of that magnificent view that Ginny had insisted on placing the seats all the way down the hill, together with a railing running the length of the stream. 'Even people who find the climb difficult should be given at least a chance to try to reach the top and enjoy the fantastic view, not to mention seeing the rare plants,' she had insisted, and eventually Lewis had allowed her to have her way, realizing from past arguments that Ginny was usually right.

Once, the kitchen garden had been her favourite spot, but now it was the grotto roof. Being there was heaven on earth to her – until her mobile phone rang and spoiled the tranquillity.

Ginny fished it from the pocket of her checked work-shirt, and winced as she saw that the call came from her mother. She was tempted to ignore it, but knew that Meredith would keep trying until she got an answer.

Sighing, she pressed the right key. 'Hello, Mother.'

'Genevieve, darling – wonderful news!'

Ginny winced each time she heard her full name. Sturdily built, with a very ordinary face beneath short black easy-to-cope-with hair, she was definitely a Ginny, never a Genevieve. 'Really?' she asked cautiously.

'You're going to be so thrilled, darling!'

I bet I'm not, Ginny thought; and she was right.

Two

'I'm still worried about being able to write an entire serial,' Helen said as she, Jenny and Marcy left Ingrid's house after their coffee morning.

'Didn't you say that you've work to do on the winning entry first?' Jenny asked.

Helen nodded. 'Someone from the editorial department's going to phone me in a day or two to talk it over and suggest changes.'

'Then relax and leave it to the magazine people to help you – after all, they're now committed to publishing it, and they'll be as keen as you are to get it just right. Use their knowledge and experience, and I'm convinced that as you're working on one episode the ideas for the next will come into your mind. It's the same with everything in life – we learn as we go along. You've got past the first and most important hurdle by being chosen as winner and now it's a case of taking things step by step. I never miss your Lucinda Keen page and I think you respond to the letters with a lot of common sense. Think of the experience of life's ups and down that that page has given you.'

'Now there's a thought,' Helen said, cheering up. 'You're such a good friend, Jenny!'

'I'm coming to Dumfries to do a play!' Meredith's voice sang into Ginny's ear.

'What! When?'

'Quite soon – we start rehearsals at the end of July and the play runs from mid-August until mid-September, which means that I can fit it in before going back to Spain at the end of October to start on the next series of the sitcom. So I'll be able to come and see you, and those nice people you work for. You haven't asked me the name of the play,' Meredith reminded her daughter.

'What is it?'

'*Blithe Spirit* – frothy but fun, and very popular with audiences, so we should get a lot of advance bookings. My name alone is sure to be a big help. I'm playing the part of Elvira, of course. Isn't it all wonderful? Must dash!'

The line went dead, and Ginny crammed the phone back into her pocket, her day suddenly ruined. After a moment of self-pity she swung down from the grotto roof, using the strong ivy as a ladder. Then she headed down the hill, taking her time in order to allow the music of the small waterfalls and the pleasure of the clumps of ferns and water-loving plants on either bank of the stream to soothe her shattered morning back into some semblance of tranquillity.

In the house below, the large kitchen table once used by uniformed servants supervised by a butler and a housekeeper was packed with young people of all nationalities, talking, laughing and eating after a morning spent out of doors, working on the estate. Jinty McDonald, the nearest these days that the Ralston-Kerrs had to a housekeeper, officiated at the large stove, while Fliss Ralston-Kerr and Kay McGregor, the backpacker on kitchen duties, served the hungry youngsters who spent their summers working their way round the world before settling down.

Lewis, the son of the house, and Duncan Campbell, the estate's one and only gardener, sat together at one end of the table, doing their best over the babble of voices to work out the afternoon's duties.

'I could do with a word with Ginny,' Duncan was saying.

'Me too.'

'Where's she got to?'

'Let me guess – up at the grotto?' Without even realizing it, Lewis was beginning to resent the time Ginny spent on her own at the top of the hill, away from everyone else, including him. 'Ever since she found those foreign plants she's spent more time there than anywhere else.'

Jinty pushed between them to dump two plates of roly-poly pudding down. 'Be fair, you two, Ginny's the best worker this place has got.'

'I'd not say that!' Duncan was offended.

'Well, I would,' Jinty retorted and rushed off to collect some food to take to the butler's pantry for Hector Ralston-Kerr, owner of Linn Hall. Hector, a man who loved peace and quiet, always went to ground when the summer workers invaded the kitchen like a plague of hungry, noisy, energetic locusts.

By the time Ginny reached the courtyard behind Linn Hall, where her beloved camper van, known as Jemima Puddleduck, stood, she was feeling a little calmer, but before making for the open kitchen door she veered off towards the walled kitchen garden, where her love affair with the estate had begun.

As soon as she stepped through the wooden door into the garden, the peace of the place, with its neat raised beds and brick paths, its vegetable beds, fruit bushes and trees and aromatic herb garden, combined with the hum of bees and chattering birdsong, made her feel, as always, that she had come home.

Four years ago this garden, like the hilltop, had been a wilderness, but now it provided enough fruit, vegetables and herbs to supply the village store as well as feeding the family and the small army of young backpackers.

Ginny had been assisted in her struggle to set it to rights again by Jinty McDonald's son Jimmy, at that time a skinny, red-haired fourteen year old. His maternal grandfather had once been the estate's head gardener, and had passed on his love of growing things to the boy, who started working on the estate during weekends and school holidays. Jimmy had learned a lot from Ginny, and now, aged eighteen and finished with school, he was in charge of the kitchen garden.

Ginny relaxed until the sound of voices and laughter as the part-time garden staff left the kitchen reminded her that she was late for lunch. Suddenly aware that she was hungry, she headed towards the exit.

'We were about to send Muffin on a search mission,' Jinty McDonald called out as Ginny entered the kitchen to be welcomed by the large, floppy, mixed-breed dog the family had inherited from a villager a few years earlier. 'Kay, be a love and fetch Ginny's dinner from the oven, will you, while I start on the dishes. Where were you?'

'Down, Muffin! Sorry, I forgot the time.' Ginny went to wash her hands in the smaller of the two stone sinks.

Lewis got to his feet. 'After you've eaten, Ginny, I'd like a bit of help with the rose garden.'

'And I could do with your advice down by the lake. There's still some planting to be done there, and I want to make sure it's what you planned,' Duncan chimed in. 'See you there when you've had your dinner?'

'OK.' Ginny dried her hands. 'Won't be long. Jimmy, are you coming to the camper this evening?'

Jimmy McDonald, on his way out, nodded his red head vigorously. 'Sure thing!' he said, and was gone.

'Gardening's best learned on the job, Ginny. There's no sense in filling that lad's head with Latin names and all that other stuff he'll never need.' Duncan disapproved of the way Ginny, who had spent the winter at horticultural courses and who loved to pore over books on gardening, was tutoring the new young gardener.

She sat down at the table, her mouth watering as she lifted the cover from her plate and was instantly wreathed in a delicious aroma. 'Sorry, Muffin,' she told the dog, who had come to sit beside her, gazing up at her with hopeful dark eyes, 'I'm going to devour the lot.' Then, to Duncan, 'Jimmy's interested in everything to do with gardening, and I enjoy trying to find answers to his questions.'

'Huh!' Duncan slammed the door on his way out.

'He's a bit of a moaner, isn't he?' Kay observed. 'Never seems to be satisfied with anything anyone does. I'm glad *I* don't work in the grounds; I don't fancy working with him.'

'Pay no heed,' Jinty advised. 'He's just annoyed because my Jimmy's mad about the estate. You're doing my lad the world of good, Ginny, and I appreciate it. Duncan's always been too lazy to learn more than he needs to.'

'Jinty!' Fliss Ralston-Kerr protested. 'I don't know what we'd have done in the past without Duncan.'

'Fair enough, Mrs F, but poor Helen Campbell has to look after her own garden, as well as the house and the kids, because

Duncan reckons that because gardening's his job he shouldn't be expected to do it at home during his time off work. Our Jimmy, bless him, has looked after our wee bit of garden since he started to help my dad when he was little more than a toddler. Growing things runs in Jimmy's blood, and in Ginny's, but as far as Duncan's concerned it doesn't run any further than his pay packet.'

'Just don't say that in front of him,' Lewis advised. 'What kept you so late, Ginny? No problems at the top of the hill, I hope?'

'Everything's doing fine. It's just . . .' She suddenly remembered the phone call and felt her spirits drop a notch or two. 'My mother phoned, and it held me back.'

Jinty and Fliss immediately looked interested. 'Oh – is she still filming abroad?' Fliss wanted to know.

While Jinty asked, 'Any chance of her coming back from Spain soon and paying another visit to Prior's Ford?'

'As a matter of fact, she's just arrived back in London, and she's coming to Scotland at the end of July to do a stage play in Dumfries.'

'Dumfries? That's wonderful! We must all go to see the play,' Fliss said at once. 'And how lovely for you, getting the chance to see her again.'

'Yes.' Ginny forced a smile. To be truthful, she hated meetings with her mother. Meredith was an artiste to her perfect fingernails, and in her eyes her only child, ordinary looking and with no interest at all in the theatre, was a massive disappointment. They had absolutely nothing in common.

'Where will she be staying?' Fliss wanted to know.

'In a hotel in Dumfries.'

'But she'll be coming here to see you?' Jinty said hopefully.

'She says that she plans to.' And no doubt as soon as she set eyes on her daughter she would start on again about Ginny improving her looks and her taste in clothes.

Kay had been following the change of subject, her brow furrowed. Now she butted in to ask, 'What d'you mean, Ginny, about your mother being in a play?'

'Didn't you know that our Ginny's got a famous mother? You've heard of Meredith Whitelaw, surely?' Jinty said.

Kay stared open-mouthed for a moment, then let out a squeal that started Muffin barking. 'Omigod! Not Meredith Whitelaw that was on the telly – Imogen Goldberg in *Bridlington Close*? She *can't* be your mother, Ginny!'

'She can. Shut up, Muffin.'

'Wow! To think we've been mates for weeks and weeks and you never said a word! Me and my mum never missed an edition of that soap, even when we were on our holidays. Why didn't you *tell* me?'

Ginny sighed inwardly. She hated it when people realized who her mother was. '*She's* the actress, not me. I'm just a gardener.'

'I know, but still . . . We both cried buckets when Imogen Goldberg was killed in that accident. Your mum's in whatsit now, that new soap about people living in Spain, isn't she?'

'*The Sun Always Shines.*' Fliss, too, was a Meredith Whitelaw fan.

'That's the one. Golly! She's so glamorous, isn't she? It's a shame you don't look in the least like her, Ginny. Did you say she's going to be in Dumfries to do a play? When's she coming?' Kay rattled on when Ginny nodded.

'In July.'

'Wow! Will she be coming here? Will I meet her? I'll need to get my hair done!'

'Wait a minute – I've had a marvellous idea, Mrs F,' Jinty interrupted as Ginny choked slightly over her dinner. 'We were just talking about the August garden fête that's always held on the estate; you know how much poor Mrs F hates having to open it, Ginny.'

'I never know what to say, and I never have anything new to wear,' Fliss agreed. When Hector Ralston-Kerr had first brought her to Linn Hall as his bride she had been a pretty young woman, and despite years of trying to cope with the large, neglected house that had been in her husband's increasingly impoverished family for generations her thin face still bore signs of the youthful Fliss. Now her myopic brown eyes darkened at the thought of the fête, and she pushed her spectacles further up her neat nose as she always did when she was worried. 'That annual fête is the one thing I hate about living in Linn Hall, but the villagers always look forward to it.'

'Wouldn't it be a wonderful idea to ask Ms Whitelaw to open it this year? Think of the people who would come just to see her in the flesh,' Jinty enthused, while Ginny's heart sank into her sturdy gardening boots.

'Me for one,' Kay chimed in. 'That would be brilliant! D'you reckon she'd do it, Ginny?'

'Oh, Jinty, that would be the answer to a prayer!' The worry lines vanished as Fliss beamed.

Ginny, already depressed by the prospect of her mother spending almost three months near enough to visit, did her best to look doubtful rather than horrified. 'To be honest, Mrs Ralston-Kerr, I'm not sure if she'll have the time. From what I've gathered in the past, stage work can be quite exhausting.'

'Of course, I never thought of that.' Fliss's face fell, and Ginny, who was very fond of her, felt like a heel.

'Perhaps someone else would be willing – Ingrid Mackenzie's back in the village; you could ask her.'

'I'd give Ms Whitelaw first refusal; she'd be bound to attract lots of people here. Couldn't you at least ask her, Ginny?' Jinty was totally unaware of Ginny's distress. 'I'm sure you could persuade her.'

'I could try, I suppose.'

'Oh, thank you, dear! Perhaps she'll do it for you, being her daughter,' Fliss said gratefully.

'We won't know if we don't try.' Ginny, who knew that Meredith would jump at the chance to hog the limelight, helped herself to a piece of bread and began to wipe up the last of the gravy on her plate. 'Thanks, Jinty, that was fantastic.'

'There's jam roly-poly for afters.' Jinty went to fetch it, saying over her shoulder, 'I heard in the village store this morning that Thatcher's Cottage's getting a new tenant, Mrs F. A man on his own, Sam Brennan said. A college lecturer or something like that. Let's hope he's going to settle into the village better than the last two lots of tenants. Poor old Doris Thatcher and her husband were such a respectable couple; they must be birling in their graves over the sort of folk that have been living there recently!'

Three

Helen's two younger children, Lachlan and Irene, still attended Prior's Ford Primary School, and so they still came home for lunch. Sadly, they were both too young to be very interested in the news of their mother's competition win, so Helen had to wait until her older son and daughter came home from their secondary school in Kirkcudbright.

Once lunch was over, Lachlan and Irene headed back to their classrooms, leaving her free, once the dishes were washed, to rush upstairs to the old computer in the bedroom she shared with her husband. Settling down with a sigh of contentment, she read, yet again, what she had written for the serial competition. Then she started to expand the storyline, working for two hours without a break before noticing the time. She counted the money in her housekeeping purse and then hurried out to the village store.

'I've suddenly realized that I should have a special meal ready tonight, to celebrate,' she told Marcy as she dumped her wire basket down by the checkout.

'You certainly should – in fact, you should get Duncan to take the entire family to the pub for a meal.'

'You're joking, of course! Can you see Duncan paying for a dinner for six when I can cook one for far less? In any case, we can't afford it – though perhaps when I get paid for the serial I'll be able to take us all out for a good meal.'

'Hang on to that thought. Eleven pounds and thirty-six pence.'

Helen handed the money over, got her change, and then checked what money was left in the purse. 'What's your cheapest wine?'

Marcy checked the shelves, glanced around to see where her partner Sam was, then selected a bottle and returned to the checkout. 'There you are.'

'How much?'

'It's on me – now hurry off while Sam's still in the back shop.'

'Thanks, Marcy, you're an angel!' Helen thrust the bottle into her bag and set off for home as the school bell rang to mark the end of the day's classes.

At last the two older children arrived home from school, and Helen was able to share her news.

'Mum, that's wonderful!' Gemma Campbell gave her mother a warm hug. 'I can't wait to brag to everyone about you. Just imagine – they must have had hundreds of entries for the competition, and my mum's the winner! I can't wait to tell my pals tomorrow. Can I tell my English teacher too? He'll be dead impressed!'

'Of course you can tell him, but I don't know about a man being impressed over a women's magazine serial.'

'I don't think he's ever published anything, so he jolly well *should* be impressed!'

Gregor, too, was thrilled for her. 'You're going to be a famous writer one day, Mum.'

'Let's not count our chickens, love. I've still to complete the serial.'

'You'll do that, and more. I decided ages ago that when I grow up and get my own house I'm going to have a bookcase in the hall with all the books you've published sitting in it, so that everyone who visits sees it first thing.'

'Oh, Greg . . .' She hugged him tightly. Gregor was her first-born, and he was only now growing out of the asthma that had plagued him from babyhood. The two of them had spent many a long night in the living room, Greg wrapped in blankets, wheezing in one armchair, Helen in the other, telling him made-up stories in an attempt to take his mind off the constant struggle for air, while Duncan and the other children slumbered through the night.

The stories they had shared, and the frightening nights they had endured together, had instilled a love of reading in him, and also meant that although Helen tried hard not to have favourites, she had a slightly stronger bond with Greg than she had with the others. He had always shown a keen interest in her writing progress, and she had no doubt that he really did plan to have that special bookcase in his own house one day. She just hoped that she would be able to fill it for him.

Duncan, on the other hand, wasn't a reader and had never shown much interest in her desire to be a writer. He grumbled about the time she spent on the computer, but put up with it because typing papers for other people brought in some much-needed money.

As it happened, he arrived home from work in a better mood than usual and came into the kitchen to wash his hands, sniffing at the aroma from the cooker.

'Chicken curry? That's unusual,' he said when Helen nodded.

'It's a bit of a special occasion.'

'What sort of occasion?'

'Remember that magazine serial competition I went in for?'

'No – did you?'

'Yes I did, and I've won it.' She handed a towel over as he turned to stare at her, scattering water over the floor. 'I'm getting a contract to write a five-part serial, and they're going to print it in the magazine when it's finished, if they like it enough.'

'That's good, love,' he said, to her surprise, then: 'How much are they going to pay you for it?'

'I'm not sure,' Helen said, mindful of Ingrid's advice. 'I won't get any money until it's published, but I'll definitely get something.'

'Good for you!' He even dropped a kiss on her cheek. 'We should go to the pub tonight for a celebration drink, if Anna next door doesn't mind keeping an eye on the kids for us.'

'I got a bottle of wine in the store this afternoon and some fruit juice for the children. I'm going to put out fancy glasses so that we can all have a drink with our dinner, then once homework's over and they're all in bed, you and I can finish off the wine.'

'Good idea,' said Duncan, beaming at her.

The news that someone was moving into Thatcher's Cottage came up for discussion that evening in the local pub, the Neurotic Cuckoo.

'It's such a nice little cottage, down by the river and with such a pretty garden,' Cissie Kavanagh said. She and her husband Robert were enjoying a drink with neighbours Dolly and Harold Cowan. 'Pity it hasn't found people able to settle in properly and make the most of it.'

'Third time lucky?' Dolly suggested.

'I'll drink to that,' Harold drained his glass. 'Same again?' He signalled to Joe Fisher at the bar and then, a rare grin lighting up his naturally lugubrious face, said, 'That young couple at the end of our row have fairly brightened up the place, haven't they, Robert?'

'Tricia was showing me what they've done to the house, and it's amazing how modern they've made the old property,' Cissie said. 'I was impressed.'

'So was Harold, but not the way you mean, Cissie.' Dolly shook her dyed blonde curls at her husband. 'He was doing a bit of gardening the other day while Tricia was sunbathing outside her back door – in a bikini.'

'And painting her toenails scarlet,' Harold added. 'She's a bonny lass, that!'

'You must have got close, to notice the colour of her toenails,' his wife commented.

'It was only polite to pass the time of day with her, same as I'd do with any of our neighbours.' Harold winked at Robert.

'I'd never have had your Harold down as having an eye for the girls, Dolly.'

'You should have seen him in the old days, Cissie – I had to fight to get him, and I'll admit,' Dolly added, looking at her husband with loving blue eyes, 'it's good to know there's still a bit of life in him yet.'

The four of them lived in a row still known locally as the almshouses, although they had been renamed Jasmine Row years ago after being renovated and turned into six little terraced houses, their front doors opening on to the Main Street pavement, and with an open area at the back with washing lines and a few flower beds. All the residents had been pensioners until some nine months earlier, when newly-weds Tricia and Derek Borland, offspring of the village's local garage-owner and butcher respectively, bought the end house after the death of Ivy McGowan, the village's oldest resident.

'I think it's nice\that we've got some younger neighbours now,' Cissie said as Joe Fisher delivered their drinks. 'They brighten up the place. And talking of new residents, Joe, what d'you know about Thatcher's Cottage?'

'The new tenant was in here for a meal when he came to look at it. Seems a nice enough chap – a professor of some sort. Late fifties, I'd say, or mebbe into his sixties.'

'On his own?'

'Seems to be, Robert. Gracie took to him.' Joe jerked his head towards his wife, behind the bar. 'She says he's like a friendly teddy bear. I think he'll settle in well enough.'

'Let's hope so.' Dolly gave a sudden shiver. 'Thatcher's Cottage needs a normal tenant.'

'You're right there, Dolly – nobody in the village would disagree with you on that one,' Joe said, and returned to the bar.

Jess McNair was sitting on the bench outside Tarbethill Farm's kitchen door shelling peas and listening to the contented clucking of the hens wandering around the yard when Naomi Hennessey arrived.

'I should be writing next Sunday's sermon in my study, but the weather tempted me out for a walk. Let me help you.' The minister, dressed as she usually was when not in the pulpit in a loose blouse and long full skirt, both a riot of colour, settled herself down beside Jess and reached out a brown hand to take some of the pods. 'So – how are you on this lovely morning?'

'On a mornin' like this I feel happy again,' Jess said, 'and that's somethin' I never thought would happen after losin' Bert.'

'How's Ewan doing?'

'It's hard tae tell with Ewan – he keeps his thoughts tae himself.'

'So he's not thawed towards poor Alison yet,' Naomi said, and Jess shook her head.

Alison Greenlees, a young widow with a small son, had moved into the village a few years earlier when her parents, Joe and Gracie Fisher, became landlord and landlady of the

Neurotic Cuckoo. She and Jess's son Ewan had become close, and at one point it seemed that shy Ewan was on the verge of proposing. Then, unexpectedly, everything went wrong for the McNairs – Victor, Ewan's older brother, decided to give up farming, and to make things worse, Victor persuaded his father to give him a small, rough field that was of no use as farming land, and then sold it on to a builder. Bert had disowned him, then killed himself during a fit of depression over the struggle to keep Tarbethill going without the help of both his sons.

Ewan, who loved Tarbethill as much as his father had, was left to cope with the near-impossible task of keeping the place going with only his mother and Wilf McIntyre, the elderly farmhand, to help him. Alison would willingly have married him and worked on the farm that she, too, had come to love, but Ewan's pride wouldn't allow her to make what he now saw as a sacrifice.

At first he had tried against all the odds to keep the failing farm operating exactly as it had for generations, but Alison, who had a business background, had, with help from Jess and Victor, finally persuaded him to make swingeing changes, such as selling off Bert's precious dairy herd and turning two of his largest fields into allotments. She had managed in this way to save more land from being sold off, but Ewan still couldn't bring himself to forgive her for what he saw as meddling.

'It's been a tough few years for the McNairs, Jess,' Naomi said now, 'but you and Ewan are survivors and I've never had any doubts that things will get better for you. I enjoyed the walk up the lane, stopping to chat with some of the folk working at either side in their allotments. I wish I'd the time to rent one of them for myself, but I'm content with the knowledge that come this year's harvest festival the church will be filled with locally grown offerings. And the rents must be a big help.'

'They are that, and it makes such a difference to me, not havin' to get up early every mornin' to milk the cows as well as goin' through it all again every night no matter what the weather's doing. At least Ewan doesnae disappear every time Alison comes to see me, and there's no doubt that he enjoys seein' wee Jamie, but I'm not getting any younger, Naomi, and I'm heart-desperate to see him and Alison settled together before I go.'

Naomi laughed the rich, warm laugh she had inherited from her Jamaican mother. 'You've got years left yet, woman; of course you'll see them settled.'

'I'd like to see some grandchildren around the farm, too, since Victor and his wife don't seem to be bothered about bairns. If Ewan had only found the courage to propose to Alison before his dad left us,' Jessie went on, a shadow passing over her face as always happened when she thought of her beloved late husband, 'they might have been safely wed. But how long does that poor lassie have to wait until he admits that he still loves her?'

'Nobody, including Alison, doubts that he loves her; he's just determined to get the farm back into profit before he takes on the added responsibility of a wife and stepchild.'

'There's determined – and there's stubborn,' Ewan's mother said flatly.

'And there's a man's pride – your boy must have found it hard to accept that Alison was right when she said that making big changes to the farm was the only way to save it. But don't you fret,' Naomi told her friend. 'He's made the changes, and even if he's too stiff-necked to admit it I'm sure he realizes that they were needed. As for Alison, she's as strong-minded as he is. She won't rest until he's placing a wedding ring on her finger under my watchful eye. Let's take it one step at a time and give thanks for all the good things that are happening in the meantime.' She popped an empty pod into her mouth and crunched it with relish.

Four

'Glad to be back home again?'

'I always enjoy coming back to Prior's Ford,' Clarissa Ramsay said into the telephone receiver.

'Does that mean that you didn't enjoy bein' with Alastair's folks?'

'Not at all. I had a lovely time. I've been there before, remember, so it wasn't at all strange. They always make me feel like one of the family.'

'So when do you see Alastair again?'

'He's going to be busy for the next few weeks because the art gallery's organizing a big exhibition in the next few months. He's asked me to spend time in Glasgow with him while it's on.'

'When you say "with him", do you mean "with", or do you mean him in his flat and you in a hotel again?'

'Amy, sometimes you can be downright nosy!'

'Sure I am, that's the only way to find things out.' Although Amy was in America her voice was as clear as though she were calling from the house next to Clarissa's.

'He insists on booking a double room in a hotel this time.'

'Well good for him! You share a room when he's in Prior's Ford, don't you? *And* you've been on holiday together in that nice little cottage for two at Loch Lomond. It's time you stopped makin' such a fuss about him bein' a little younger than you.'

'A lot younger than me.'

'Hey, love knows no borders. Did you have separate rooms when you stayed with his parents?'

'If you must know, we shared a room this time, because the house was filled with people who had arrived for his sister's wedding.'

'Sounds as though his parents are more with it than you,' Amy suggested. 'Good for them. They're probably glad he's fallen for you instead of some fluff-brained kid. So – when do you see him next?'

'We're going back to that nice wee cottage by Loch Lomond in July for a week.'

'Good – enjoy!'

'We will. Are you planning a trip to Scotland this year?'

'I'd love to, but not at the moment. Gordon's cousin Patsy, the one he grew up with, has to get a new hip next month, and I've said I'll see her through it an' stay on until she's fit to be on her own again. She hasn't got anyone else, an' I know it's what Gordon would want me to do, bless him, me havin' been a nurse an' all.'

'Amy, you were a midwife.'

'So I'll come in handy if she happens to fall pregnant as well.'

'That's not likely at her age, is it?'

'Oh, I don't know about that – Patsy was always a feisty girl. She was married three times, you know. Outlived every one of 'em. P'rhaps once she gets that new hip she'll get her old zest for life back an' go on the lookout for Number Four. Which reminds me – how's Stella?'

'She seems to be fine, but you know Stella, she doesn't say much about herself.'

'Poor girl, it's such a shame that that romance didn't work out.'

During a previous visit to Prior's Ford, Amy had befriended Stella Hesslet, the shy librarian who drove the mobile library that served the village. On a visit to a friend's B&B in England, Stella, a middle-aged spinster, had met a man who seemed interested in her. Amy had approved of him, but unfortunately he turned out to be as shy as Stella, and when it came to the hoped-for proposal he had taken cold feet, leaving Stella on her own again.

'It's my belief that Stella never really expected it to work out,' Clarissa said. 'I suspect that she sees herself as someone unworthy of happiness.'

'I'm goin' to have to do somethin' about that woman when I next visit Scotland. If only Patsy's hip could have kept workin' for another six months,' Amy mused. 'Oh well, next time you speak to Alastair say hi from me. I love that guy of yours to bits.'

As the call ended, Clarissa glanced in the mirror above the telephone table and was surprised to see how well and how young she looked; much younger than five years ago, when she was in her early fifties and married to her husband Keith, also a teacher. In those days she looked, and felt, her age. But so much had happened to her since then – the move, when Keith retired, from England to Prior's Ford; his sudden death not long after that; and her confusion at being suddenly without the overbearing man who made all the decisions.

Then all at once her life had been completely turned around by Alastair, the young artist who had found her sitting alone on a stile in the pouring rain and had taken her to the tumble-down farm cottage he rented. He had not only saved her sanity, he had also restored the self-confidence that Keith had whittled away bit by bit. They became close friends, and then came the most incredible thing of all – the realization that she had fallen in love with him. Even more incredible was the fact that he had fallen in love with her. And thanks to her American friend Amy Rose, who recognized the mutual attraction and forced them both to recognize it too, they were now together.

She was indeed a very lucky woman!

Police Constable Neil White reversed his car out of the driveway and travelled the short distance to his estranged wife's house at the top of Clover Park, where he parked, grabbed a bag from the passenger seat, and hurried to the front door.

Normally, when it was his turn to drive them both to work, Gloria opened the door as soon as he arrived, but this time it remained closed. He rang the bell, then hearing her voice, unusually animated, realized that she must be on the phone. After a few seconds, she laughed. As it had been a long time – too long – since he had heard that musical laugh, Neil leaned slightly towards the door, straining his ears, then stepped back swiftly as the handle began to turn.

The faint smile lingering from the phone call disappeared when Gloria saw him, to be replaced by her 'Sergeant Frost on duty' look.

'Your driver reporting for duty, ma'am.'

'Very funny. Don't tell me . . .' she said as her eyes fell on the bag, 'more fresh vegetables for my mother, grown on your very own allotment and plucked from the soil by your very own hands. Have you never heard of fruit and veg shops, or supermarkets?'

'Your mother appreciates fresh home-grown veg. I'd give them to you if you liked cooking, but as I recall from our brief time together, you don't.'

'There's more to life than cooking.'

'It's a mutual support thing. I grow vegetables, your mother cooks them, and you eat them. I presume your mother's visiting you tonight, this being Tuesday?'

'Put them in the kitchen.' Gloria stepped back, then as he passed her she went out to the car, saying over her shoulder, 'And make sure the door's properly shut when you come out.'

She was in the passenger seat by the time he got back to the car, slipping her wedding ring on to the third finger of her left hand.

'Got your ring on?' she asked.

'Of course.' He started the car. 'I'm sick of this business of having to remember when to take it off and when to put it on.'

'You wouldn't need to bother if you would only apply for a posting to another station.'

'I don't see why I should.'

'Apart from the fact that as sergeant I'm the senior officer, sheer male courtesy means that you should make the move.'

'I wasn't the one who walked out on our marriage,' Neil retorted. 'I put the veg into your refrigerator,' he added as they headed away from the village. 'Don't forget them tonight.'

'Talking of vegetables, how's your little Swede?'

'If you mean Anja, she's Norwegian. And she's fine as far as I know.'

'Talking about marriage yet?'

'I don't think she's the marrying type.'

'Oh, I disagree. I've seen the way she looks at you.'

'I didn't know you were interested enough to bother about the way anyone looks at me. And in any case, I'm already married, or have you forgotten?'

'I try to. And it wasn't so much the way she was looking at you last weekend but the way she was hanging on to your arm when I saw you going into the Neurotic Cuckoo together. Difficult to miss. Ease your grip on the steering wheel,' Gloria went on sweetly as the car turned on to the road to Kirkcudbright and picked up speed, 'your knuckles are terribly white.'

Neil bit back a retort, wishing he didn't love her so much. He was sick of the arguments they went through every time they were on their own together. It wasn't his fault that within a year of their marriage Gloria's hunger for promotion had made her decide that she would be better on her own, nor was it his fault that since the police service demanded total professionalism from their officers the two of them had only managed to retain their jobs by agreeing not to let their colleagues know that they had split up. On duty, they wore their wedding rings and were civil to each other. Off duty was a different matter.

To make things worse, they had each, without realizing it until too late, bought a house in Clover Park, which meant more juggling – while their work colleagues thought they were still married, their neighbours in Prior's Ford thought they were both single. It made life complicated.

They drove the rest of the way in silence, and by the time they reached the police station Neil felt like a piece of limp lettuce. It certainly wasn't the best way to start a day's shift.

Following Kevin Pearce's untimely death the popular drama group he had founded when he and his wife Elinor first arrived in Prior's Ford had almost collapsed without him. First attempts to find another director proved fruitless, and it wasn't until they were about to admit defeat and disband that Lynn Stacey, the primary school's head teacher, took pity on them and admitted to an amateur drama background that included acting, stage management and directing.

'I really had to wrestle with my conscience,' she told her good friend Ginny Whitelaw. 'I love amateur dramatics, but when I first came to the village I was determined not to become involved, because poor Kevin seemed to me to be rather pompous. Working with him didn't appeal to me at all, and in any case, I've been kept busy enough with the school. But give Kevin his due – he did run a good group and I'd hate to see it end.'

Lynn had proved to be both efficient and encouraging, and

once her offer was accepted it was decided to continue to rehearse *The Importance of Being Earnest*, the play that Kevin had been keen for them to perform. Rehearsals had progressed swiftly, and the play was due to be staged at the end of September. Everyone found Lynn easy to work with – everyone, that is, except leading lady Cynthia MacBain, who missed the special – some called it fawning – attention she had always enjoyed from Kevin.

'He was so appreciative of my work, and so encouraging,' she complained to her husband Gilbert as they walked to the village hall. 'He and I had a special rapport, didn't we?'

'You did indeed, my love, and that was because Kevin knew how fortunate he was to be working with an actress of your calibre.'

'Until that dreadful time when he was so besotted with Meredith Whitelaw that he actually took the lead part from me and gave it to her,' Cynthia suddenly remembered.

'That wasn't really Kevin's fault; he was bewitched by Meredith. I suspect that he was secretly relieved when she let him down and went off to film that television play. But you saved the day, didn't you?' Gilbert genuinely loved his sometimes-difficult wife, and finding the right words to soothe her when her ego was bruised had long since become second nature.

'I suppose I did.'

'There's no doubt about it. A lesser woman would have refused to take the part back, but you're a real trouper – you swallowed your pride and stepped in to save the show, just as you're doing now that Lynn's taken over. I swear that Kevin's admiration for you doubled on that day.'

'What else could I have done?' Cynthia began to brighten up again. 'I could never have let him down – as *she* did.'

'You were, as ever, professional to your fingertips,' Gilbert assured her as they reached the hall to find that several members of the drama group were already there.

Jinty McDonald, who cleaned the village hall and the primary school as well as helping out at Linn Hall, was pinning up a notice proposing a village outing to see Meredith Whitelaw onstage in *Blithe Spirit*.

'Did you know about this?' Jinty asked when the MacBains appeared. 'Ms Whitelaw's playing the part of Elvira, and most of the Women's Institute are going. Put your name down now to avoid disappointment.'

'I'm not a great fan of Noel Coward's work,' Cynthia said dismissively.

'I love that play,' enthused Jinty's daughter Stephanie, a talented young amateur actress. 'I can't wait to see Meredith Whitelaw on the stage. She was very kind to me when she was here last time and came to our rehearsals. I learned so much from the few acting lessons she gave me.'

'Gilbert, let me know when Lynn arrives; I'm just going into the kitchen to work on my lines, away from the chatter,' Cynthia said through gritted teeth.

'Well done, everyone,' Lynn enthused halfway through the rehearsal. 'I'm impressed by the progress you've made already.'

'Kevin was an excellent director – he managed to get the best out of everyone, even those of us with less experience than others,' Cynthia told her sweetly.

'I can see that he's done an excellent job. It makes my work so much easier,' Lynn was saying when Neil White burst into the hall.

'Sorry, I had to do a late shift. Hope I haven't missed much.'

'We've been concentrating on the scenes without you,' Lynn told him. 'We'll resume in ten minutes, everyone, and catch up on Neil's scenes.'

'Neil, I have brought coffee for you,' Anja Jacobson said in her lilting Norwegian accent as she looped a hand through his arm. 'Come to the end of the hall and we'll go through your lines.'

Five

Because Jinty cleaned the primary school and the village hall as well as helping out at Linn Hall and in the village store when required, she tended to know all the village gossip before anyone else did. During the rehearsal break she chattered away about Meredith Whitelaw agreeing to open the Linn Hall garden fête in August, and about the new tenant about to move in to Thatcher's Cottage.

'Is it true that he's a retired university lecturer?' Cynthia asked.

'So I've heard. He's a Doctor, not a Mister. He does a lot of writing and wants peace and quiet. He's not bought the cottage, just rented it for a year with a view to buying if he likes the place. I think he's on his own,' Jinty added.

'I just hope that he's better than the people who rented it before,' Hannah Gibb said with a shiver.

'I wonder . . .' Cynthia MacBain said as she and Gilbert walked home from the rehearsal.

'I don't think that it would be a good idea for us to hold a welcoming party for the new tenant who's moving into Thatcher's Cottage,' said Gilbert, who knew how his wife's mind worked.

'Why not? A retired professor, on his own – he might like to be welcomed to the village. And you can't deny that we hold very good parties.'

'I'm not disagreeing with that, Cynthia, but this is the third time Thatcher's Cottage has had new tenants since Doris Thatcher died, and so far the old building hasn't had much luck, has it?'

'But a retired lecturer, dear. An educated man!' Cynthia taught English at Kirkcudbright Academy and considered educationalists like herself to be the crème de la crème of their communities.

'The first couple to take over the cottage after Doris's death were filthy rich, and as far as I recall, they turned out to be more "filthy" than "rich",' Gilbert reminded her. 'And the second couple consisted of a retired high-ranking police officer and a well-known cookery expert who turned out to be a murderer. Just because this new man has lectured in some university, it doesn't follow that he's as respectable as you'd like him to be.'

'Mmm. Perhaps we should wait for a few weeks before making a definite decision.'

'Or a few months. For all you and I know, this academic man might be a reincarnation of Jack the Ripper,' Gilbert said as he opened the garden gate for her.

*   *   *

'I can't wait to see her again,' Fliss said excitedly as she and
Jinty got a room ready for Lewis's daughter, Rowena Chloe.
The little girl lived with her grandparents in Inverness most
of the time, but spent the summers at Linn Hall. Rowena
Chloe's visits were looked on as the highlight of the year.

'Neither can I – she brings this place to life, doesn't she?
It's great to see her playing in the gardens.'

'It's just a pity that we have to put up with a visit from the
Ewings when they bring her here,' Hector put in from the door.

'Only for a little while, Hector. They never stay for long,'
his wife reminded him. 'They're always in too much of a hurry
to get off on their holidays, or to get ready for their holidays.
I've never known a family for holidays like the Ewings!'

'I came to say that I've just remembered the big old rocking
horse upstairs – d'you think that Rowena Chloe might like to
have it in her bedroom? Now that she's four, she could probably cope with it, so I wondered if Lewis and I should bring
it down to her room.'

'Good heavens, I'd forgotten about that old horse. Lewis
used to love playing on it.'

'So did I when I was a child. There's nothing like a rocking
horse, is there?' Hector's clear blue eyes grew misty with
memories.

'When did you last go on holiday, Mrs F? I don't ever
remember you being away from Linn Hall.'

'Well – I think Lewis must still have been at school the last
time we had a family holiday.'

'Not that we've had many either, with all our kids to cater
for. There's never enough money to spare on luxuries. Not
that I mind – I love living here.'

'We spent a couple of days in Glasgow when we went to
Lewis's university graduation – that was nice, wasn't it, Hector?'

'It was all right. The rocking horse – d'you want it brought
down here?' Hector prompted.

'I don't think we should put it in her bedroom, dear – she'd
probably spend half the night on it instead of in bed, and in
any case, I remember it as being quite big for a four-year-old.
We'll ask Lewis's advice when he comes in, and if he thinks
she could manage it, we might take it down to the kitchen,

where there's always someone to keep an eye on her, just in case she falls off and bangs her little head. D'you think she'll be all right in a room of her own, Jinty?'

Until now, the little girl had slept in a cot in Lewis's room, which had its own small dressing room. The dressing room had been used as a store for years, but this year they had decided to clear it out and give Rowena Chloe a room of her own.

'I should think so. There's the connecting door – Lewis can always leave it open at night, then he'll hear her if she wakes up. And you've got that nice little bunny rabbit night-light that she loves.' Jinty cast an eye around the room. 'I think she's going to like this!'

'Please can we go to the farm to see Tommy?' Jamie Greenlees begged as he ran across the playground to join his mother at the school gates. '*Pleeease?*'

'Wouldn't you be better to go home and change into your play clothes first?'

'I don't want Tommy to forget me. I don't think rabbits have very long memories. I'll not get my school clothes dirty – promise!'

'All right then, but just for a little while because I have to help Grandpa behind the bar later.'

When they reached the farmyard Jamie burst in through the open kitchen door like a small tornado, yelling, 'Auntie Jess, it's me!'

'I can see it's you and hear that it's you.' Jess's face lit up, as always, at the sight of the little boy. She and Ewan were sitting at the table, together with Wilf, the farmhand. 'Ready for a glass of milk, are you?'

He nodded and scrambled on to a chair as Alison arrived. 'I wanted to make sure that Tommy's all right.'

'He's doing fine, Jamie,' Ewan assured him. The rabbit had been a birthday gift to the little boy from Jess and Ewan, who had made a large hutch and run for it.

'You'll have a cup of tea, Alison?' Jess asked, then, as Ewan gulped down the last of his own tea and put the mug down, 'and you'll have your usual second cup, Ewan.'

'We should be gettin' back to—'

'We've time for another cup, surely,' Wilf cut in, winking at Alison. 'There's no rush. I'll have more, thank you, Jess.'

'Aye, well . . .' Ewan muttered, looking everywhere but at Alison as Jess set a glass of milk before Jamie, then picked up the huge teapot and poured tea for herself and the others before sitting down again.

'Help yourself to the pancakes, there's plenty of them,' she invited everyone.

'How are the hens doing?' Alison wanted to know.

'Och, they're fine. That deep-litter house suits them, and they're layin' steadily. I'm workin' up quite a wee business of my own,' Jess said proudly.

'That's good.' Alison reached out to stay her son's hand as he tried to take two pancakes at the same time. 'One's enough, Jamie.'

'I need one for Tommy.'

'I've put some lettuce aside for him. He'll like that better than pancakes,' Jess told him. 'It's in that bowl by the sink.'

'Finish your milk and then take the lettuce to Tommy,' Alison suggested. 'I've to get back soon to help Grandpa.'

'I'm going to deliver some stuff to the village store in a half hour or so; I can take Jamie back home then if you like,' Ewan offered unexpectedly.

'Are you sure?'

'Of course. It'll give him a bit longer with his pet.'

'Ewan's more comfortable with you now, d'you not think so?' Jess asked when the others had gone – Jamie to feed his rabbit, the two men to finish off whatever they were working on.

'At least he doesn't make some excuse and rush out every time I appear.'

'It's all about pride – his father was just the same.' Jess began to fill the big sink with hot water. 'Bert always felt that he should be able to run the entire world. That plan you thought out to save the farm's working a treat, but Ewan's just not ready yet to admit it. Mind you, he'd never have been able to think it through the way you did.'

'That's because he's a hands-on person, and he felt as if he should try to keep things going the way his father had done – and his grandfather too.' Alison finished bringing the used plates and mugs to be washed, and picked up a dish towel. 'I couldn't do what Ewan does, but when I lived in Glasgow I worked for a firm where I was expected to plan ahead, using my brain instead of my hands. So you'd say that things are beginning to work out here?'

'It's all going well, and Ewan knows it now. As for me, I love havin' more hens to look after and more eggs to sell,' Jess said happily. Once, she had cared for about thirty hens, but now, thanks to Alison, there were another two hundred birds in the new deep-litter house and even more inhabiting a dozen small henhouses in a fenced-off corner of a field near to the farmhouse.

Jess had always looked on her hens as the feathered equivalent of the Prior's Ford community, some tending to group together like old friends gossiping happily while others indulged in complaining, bossing and tale-tattling. But now they were more like a hen town than a hen village, and more like a business than a little family. Added to her usual tasks – housework, laundry, mending, cooking, looking after the farm allotment and baking at least twice a week, the extra hens meant more work, but she didn't grudge a moment of it. She had spent most of her life working from dawn to dusk and that was the way she liked it.

'How's your own work?' she wanted to know. Now that Jamie was at school until three in the afternoon, Alison had taken on morning work as bookkeeper in a small office in Kirkcudbright.

'I'm enjoying it, but like Jamie, what I like best is being here, at Tarbethill. We may both be Glasgow-born, but we're turning into real country folk.'

'If it hadn't been for Victor deciding to marry a town girl and give up on bein' a farmer, you and Ewan could have been married by now, and that wee lad livin' here instead of just visitin'.'

'I know.' Alison put a comforting arm about the older woman's shoulders. 'When my Robbie was killed I never thought I'd love another man, but Ewan proved me wrong. Now I'm just going to have to wait until he realizes that he can have me and Jamie as well as Tarbethill – no matter how long that might take.'

'I hope it won't be much longer because I want a whole lot of grandchildren runnin' about this place with Jamie!' Jess ran the cold tap hard to swirl the last suds down the drain.

Alison laughed aloud. 'Just don't tell Ewan that; your expectations might be too much for him to bear. Let's go and see how that boy of mine's doing before I head back to the pub.'

As they went out into the sunshine together, she added, 'With your help I'm learning what it's like to be a farmer's wife. Before you know it, Ewan will suddenly discover that I'm indispensable!'

The three Ralston-Kerrs, Muffin the dog, Jinty and Ginny all spilled out of the kitchen door as they heard Tony Ewing's big people-carrier turn the corner into the stable yard.

When it came to a standstill Val Ewing jumped out of the front passenger seat, blowing kisses. 'Here we are again, lovely to see you! Fliss, you look tired, dear, don't you think it's time you had yourself a good long holiday? Hector, sweetie – and Lewis, as handsome as ever. Give me a hug!'

She threw her arms around Lewis, intercepting him as he tried to get to where Rowena Chloe, strapped into her child seat, was banging impatiently on the rear window. It was left to her husband Tony to emerge from the driver's seat and go round the car to open the door and unfasten his granddaughter.

'Daddeee!' She bounced out of the car in such a hurry that she would have fallen head-first on to the ground if Tony hadn't caught at one arm to steady her. Then she raced towards Lewis, yelling, 'Daddy-daddy-daddy-daddy-*daddy*!' and threw her arms around his legs.

'Hello, sweetheart!' He picked her up and hugged her, laughing as she showered his face with kisses, her red curly hair bouncing against her neck. 'Welcome back!'

'Daddy, I haven't seen you for *ages*!'

'I was at your fourth birthday party just last month. Don't you remember? So was your mummy.'

'That was years and years ago,' she said firmly, squirming round in his arms to look about. 'Muffin! Put me down now,' she ordered, and when Lewis did so she rushed towards the dog, arms outstretched.

'Weena, don't,' Val screeched as the two met, Rowena Chloe's arms going round the dog's neck while Muffin did his best to cover her face with sloppy dog kisses. 'Tony, make them stop – it's unhygienic!'

'It won't do her any harm,' Lewis protested, and then as Val continued to fret he caught Muffin by the collar and pulled the dog back. 'Settle down, Muffin, you'll be able to play with her later.'

'There are wet wipes in the car, Tony,' Val began to say as Jinty stepped forward and wiped the little girl's face with a handful of her apron.

'There now. Hello, pet.' She dropped a kiss on Rowena Chloe's face. 'Say hello to everyone, then we can go in for a nice cup of tea.' She released the child, who immediately rushed to hug Fliss's knees.

'Granfizz!' she said, then, to Hector, 'Grandpa!' moving on to, 'Ginny! Muffin!'

'You've already said hello to Muffin.' Lewis picked his daughter up and carried her into the kitchen, followed by the others.

Six

'What did Rowena Chloe just call me?' Fliss asked when they were all settled at the big kitchen table.

'She's decided that as I'm Gran, you're to be Granfliss – isn't that clever of her?' Val said. 'It means that we all know who she's talking about. She calls Tony Papa, so that means that you can be Grandpa, Hector. Oh, it's so nice to be back here! I've said it before, Fliss, and I'll say it again – I think our Molly was silly to give up the chance of living in a lovely big house like this. We were just saying, weren't we, Tony, coming through those gates and up the drive, what a shame it is. I was looking forward to seeing my daughter as the lady of the house! And the gardens are all looking fantastic.'

'How is Molly?' Fliss asked.

'Happy as a sandboy from what we hear, which isn't often because that girl's always been one to live for the moment – hasn't she, Tony? – and it's a case of out of sight, out of mind where she's concerned.' Val fluffed up her short curly hair, which was more auburn than Molly's vibrant red curls. 'She and Bob seem to be very happy together, though. They're still in Portugal, both working in a British-style pub. It was nice to see them home for Weena's birthday but they didn't stay long. They gave her a lovely doll, didn't they, Weena? A Spanish-type doll called Carmen.'

'Where's Carmen?' Rowena Chloe asked anxiously.

'In the car, pet. Papa will bring her in later, with the rest of your things.'

'So they're not thinking of coming back to settle in Scotland?' Jinty asked as she poured tea.

'Not at the moment, but then Molly never was one for staying home for long.'

'Are they likely to want Rowena Chloe to go over there to live with them?' Fliss asked, and saw her son's head turn sharply.

'I don't see it, myself. I mean, they're both working, and living over the bar. Not really the right place for a little poppet like our Weena.'

'She'll be starting school next year in any case,' Lewis said.

'Exactly. They grow up fast, don't they? We're heading for Portugal ourselves in a couple of weeks. Not the same area as Molly and Bob are, but we'll manage to see them while we're there. This chocolate cake's lovely, Fliss, did you make it yourself?'

'Jinty did. She's a fantastic baker.'

'Can I have another piece? Tony, you've got to try this chocolate cake, it's gorgeous!'

'And what about Stephanie?' Fliss asked politely. 'She must be just about ready to leave school now.' Stephanie was Molly's young sister, and the two girls were completely different. While Molly, like her parents, loved travelling and enjoying life, Stephanie was the academic of the family.

'Oh she's still the same Steph – a bit of a stick-in-the-mud, never happy unless she has her nose in a book. She's just finished school, and she's off to university in the autumn, would you believe? If she didn't have our Molly's green eyes and my auburn hair I'd swear that someone switched babies in the maternity hospital where she was born.'

'Is she going to Portugal with you?'

Tony, overhearing, shook his head. 'She's not one for sunbathing and nightclubbing.'

'Not like us at all,' Val agreed. 'She's going off to some African state with friends, to do voluntary work.'

'Sometimes I wonder if that girl's all there,' Tony put in.

'Don't say that, honeybun,' his wife protested. 'Steph's a lovely girl really, just not like Molly. Each to their own, eh, Hector?'

'I s'pose. We'll have to watch our time, Val,' Tony reminded her, taking the final piece of cake.

'So we will. We're going out with friends tonight. Karaoke – we love it, and now that this little minx is with her daddy, we don't have to worry about her. We know she's in safe hands.'

'When you bring her things from the car, you'll have to come upstairs to see Rowena Chloe's room – it's small, but it's right beside Lewis's room, and there's a connecting door. We thought that now she's four she needs a proper bed instead of Lewis's old cot, and a room of her own.'

'Ooooh, did you hear that, Weena? Granfliss and Grandpa and Daddy have got a special little bedroom just for you, right beside Daddy's. Isn't that exciting?'

'Can Muffin sleep in my room with me?' asked Rowena Chloe, who was sitting on the floor so that Muffin could lick the chocolate from her face.

'So this is where you grow all those vegetables.'

Neil White, checking the progress of his first batch of leeks, looked up to see his mother-in-law step from the farm lane into his allotment. On this warm June day, she looked cool and fresh in a blue and white short-sleeved linen jacket over pale-blue cropped trousers that revealed shapely ankles and bare feet clad in dark-blue sandals.

'Rosemary?'

'Don't look so nervous, darling, I'm not checking up on you;

I just wanted to see what this allotment of yours looks like.' She patted the bag slung over one shoulder. 'I come bearing cream buns and a Thermos of tea – is there somewhere to sit down?'

'Over by the hut.' He led the way to the bench along the side of his small hut, aware of the inquisitive and envious glances being thrown their way by some of the other allotment holders. He couldn't blame them; even though she was his wife's mother he had to admit that Rosemary looked fantastic.

'Gloria didn't send you, did she?' he asked as she produced a Thermos and sturdy paper cups, each in a plastic holder, from her bag.

'If my daughter has anything to say to anyone, she's quite capable of speaking up for herself. I'm here to see your allotment, as I said. Also, we need to talk, you and me. Hold these.' She handed the cups to him and unscrewed the top of the Thermos. 'Isn't this nice?' she went on as the two of them leaned back against the hut's warm walls, with a large cream bun in one hand and tea in the other. 'Are you enjoying being an allotment-holder?'

'As a matter of fact, I am. It's relaxing.'

'It feels relaxing. Gloria needs to do something like this. It might slow her down a little.'

'I don't see her digging and planting for pleasure.'

'I suppose you're right. Pity, really. So – how are you, Neil? We haven't had a chat for ages.'

'I'm all right.'

'All right,' Rosemary said, 'isn't good enough, is it? When are you and Gloria going to sort out your differences and get back together again?'

'You'd need to ask her that. Splitting up was her idea, not mine.'

'D'you want to get back together again? And don't prevaricate,' Rosemary said crisply as he hesitated. 'A straight yes or no, please.'

'I find it difficult to discuss my marriage with my mother-in-law.'

'Rubbish – who else can you discuss it with? Certainly not Gloria, because she's as stubborn as her father. That's why I came here today,' Rosemary swept on. 'To be honest, Gordon and I are sick of this will-you-won't-you-sort-your-problems-out business – at least, I am, and I suspect he is as well, but trying to get my husband to bare his inner soul's like trying to coax a tortoise to come out of its shell for a spot of sunbathing. As for Gloria . . .' She heaved a sigh. 'She takes after him. Every time I try to get her to talk things out, woman to woman, she does nothing but bad-mouth you.'

'It's all she does to me too. She loathes me.'

'Oh, tosh, she's still mad about you. Don't tell me that you don't know that,' she said as Neil's arm jerked and some tea slopped over the side of his cup.

'She's got a strange way of showing it.'

'I'll grant you that she's very career-minded and always has been. Even in primary school she had to be the best at everything – just like her father, poor soul. But,' she swept on while he was still trying to work out whether the poor soul was Gloria or her father, 'beneath that hard exterior there's a soft centre. She's made sergeant, and that'll keep her happy for a while at least. But if I know my daughter – and I know her better than she knows herself – I'd say that now she's won the prize she's realizing what she gave up in order to get it. I mean you,' Rosemary said as Neil's brow furrowed.

He felt a moment's hope. 'How can you be sure about that?'

'If she wanted another man in her life she'd probably have found him by now. It's my belief that she misses you but she can't work out how to get you back without losing face. You're the problem, Neil. You're too gentle with her. I know that she's my only daughter, and I truly am against domestic abuse,' Rosemary said, 'but sometimes I think that you'd still be together if you had even once put her over your knee and given her a good spanking.'

'I couldn't do that!'

'I know,' she said sadly. 'You're too much of a gentleman, and she takes advantage of that. Perhaps you should make her jealous. What about that pretty young woman we saw you with the day Gloria and I came to look at her new home and discovered that you were living in the same estate?'

'I told you then that Anja's an interior decorator. She helped me to furnish the house.'

'She seemed to want to be more than your interior decorator, and Gloria knew it.'

'We're seeing each other,' Neil admitted.

'Do you sleep together?'

He felt a wave of heat flood his face. 'Certainly not!'

'Why not?'

'I'm married!'

'My poor Neil, you're such a stickler for propriety, aren't you?' Rosemary threw her last piece of cream bun to a small bird hopping about nearby. 'That's why you keep letting Gloria have the upper hand. I bet that if she thought you were getting really serious about this Anja, she'd do her best to get you back.'

'I like Anja too much to use her.'

'Again,' Rosemary said, 'we run up against the fact that you're too decent.'

'Not entirely. If Anja thought I really cared for her she'd not let go.'

Rosemary glanced at her watch then stood up. 'I have to leave now; Gordon will be wondering where I've got to. Think about what I've said, Neil. If you can find a way to let Gloria think she's losing you, it would force her hand.'

She picked up her bag, slung it over her shoulder, and then added, 'The first time I met you I knew that you were the right man for my daughter, and I still think so. I just wish that you had the sense to know it too. Please bring her to her senses soon, if only because Gordon and I are being snowed under by all those vegetables you keep giving her. She needs a rude awakening rather than an avalanche of carrots and potatoes. You've got some cream on your chin.'

She reached down and scooped the cream up with one finger, which she then put into her mouth and sucked, before withdrawing it slowly. It was an incredibly sexy gesture.

'Mmm, nice,' she said. 'Ciao . . .'

Then she was gone, leaving Neil's pulse racing.

'Wouldn't you like to just live here for good?' Alastair Marshall said as he and Clarissa arrived back at the small cottage following a day exploring the hillside overlooking Loch

Lomond. They were spending a week in the cottage by the water, where they had first stayed shortly after finally admitting to the way they felt about each other.

'I don't know if I'd like it so much in the winter,' Clarissa admitted. 'All alone out here, snowed in.'

'I'd keep you warm.' He pulled her into his arms and held her close, kissing the top of her head.

'While we starved to death?'

'It's well seen that you were a teacher – you tend to look at the practical side of everything.'

'And it's well seen that you're an artist – ignoring the practical side of everything. Who would ever have thought,' Clarissa marvelled, 'that two people so different in outlook and age could ever have got together?'

'God bless Amy Rose, that's what I say. If she hadn't noticed that we were attracted to each other so strongly, and both trying so hard to deny it, look at what we would have missed. Let's go along to that superb restaurant tonight for dinner – after a day in the fresh air I'm starving, and I feel too lazy to cook. And don't say you'll cook,' Alastair added as Clarissa opened her mouth to speak, 'because I'm in the mood for a really good steak, and I don't think we've got any in the fridge. But before that, let's enjoy a glass of wine.'

'Lovely.'

'You phone the restaurant and book a table for whenever suits you, and I'll see to the wine. What are you smiling about?' he added.

'I was just thinking how very lucky I am, and how I never thought that someone like you would happen to me.'

'I think that all the time, about you.'

When they were in the restaurant, he asked, 'Looking forward to coming to Glasgow in September for the art exhibition?'

'Are you sure you want me to be there? I know nothing about art!'

'You *must* come, Clarissa. I've never been given entire responsibility for setting up an art exhibition before. The artist concerned has got an exceptional talent and I want to do my best for her. It's going to be a nerve-wracking time for me, and I need to know that you're there.'

For a moment, Clarissa's breath caught in her throat. Nobody had ever needed her so much, or so openly. 'Of course I'll be there.' She reached across the table to put her hand on his. 'Despite my total lack of artistic intelligence.'

'Good,' he said. 'Even if you don't know a Picasso from a newspaper cartoon, you're my lucky charm.'

Seven

When the few pieces of furniture he had brought to Thatcher's Cottage were in place and the removal men had been thanked both vocally and financially and driven off in their van, Dr Malcolm Finlay lit his pipe and set off to survey his new home.

Ever since retiring from work as a lecturer two years earlier he had been looking for the perfect bolt-hole, and he reckoned that he had found it in Thatcher's Cottage. Small and compact, it consisted of three rooms downstairs – a living room, a small dining room and an even smaller kitchen – and two bedrooms and a bathroom upstairs. A little niche in the kitchen, which he guessed had once been a coal cellar, was the perfect size for a man used to eating on his own at a small table, which meant that the dining room could be turned into a library for his many books, and since he had no intention of ever inviting anyone to stay, the second bedroom was his study. Already, he felt totally at home.

He wandered out to the neat front garden and walked round the side of the cottage, past the small garage that already housed his beloved Mini, to the back garden, where he stood watching the river below, puffing pipe smoke towards the blue sky above.

It had been a while since he had known such contentment. After retiring he had felt unsettled, but didn't know why. It took his strong-minded older sister Daphne, who had left home in her late teens, married, and raised three children now busy raising their own children, to point out that it was time for a move.

'You're rattling round that big house like a lonely marble trapped in a large box, Malcolm. And I use the term "marble" advisedly, given that you're such a roly-poly of a man. You're still living with Ma and Pa, even though they've been dead for yonks. When were you last upstairs?'

'I don't need to go upstairs. I've got everything I need here on the ground floor.'

'My point exactly.' Daphne was an organizer; she had organized her children until they grew up and escaped the nest, and now she organized her doting husband and the Labrador dogs she bred, worked part-time in her local Citizen's Advice Bureau, made her own jam and was in three book groups. She and Malcolm were as different as chalk and cheese. 'You should have married – you need someone to organize you.'

'I'm quite happy as I am.'

'But are you happy *where* you are?'

'No.' The word had popped out of Malcolm's mouth before he had time to consider his answer. 'Come to think of it, I'm not,' he said slowly.

'There you are. At work, you were a man of importance – you still are, with your articles selling to all those academic publications. But in that house you're still Ma and Pa's son. D'you see what I mean?' she drove on. Then, when he was silent, said, 'Malcolm, have you fallen into one of your daydreams?'

'No, I'm just beginning to think that I do see what you mean,' Malcolm said slowly. He had never realized until she confronted him with the truth that as he still lived in what had been his parents' home, he still lived by their rules.

'There you are, then – you need to move. I'll find somewhere for you.'

'No,' he said swiftly. 'I'll do that – but you'll have to help me to empty this house and get rid of it.'

'Of course. Start looking – now!' Daphne said. 'I'm coming round to see you next week – Monday afternoon would suit me best, so put it in your diary. Over the next few weeks, while you're house-hunting, I'll go through all the rubbish that's gathered over the years in that mausoleum we used to call home and get rid of it. Must go, I'm chairing a meeting in ten minutes.' And as usual, she hung up without saying goodbye. Daphne was always too busy to bother with niceties.

★   ★   ★

By the time Malcolm found Thatcher's Cottage, in what seemed to him to be a pleasantly sleepy little village where nothing ever happened, his sister Daphne had cleared everything out of the family home – their parents' clothes and books, his mother's jewellery, a vast collection of ornaments and most of the furniture – only leaving the bare necessities required by her brother.

What was left fitted into the furniture van hired by Daphne to take it and his main book collection, while he and the essential reference books that he could never bear to be without travelled in his little Mini.

The sense of freedom he experienced now, standing out in his very own garden, listening to the river purling contentedly below, was positively heady.

It seemed to Malcolm that one of the pleasures in living in a village must surely lie in visiting the local public house, so on his first evening he strolled along to the Neurotic Cuckoo, where he found the bar half-full.

Heads turned as he went in, and the buzz of conversation ebbed slightly. Malcolm, a loner by nature, but used, after years of being a college lecturer, to a bit of necessary socializing, beamed on everyone as he made his way to the bar.

'Evening,' he said amiably to the man behind it. 'Malcolm Finlay. I've just moved into Thatcher's Cottage, and I'm keen to sample your beer. A pint, please.'

'Joe Fisher, landlord. Welcome to Prior's Ford.'

'I'm Robert Kavanagh.' The man beside Malcolm held out his hand. 'And this is Bill Harper; he runs the garage near to your cottage.'

'I've seen your Mini going by. Well cared for.' Bill shook hands as Joe Fisher set a brimming glass down on the counter.

It was a promising start, Malcolm thought as he settled down to a chat. And the beer was good into the bargain.

By the time he wandered back to his new home through the peace of a pleasant July evening, he was beginning to congratulate himself on choosing Thatcher's Cottage. He had admitted to his new-found friends that he would need a gardener, as he knew nothing about growing plants or vegetables, and enquired about the possibility of finding someone willing to keep the cottage tidy, and do a bit of cooking as well.

'I'll ask my wife to talk to Jinty McDonald,' Robert offered. 'I doubt if Jinty herself can help, because she already works in Linn Hall – that's the big house on the hill – and cleans the school and the village hall . . .'

'And works here when we need an extra pair of hands,' Joe Fisher cut in. 'I don't know what this village would do without Jinty.'

'Joe's right, but she's a good sort and she's lived in this village all her life. She'll be sure to find someone suitable for you,' Robert said, nodding. 'And if you need a gardener, a couple of her lads might be able to help out. Her dad was the head gardener at Linn Hall in its heyday, and one of her boys, Jimmy, works as a gardener there now that he's left school. But his young brother Norrie helps out in the Linn Hall gardens now, and from what I've heard, he's showing as much promise as Jimmy. I'll ask Jinty about him, too.'

Daphne was right, as usual, Malcolm thought at he reached his new home and started making himself some supper; the move to Prior's Ford looked like being a good idea.

Neil White checked his shoes to make sure that they shone before knocking on DI Cutler's door.

'Come in. Ah, Police Constable White.'

'You wanted to see me, sir?' Neil hadn't the faintest idea why, and he'd worried about it all the way upstairs, trying without success to think of any recent misdemeanours.

'Yes, I did. How do you fancy attending a course at Tulliallan?'

'Me sir?' Sheer astonishment made Neil's voice squeak. Tulliallan was the Scottish college where all police personnel, from new recruits to command level, were trained. 'I mean, yes, sir!'

'There's a place available on an Initial Investigators Course lasting four weeks; the only drawback is that it starts next Monday. They've had a cancellation, and I put your name forward because you did well in that murder enquiry we had last year in the village where you live. Do well there and you'll come back to us as a Detective Constable with CID. Can you manage the short notice?'

'That isn't a problem, sir.'

'Then it's decided. Here's the rundown on the course. Good luck – and don't let me down, lad.'

Neil left the office in a state of dazed euphoria, unable to keep the grin from his face. On the way downstairs he paused on the landing to snatch a quick glance at the papers he had been given.

It was going to be a tough course, but if it all went well he'd end up in CID.

Suddenly life had taken on a rosy glow.

It was Gloria's week for transport, and she was very quiet on the way home after their shift. Neil finally had to break the silence.

'I take it that you knew what was going to happen before I did?'

'Tulliallan, you mean? As your sergeant, I was naturally consulted. So what did you decide?'

'To grab the chance, of course.'

'You're going for it?'

'Of course. You didn't think that I would turn down an opportunity like that.'

'I thought you were happy enough as you are.'

'Oh come on – you must know me better than that!'

'You've never talked about wanting to climb the ladder.'

'I didn't get the chance because you were always talking about your personal ladder,' Neil rapped back at her.

They were both shocked by his reaction. The car swerved slightly, and when he glanced at her hands on the steering wheel he noticed that her knuckles had gone white. He opened his mouth to apologize, then shut it again, and the rest of the journey passed in silence.

When they arrived in Clover Park and she stopped the car outside his gate, he opened the passenger door, and then glanced over at her set profile.

'I'm off to Tulliallan at the weekend. Fancy a drink in the Cuckoo on Friday evening? I feel like celebrating.'

'Won't you be seeing your little girlfriend on Friday night?'

'She's not my – no, I'm not seeing her.' At a time like this, he felt too euphoric to get involved in another squabbling match. 'I'll be there at seven, on my own, if you feel like joining me. It's up to you, Sergeant,' he said and got out of the car.

'Seen the notice in the window?' Sam Brennan asked as he took the items from Cynthia's basket, running up the charge for each one. 'The WRI's organizing a bus trip to Dumfries in September to see Meredith Whitelaw in that play. We're taking names for them – just about everyone's thinking of going. Do you want me to put you and Gilbert down for tickets?'

'I'm not sure if we'll manage,' she snapped, packing her shopping bag as fast as she could. 'We're both very busy.'

'Don't take too long to decide or you'll miss out. That'll be thirteen pounds and twenty-seven pence, please. Oh – and could you ask Gilbert if he could let me have another half dozen jars of honey? The last lot sold out fast.'

As she left the shop, Cynthia glanced across the village green at the Neurotic Cuckoo, deciding to have some coffee there before going home. The mobile library was parked near to the pub, and as she passed by it Cissie Kavanagh came down the two steps, several books tucked under one arm.

'Hello, Cynthia, looking forward to the long summer school break? Not long now.'

'I certainly am.'

'I'm going to treat myself to a coffee.' Cissie indicated the pub. 'Care to join me?'

'That's exactly what I'd decided, too.'

'Have you met Dr Finlay yet?' Cissie asked as they fell into step together.

'Who?'

'That new man who's moved into Thatcher's Cottage. He's very interesting; Robert spent the best part of last Saturday with him at the old quarry, watching the peregrine falcons. Their young are beginning to fly now.'

'So your husband's actually met him already?' Cynthia sensed a stab of jealousy.

'We both have. Robert brought him back from the quarry

for his tea. He's a big man, with a big man's appetite,' Cissie
went on with the pleasure that women fond of cooking and
baking tended to display towards men who enjoy their food.

'I thought I might call in at Thatcher's Cottage on my way
home,' Cynthia lied. 'A quick courtesy visit to welcome him
to our little village.'

'He's in the library van at the moment, registering as a
borrower and ordering a whole list of academic tomes. It looks
as though he's going to keep Stella busy. Here we are.' Cissie
started to go into the pub, then halted as Cynthia caught at
her arm.

'That reminds me – I wonder if Stella has the latest Joanna
Trollope in stock yet. If so, I'd better get it before someone
else does. I'll join you in a minute – order a black coffee for
me, will you?' she said over her shoulder as she swung round
and headed back towards the mobile library.

The van's interior consisted of a counter behind the driver's
cab and two long walls packed with bookshelves, with a
passageway running the length of the van between them. When
the library was busy, as often happened, borrowers had to wait
outside for their turn to go up the two steps. On a mild and
sunny day, the wait was a welcome opportunity to chat to each
other.

A few people were heading across the village green towards
the van, and Cynthia had to break into a sprint in order to
reach it before they arrived. Two readers were browsing along
the shelves, and Stella, at the counter, was blocked from sight
by the well-built man talking to her.

'I realize that my list is rather long,' he was saying as Cynthia
arrived behind his comfortable old tweed jacket. 'If it's going
to make things difficult for you I'm quite prepared to drive to
Dumfries for them. Perhaps I'm asking too much – I have no
previous experience of the duties of a mobile librarian, you
see.'

'Not at all,' Stella assured him in her fluttery voice, 'though
it may take a few weeks before I get them all. There's not
much call for titles such as these.'

'I quite understand – I'm too used to university libraries,
I'm afraid. If you're going to be here next Monday afternoon

I'll make a point of looking in to see if you've managed to get one or two from the list, but please don't worry if you can't. In the meantime, good afternoon, and thank you for being so helpful, Miss – er—'

'Hesslet. Stella Hesslet.'

'Stella – a pretty name. Thank you.' He began to turn and came up against Cynthia, who had been fidgeting at his back. 'I do beg your pardon, madam, I didn't realize you were there. I'm rather too large for narrow spaces.'

'Not at all. I take it that you're Dr Finlay, our new resident?' When he nodded his large head, massed with grey curls, she tried to hold her hand out but failed because it was trapped between her body and his tweed-covered belly. 'I'm Mrs Cynthia MacBain.'

'How do you do? Excuse me –' he began to ease past her – 'I must get outside to make room for all the other people wishing to make use of the library.' Then he was on his way down the passage, apologizing profusely as he crushed past the few people he met on the way.

'Good morning, Mrs MacBain,' Stella said.

'I wondered,' Cynthia asked hurriedly, eager to follow him, 'if you have the new Joanna Trollope in yet?'

'Yes, but Mrs Parr stamped it out half an hour ago. She's a quick reader – she may well bring it back next week. Would you like me to put your name down for it?' Stella reached for a form and a pen.

'Would you, please? And could you fill the form in for me? I'm in rather a hurry at the moment,' Cynthia said and fled from the van as quickly as she could.

As she eased her way down the aisle she heard the next woman in the queue ask Stella, 'Do you know when the next Lilias Drew book's coming out? I love her stories!'

Eight

Malcolm Finlay, lumbering across the village green, turned when he heard Cynthia call his name.

'Oh dear, did I forget to leave the right information with the librarian?' he asked as she caught up with him. 'I'm not very good with things like that.'

'No, not at all. We met a moment ago in the van – I'm Mrs Cynthia MacBain,' she said as he peered down at her through thick-lensed glasses that made his astonishingly green eyes seem huge in his round face.

'Er – oh yes, I remember.' He gave her a kindly smile.

'I was just wondering if you're settling in all right.'

'Oh yes indeed, thank you for asking. People have been most kind. If you want to know if I've found a cleaning lady, Mrs McDonald was kind enough to find someone who seems eminently suitable, so the position's filled. I'm sorry,' he finished apologetically as she stared at him.

'No, I'm not looking for a post as a cleaning lady,' she said, only realizing when he recoiled slightly that she had snapped at the man. 'I mean – I only wished to say that my husband Gilbert and I would be delighted to host a welcoming party for you in our home. Not many people, just a select gathering, with you, of course, as the guest of honour. We have always made a point of welcoming strangers to Prior's Ford. We find that it breaks the ice for them, so to speak.'

'Oh.' Again he seemed utterly taken aback. 'Er – to tell the truth, Mrs – er–'

'MacBain, Cynthia MacBain.'

'Mrs MacBain, yes . . . to tell the truth, I'm not very good at parties and gatherings. Not what you might call a social animal at all. So – thank you for the kind thought, though,' said Dr Finlay, and then turned and went on his way, leaving Cynthia so dumbfounded that she was halfway home when she suddenly remembered that she was supposed to be having coffee with Cissie Kavanagh.

Cissie was at a table by the window, chatting to Gracie Fisher when Cynthia arrived, almost out of breath.

'There you are! Lucky I told Gracie to wait until you arrived before she brought your coffee.'

'Black, isn't it?' Gracie said, and when Cynthia nodded, 'I'll fetch it right now. You look as though you could do with a cup.'

'Bring another for me, please, Gracie, I've almost finished this one. I saw you rushing after Dr Finlay, Cynthia, then heading off in the opposite direction when you left him,' Cissie remarked as Gracie bustled to the kitchen. 'Forgot something, did you?'

'I had to pass a message to him from Stella Hesslet – he'd forgotten to provide some information that she needed for his library ticket,' Cynthia improvised. 'Then I suddenly wondered if I'd left something on the stove. I was on my way home when I remembered that I hadn't.'

'It's not like you to be forgetful – is playing the lead in the drama club's new play beginning to get too much for you? After all, none of us are getting any younger.'

'Absolutely not – I'm a schoolteacher,' Cynthia said shortly. 'There's nothing wrong with my memory!'

'Of course not. Talking of plays, do you know that the WRI are getting up a bus to go to the theatre in Dumfries? Meredith Whitelaw's going to be starring in *Blithe Spirit*. We're all very excited about it. You should put your name down.'

'I'll need to check my diary first,' Cynthia said.

'Here we are – one white coffee, and one black coffee,' Gracie said cheerfully. Then, as she set down the cups, she added to Cynthia, 'Have you heard that there's going to be a bus organized to go to Dumfries to see Meredith Whitelaw in *Blithe Spirit*? We'll probably need two buses – there's a lot of interest being shown, so I'm told.'

'I saw that new chap talking to someone outside the village store today,' Gilbert MacBain told his wife later. 'Looked like quite a friendly sort of person. Are you still thinking of us holding a welcome party for him?'

'I thought you didn't like the idea.'

'I just felt as though we should see what he was like first.'

'As it happens,' Cynthia said on her way to the kitchen, 'I met him briefly in the mobile library this afternoon – I don't really think he's our sort of person.'

'Congratulations, Neil, what wonderful news!'

'Thanks, Rosemary. So Gloria told you about the Tulliallan course?' Neil was just stepping out of the bath when the phone rang; he had hurtled into the bedroom, grabbing a towel as he went and wrapping it around his waist.

'Of course. I think she's got mixed feelings about it – partly pride, and partly apprehension. Am I right in assuming that if you sail through this course and move to CID, you'll be able to pull rank over her if the two of you find yourselves at a crime scene?'

'That's right – if I sail through.'

'Of course you will! What has my daughter said to you about it?'

'Not much. I invited her to join me for a drink in the local pub on Friday, but she hasn't actually said yes – or no.'

'That could be a good sign.'

'Mmm,' he said doubtfully. 'I'll be there, just in case.'

'Want me to look after your allotment while you're gone?'

'Would you?'

'I'd love to. How would it be if I came along on Saturday afternoon so that you can show me what to do? Around two thirty?'

'That's grand – thanks.'

'See you then,' his mother-in-law said and hung up, leaving Neil thinking of how pleasant life would be if Gloria had only been born with her mother's nature rather than her father's.

It was embarrassing when Anja, too, offered to take care of the allotment during his absence and he had to tell her that an arrangement had already been made with a friend.

'You must have known that I would do that for you,' she said, pouting.

'To tell the truth, it's all happened so quickly that I didn't have time to think things through.'

On Friday evening he walked into the pub at seven prompt, not at all sure if his prickly estranged wife would decide to accept his invitation to a celebration drink. But she was already there, looking gorgeous and with two drinks on the table.

'I've booked dinner here for half past seven,' she said as he joined her. 'My treat. You've earned it.'

Meredith Whitelaw's chauffeur-driven limousine drew up on the wide sweep of gravel before Linn Hall's front entrance one morning in late July.

Although she was expected, Fliss and Hector Ralston-Kerr, who, with Jinty and Kay, were enjoying a mid-morning cup of coffee now that the estate workers had finished their break, jumped when the front doorbell jangled high on the kitchen wall for the first time in years.

'What's that awful noise?' Kay squealed. 'Is it a fire alarm?'

'It's only the front doorbell. Who on earth can it be?' Hector's eyes widened with alarm behind his reading glasses.

'I can't remember the last time that bell rang.' His wife looked just as nervous, and it fell to Jinty to say, 'The only person you're expecting is Ginny's mum, so it's probably her.'

'Meredith Whitelaw – at the front door, in person?' Kay gasped.

'Ah. I think I'd better . . .' Hector, a shy man, scooped up his paper and made for the butler's pantry, his refuge when strangers were around.

'Don't leave me alone with her, Hector – oh dear,' Fliss said as the pantry door closed, 'now what do we do?'

'I'll answer the door, and you could fetch Ginny, Kay.'

'Have I got time to brush my hair and put on a bit of lippie first?'

'No, you haven't – just go and get Ginny. I think you'll find her in the kitchen garden.' Jinty hurried through the inner door leading to the entrance hall while Kay made for the back door. Fliss, left on her own, paced the floor, wishing that she could take refuge with her husband.

Ginny was browsing contentedly through the kitchen garden when Kay arrived at a run. 'Ginny, there's someone at the front door and we think it's your mum. You'd better come quick!'

'Oh, bother!' Ginny said under her breath. Then, aloud: 'The front door? Then it probably *is* my mother.' Who else but Meredith Whitelaw would insist on using the front door?

'That bell gave me a dreadful fright,' Kay panted as the two of them ran into the courtyard. 'It must have been awful for servants in the old days, hearing that clamour every day.'

'Hector fled to the pantry,' Fliss said apologetically as the two girls arrived in the kitchen. 'You know how shy he can be, dear. Should I try to get him to come out?'

'No, let him be.' Ginny, like Fliss, wished with all her heart that she could join him for the duration of her mother's visit. 'You'd better go to meet her, Mrs Ralston-Kerr. I'll come with you.'

'I'll put the kettle on, shall I?' Kay suggested. 'She'll be ready for a cuppa.'

'Make it coffee – filtered, not instant,' Ginny advised her before following Fliss through the inner door and along the corridor. They arrived in the large entrance hall to find Jinty hovering outside the open dining-room door.

'Ms Whitelaw insisted on having a look round. I did tell her that the rooms on the ground floor are never used and never dusted.'

'Oh dear,' Fliss said faintly. 'I suppose we'd better join her.'

Meredith was opening the curtains when they went in, allowing sunshine to fill the room and highlight the dust motes fleeing in panic from the heavy material. As the three women entered she swung round to face them, dusting her beautifully-manicured hands together.

'Genevieve, darling!' She swooped gracefully across the carpet to embrace her daughter, kissing the air several inches away from either cheek before holding Ginny at arm's-length. 'It's been *ages*! Let me look at you.' Then, her professional smile fading a little, 'Darling, you look so – workmanlike.'

'I'm a gardener, Mother.'

'I know, but do you *have* to *look* like one?'

Ginny looked pointedly at Meredith's floaty, multicoloured dress and sky-blue linen jacket. 'The sort of clothes you wear wouldn't suit me. I suppose I could try to hire a pretty milk-maid outfit from a costumier's . . .'

'We'll talk about that later, dear. Fliss, how lovely to see you again!' Meredith turned to Fliss, who took an involuntary nervous step back before submitting herself to be hugged and air-kissed.

'And you,' she faltered.

'Can I just say how very honoured I am to be invited to open your garden fête? I get so many invitations to do things like that, and I usually have to turn them down, but I couldn't say no to the village where I once spent many happy months.'

'We're glad that you've agreed. Come to the kitchen and have some coffee.'

'Could I come up with a teeny little idea first? This . . .' Bracelets tinkled as Meredith indicated the dining room's long table with an elegant sweep of the arm. 'This is a magnificent room, and it would make the perfect setting for dinner once the fête is over. A few friends from the theatre will be coming with me that day, and I'm sure they would love to eat here afterwards with some of your own friends.'

Fliss swayed slightly. 'But we haven't used the ground floor rooms for years – and they're all so dusty . . .'

'But darling, it's such a perfect setting to round off what I know will be a perfect day! I don't know *how* you can sit in the kitchen when you have rooms like this to relax in. Where's the drawing room?'

'Across the hall.'

Meredith made for the door, saying over her shoulder, 'I'm sure we can find time for a quick tour of the place. I've been *longing* to see it all! Now that you're opening your gardens to the public,' she went on as she swept across the hall, 'you really must start opening up the house as well.'

'The large rooms are difficult to heat,' Fliss ventured. 'We find the kitchen much warmer.'

'But you can't *possibly* be happy in a kitchen! After all, you're nobility.'

'I wouldn't say that . . .'

'What a superb staircase! I can't wait to see what's up there,' Meredith said as she swept on. Fliss, Jinty and Ginny had no option but to follow her into the gloomy, dusty drawing-room, glancing helplessly at each other.

'People would *adore* this place. Everyone loves to see round stately homes,' Meredith said as they finally returned to the hall having done a tour of every ground floor room.

By the time they arrived in the kitchen, Hector, wrongly assuming that their absence indicated that the coast was clear, had ventured out and was too far from the pantry to scurry back before Meredith spotted him.

'How lovely to see you again!' She pounced, grabbing his hand and shaking it vigorously while Jinty went to help Kay pour coffee. 'Thank you for inviting me to open your garden fête – I'm thrilled!' She drew him to the table, thrust him into a chair, and settled herself beside him. 'I was saying to your wife that you really should open this house to the public. Of course, it would require a complete makeover first, but make-overs are all the rage just now.'

'Makeover?' Hector clearly hadn't the first idea what she meant.

'Doing the place up – and that costs a lot of money,' Jinty pointed out.

'If this house could only be restored back to its former glory I'm sure you would be able to hire it and the gardens to a film company. I would *love* to make a film here!'

'Coffee, Ms Whitelaw?' Kay had found a tray cloth from somewhere and covered the work-worn tray with it before setting out cups and saucers instead of the everyday mugs. There was even a plate of biscuits, and sugar in a bowl instead of the usual tin.

'Thank you, my dear. I don't believe I've met you before . . .?'

'I'm Kay McGregor. I'm working in the kitchen for the summer, and can I just say that my mother and father and I loved *Bridlington Close*. It hasn't been the same since you left.'

'How kind of you to say so! Tell your parents that I thank them, too.'

'They both died last year.'

'Oh dear! You have very good bones, and good skin. Do you take after your mother?'

'I'm not sure.'

'Take my advice, dear, and always use a decent skin cream, it's worth every penny,' Meredith said sweetly, and Kay flushed with pleasure and promised to use only the best skin cream in future.

Nine

Recalling that Ginny's overpowering mother was due to visit that day, Lewis Ralston-Kerr had had the sense to scoop up Rowena Chloe and head for a distant garden centre. While his parents were having an uncomfortable time he was wandering happily round the centre with the little girl chattering non-stop beside him.

He returned in the late afternoon to find his parents recovering from Meredith's visit while Kay and Jinty prepared vegetables for the evening meal.

'Ms Whitelaw arrived in a limousine driven by a chauffeur,' Jinty informed him. 'Isn't it exciting, to have someone as famous as she is right here in our village? I told her how much everyone loved her new television sitcom and she let us in on some little bits of gossip from the set. And she's going to bring some of her actor friends to the garden party,' she rattled on excitedly as Rowena Chloe and Muffin embarked on a noisy welcome after a day apart. 'I'm going to ask Helen Campbell to let the *Dumfries News* know about it – it'll bring folk in from all over the place!'

'She's asked if we can give her and her friends dinner after the fête –' Fliss's brows were furrowed – 'and she wants us to open the dining room for the occasion. I don't really see how we can possibly entertain a whole lot of people to a meal. That room's not been touched for years!'

'Of course you can, Mrs F. I'll get the Women's Rural Institute members to help me to put the room to rights, and the drawing room too, for coffee afterwards.'

'I'll help as well,' Kay offered at once.

'And Gracie and Joe down at the Neurotic Cuckoo will

probably be willing to do the catering. I'm sure that the WRI
would be willing to assist with serving the meal, too.' Jinty had
everything planned already. 'If you ask me, getting the chance
to meet some famous actors will be a right treat for them.
Leave everything to me.'

'There's another thing, Lewis.' Hector's brow was furrowed
with anxiety. 'The woman's talking about getting someone to
make-up the house . . .'

'Do a makeover,' Kay corrected him. 'Get the place all sorted.
She thinks people would be willing to make films here –
imagine that!'

'Good grief! Where's Ginny?' Lewis wanted to know.

Hector glanced vaguely round the big old-fashioned kitchen.
'She went to see her mother off, but she didn't come back
afterwards. She must have decided to return to work.'

'She'll either be up at the grotto or in the kitchen garden,'
Jinty advised, noting with interest that Lewis always seemed
to enquire about Ginny's whereabouts when he had been away
for a while.

Lewis found Ginny sitting on a large upturned flower pot by
the kitchen garden polytunnel, staring into space and chewing
on some parsley.

'Hi. Jinty's going wild with excitement over your mother's
visit, but my folks look a bit shell-shocked. Come to think of
it, so do you.'

She hunched her shoulders, turning slightly away from him.
'I'd better warn you that I've been mother-ridden to bits and
I'm not good company. Flee while you still can.'

'I'll take a chance.' He turned another empty pot over and
sat down. 'So you didn't have a good visit.'

'She just walked in and took over, the way she always does.
I don't interfere with *her* lifestyle, so why does she keep trying
to interfere with mine? Why can't she understand that I'm a
gardener, not a blasted fashion model? She seems to think that
I ought to go to work wearing a pretty frock and high heels,
with my hair immaculate and my nails manicured. It's not
funny!' she snapped as he started to laugh.

'Sorry, I know it's not. It's just that I got a sudden picture of you knee deep in the lake as you were almost all of last summer, clearing out mud and pondweed while wearing a frock. Don't let her bother you, Ginny.'

'It wouldn't be so bad if she was just paying one of her flying visits, but she's going to be here for ages because of that blasted play.'

'Doesn't she have to get back to Spain for the next series of her sitcom?'

'Not until October. That means that she'll be here for something like six or seven weeks. How am I going to stand it?' Ginny burst out in despair. 'She's going to be in her glory, opening the garden fête. She's bringing a bunch of actors from the play. Jinty's beside herself with excitement.'

'Yes, I heard all about that from her, and from Kay. But once the fête's over you'll not see much of your mother because she'll be kept busy with the play. You'll get by with a little help from your friends,' he consoled her. 'Me, for one – we're mates, Ginny, and I'll do my best to act as a buffer between you.'

'Thanks,' she retorted, but without much conviction, adding, 'though I notice that you made yourself scarce this morning before she arrived.'

'I thought it was best to keep Rowena Chloe out on the way, and I managed to get everything you wanted from the garden centre. I couldn't get it all in the car – I kept losing Rowena Chloe among the greenery on the drive home as it was. But they're delivering the rest tomorrow morning. The time's definitely come for me to find the money to buy a van or a small truck.'

'Did you hear about her crack-brained idea of the Hall being used for filming?'

'Kay said something about that. D'you think she really meant it?'

'Oh yes – when she said it. Don't worry, she's probably forgotten it by now. My mother's always grabbing at interesting schemes that never happen – like turning me into a fashion model. It's a daft idea anyway – Linn Hall is a beautiful family home, not a film set! I just wish she hadn't barged in and upset everyone,' Ginny said mournfully. 'This is where I live and work, and I hate it when she tries to take over. I don't walk on to her film sets and try to tell *her* what to do, do I? I wish Jinty had never come up with the idea of asking her to open the fête!'

'Don't get upset about it – she'll bring in extra visitors, which will be good for us financially, then she'll go back to Spain and you won't have to see her again for ages.' He got to his feet and reached a hand down to haul her up. 'Come and help me unpack what I brought back.'

'In a minute.'

'OK,' Lewis said, and ambled off, unaware of the real reason for her misery. On one hand she had a mother who wanted her to give up the work she loved and become girly in feminine clothing, with her short black hair coaxed somehow into a fashionable style; and on the other she had Lewis, the man she adored, who accepted her as the gardener she was but never seemed to notice that she was a woman as well.

'Why don't you make yourself useful?' she asked a bird foraging in a nearby vegetable bed for worms. 'Try turning yourself into a fairy godmother ready to grant me three wishes. Two would do – the first one would be to swoosh my mother back to Spain and keep her there, and the second would be to make Lewis notice me as something more than a pal in jeans, handy for scooping mud out of the lake!'

Sadly, the bird had just located a worm and paid no attention.

Thanks to Jinty, the news that Meredith Whitelaw was going to open the Linn Hall Garden Fête spread round the village like wildfire. Helen Campbell, who wrote a weekly column about village happenings for the local newspaper, put it into her next column.

Fliss panicked when she read it.

'But you already knew, Mrs F,' Jinty pointed out. 'It can't have come as a shock, surely.'

'It's just that it didn't seem real until I saw it in print for everyone to read. Now there's no going back!'

'There wasn't any going back once Ms Whitelaw had agreed. Think of the publicity – it'll bring in people who've never thought of coming to our little fête before, especially as the paper says that some of the other actors from the play will be coming with her. And the gardens are looking splendid now, so the visitors'll have lots to see. I bet the stable shop will do well *and* the afternoon teas here in the kitchen.' Jinty's eyes shone with excitement. 'We're going to be put on the map!'

'I don't know if Hector and I are ready to be put on a map. And Ginny's mother wanting a dinner afterwards, in this house – however are we going to do that?'

'I've already told you that we'll manage, with help from the village. And everyone's willing to do what they can – I've already put out some feelers. The dining room table's big, so you need enough guests to make it look presentable. We can find out how many of Ms Whitelaw's people will be coming to the fête with her, and then there's you and Mr Ralston-Kerr and Lewis – and Ginny, of course. And you can invite some of the village people such as the school headmistress and Mr and Mrs Kavanagh, since he's chairman of the Progress Committee. You could include Elinor Pearce, since Ms Whitelaw took such an interest in the drama group when her poor husband was running it, rest his soul.'

'But the dining room hasn't been used for years . . .'

'Alma Parr's still chairwoman of the WRI, and I've spoken to her about them helping you out. If you include her and her husband George among the dinner guests, I'm quite sure that Alma will set the entire Rural to work to lick the dining room into shape, and the drawing room too. It's amazing what polished furniture and clean windows and lots of flowers can do to a room. And,' said Jinty, getting into her stride, 'it'd give us a great chance to use that lovely china and silver stored away in the butler's pantry and in the upstairs rooms; there's plenty of it. Don't you worry, Mrs F, we'll get the place looking lovely before we're done,' she ended happily.

'Who's going to serve the dinner?'

'Me, for one,' Kay McGregor put in from the sink, where she was preparing vegetables for the backpackers' lunch. '*Please* let me – it would give me a chance to be near Meredith Whitelaw!' Her hazel eyes sparkled behind their spectacles.

'There you are, Mrs F, our first volunteer, and I reckon that some of the other local youngsters like my girls and their friends would be willing as well – with some of the Rural to oversee them. They'd all do it just for the thrill of seeing Ginny's mother and her actor friends, like Kay here. I'll organize a team and supervise them, like the housekeeper here probably did in the old days,' Jinty offered. 'Every question has an answer, my mum used to say, and she was never wrong.'

'Oh no!' Cynthia MacBain peered over the top of the *Dumfries News* at her husband, who was peacefully reading a book on bee-keeping and enjoying the last piece of toast spread with honey from his own bees. 'Have you seen this?'

'What, dear?'

'The Ralston-Kerrs have only gone and invited Meredith Whitelaw to open this year's garden fête!'

'She's appearing in a play in Dumfries, isn't she? And since she's Ginny Whitelaw's mother I suppose it's only natural that they've approached her to do something for the village. She's a big name – well,' Gilbert said, hurriedly amending the comment as his wife's eyes narrowed dangerously, '*quite* a big name.'

'So *she* seems to think. I hope she doesn't come poking her nose into the drama group's business again. If you ask me, she can't act her way out of a paper bag. She's nothing but a hack, Gilbert! Don't you remember the carry on we had during rehearsals when Kevin was besotted enough to let her appear in one of our plays?' Cynthia was still stinging from Meredith's first appearance in Prior's Ford, when the actress, 'resting' after being axed from a television soap, had charmed her way into the local drama group and persuaded Kevin Pearce, its founder and director, to offer her the lead part in their play – a part which was already Cynthia's. 'She made a mess of it – and then off she went as soon as she was offered a part in that television play, deserting Kevin—'

'And you, my love, stepped into the breach and saved him by returning to the play and making a huge success of it,' Gilbert reminded her. 'I doubt if she'll have time to get involved in our drama group this time. After all, she *is* a professional actress.'

'And I'd like to know how she managed *that*,' Cynthia snapped. 'On second thoughts, I'd rather not know. We've all heard of casting couches, haven't we?'

'I've always wondered if that casting couch rumour was true.'

'I'm quite sure it is – for Meredith Whitelaw, at any rate. Good heavens, is that the time?' Cynthia said as the grandfather clock in the hall chimed. 'I'd better be off.'

'You don't want to be late only days before the end of term,' Gilbert agreed. 'I've left your briefcase and the car keys at the front door, as usual.'

Once Cynthia had gone he stacked the dishwasher and switched it on before pouring another cup of coffee to drink at his leisure while wandering round his beloved garden. The seven-year difference in their ages meant that Cynthia was still teaching while he himself had retired; he enjoyed keeping the garden in good shape, reading the daily newspaper from end to end over a leisurely cup of coffee, playing the church organ for services, taking small parts in the local drama club, nurturing his beehives and having the house to himself five days a week.

It was a peaceful existence, and much as he loved his wife, he tended to believe that the school summer holidays were over-long.

As ever, he kept his favourite spot, the three beehives at the end of the long garden, till last on his tour. The bees, on this lovely summer's day, were already hard at work.

'Let's just enjoy ourselves while we may,' Gilbert told them, settling on a rustic bench.

Ten

Now that Rowena Chloe was back at Linn Hall, it seemed to all who lived and worked there that the place had taken on an extra sparkle – even Duncan was seen to smile when she paused on her busy way from here to there to talk to him.

She flitted around the house and gardens from breakfast to bedtime, old enough now to look after herself – not that she needed to look after herself because Muffin, her devoted slave, accompanied her everywhere.

'Like that big dog called Nana in Peter Pan,' Kay said in wonder. 'He always seems to know where she is, even if she manages to slip away while he's eating his dinner or having a nap.'

The big old rocking horse had been brought down to the kitchen from the top floor of the house; on wet days she rode it almost non-stop, rocking so vigorously that there were times when Muffin, Fliss and Hector all feared that she would come flying off – but she never did. When the weather was good she was out of doors, chattering to visitors on open days, playing with the children who accompanied their parents, and even showing people around.

She adored the grotto and soon learned how to use the thick ivy stems as a ladder so that she could scramble up on to the roof and back down again with ease. She and Ginny spent many hours up there, making up stories and jokes.

Ginny and Jimmy McDonald had set aside a small corner of the kitchen garden especially for the little girl, and she spent ages there, digging, planting, weeding and hoeing a motley collection of herbs and flowers, using the set of children's gardening tools that Lewis had bought for her.

'I'm playing at being Ginny,' she informed her father when he found her working at her little patch of ground.

'How on earth,' Jinty said as she and Fliss, washing and drying the lunch dishes, watched the little girl playing in the stable yard with Muffin, 'can that child's mother bear to be away from her? The first years before they start school are the best years in a mother's life, and I wouldn't have missed a day of them for all the tea in China.'

'I know. Little ones have to learn so much so quickly – how to smile, and to recognize people, and crawl, then walk and talk. Then it all changes when they go to school, and they have so many more new things to learn. I often think that if we could keep the learning ability that children have in their first five or six years for all of our lives, we'd be geniuses.'

'Just as well that we don't, Mrs F. Can you imagine what it

would be like to have to live with a bunch of geniuses? I don't understand Molly Ewing, really I don't!'

'I think she genuinely loves her little daughter – remember the way she was when Rowena Chloe was younger?'

'That's true. Perhaps Molly thinks of her like a baby doll that she was able to dress up and play with, but now she's almost reached school age she's not so interesting. It's a good thing that that child's so relaxed about being passed from one family to the other.'

'What's going to happen if Molly and this young man she's with now have a baby of their own? Are they going to come back here to live, and perhaps take Rowena Chloe away from us? Lewis would be heartbroken!'

'We all would. But I don't think you need to worry about it,' Jinty said. 'Remember when Molly's sister told me that Molly got pregnant by this boyfriend of hers when they were school sweethearts and she had to have an abortion? I'm quite sure that that young madam's well aware of when to have a baby and when it doesn't suit.'

'What d'you mean?'

'I mean that I think she deliberately fell pregnant with Rowena Chloe in order to get engaged to your Lewis. She'd know full well that he would do the right thing by her, and at that time she was full of the idea of being the mistress of Linn Hall one day.'

'Well, whatever the reason, I'm glad that Rowena Chloe got born, for I can't imagine life without her now,' Fliss said as a peal of childish laughter, to her mind the most beautiful music in the world, floated through the open window.

Stella Hesslet was leaving the village store, a shopping basket over her arm, when she met Malcolm Finlay on his way in.

'Ah, it's Miss – er – um – the library lady.' He doffed his hat. 'My apologies, I'm not good with names, only faces. I link them with objects, and with you, it's books.'

'Stella Hesslet. Are you settling in to the village, Dr Finlay?'

'Yes indeed. I'm glad I met you, Miss Hesslet, because I had intended to ask for your advice when the library next came to the village. You don't mind if I do so now? After all, you're off duty and here to enjoy yourself. I shouldn't really be troubling you on a professional matter—'

'Not at all,' Stella fluttered.

'Thank you. In fact – if you're not in a hurry, could I offer you a drink, or perhaps a cup of tea or coffee, at the local hostelry?'

'That's very kind – a cup of tea would be welcome.'

'Good,' he said and took the basket from her, confiding as they began to cross the village green, 'I'm enjoying village life even more than I had hoped. The people here are so kind, and the whole pace of life suits me better than the busy town life I've been used to for so many years. Not only that, but the landlady of the Neurotic Cuckoo is a wonderful cook. I find myself tending to eat there more frequently than I should, given my waistline.'

It was clear to Stella, from the warmth of the welcome he received from the Fishers when the two of them went into the pub, that he was a frequent visitor. She herself rarely went into the place, being on her own most of the time.

'I shouldn't really be troubling you with my problems on what I assume is your day off,' he said when they had given their orders.

'Not at all – please go on.'

'Thank you, you're very kind. It's a professional matter – I write articles for various academic publications, but I've never learned to master the art of typing. My hands always seem to be too big for the keys.' He brandished the guilty hands, large and with fingers as thick as sausages, at her. 'For many years a very efficient lady has been typing them out swiftly and neatly for me. We had arranged that when I moved here I could post my handwritten work to her, and she would post the typed results back to me, but unfortunately she's now suffering from something called repetitive strain injury. I have to find another typist until she recovers, and I wondered if you might know of someone locally, or if there's an agency of some sort in the area that could help me?'

At that moment Gracie arrived with tea for Stella and coffee for Malcolm; when they had settled with their drinks, Stella said, 'I know that Helen Campbell's done quite a lot of typing for people, including college and university students and lecturers. She lives in Slaemuir, the council estate near your cottage.'

'You think she might be willing to help me out?'

'Possibly – she's a very pleasant young woman, and most capable, too.'

He produced a diary and pen from his jacket pocket, found an empty page, and handed book and pen across the table. 'If you can give me her address, I'll call on her.'

Stella wrote the address down. 'And if she comes into the library van before you see her, I'll let her know that you'd like to speak to her.'

Gilbert MacBain returned from a trip to a shop in the nearby town of Kirkcudbright, where he was delivering jars of honey, to find his wife busy at the computer.

'I've just booked us a ten-day holiday in Sardinia,' she announced triumphantly as the printer spat out sheets of information.

'What? When?'

'At the beginning of August. We'll get back home before the new term starts.'

'But you don't like going on holiday – you always say that you prefer a quiet time at home between terms.'

'I suddenly felt like having a change of scene. You don't mind, do you?'

'Of course not; you know that if it makes you happy, it makes me happy. What about the drama rehearsals?' he suddenly realized.

'We'll only miss four, and it's for the first time ever, unlike any of the others. You and I are already word perfect, and our holiday will give Lynn the chance she badly needs to concentrate on getting the others up to our standards – if that's possible.'

'We'll miss the Linn Hall garden fête as well.'

'Will we? I didn't think of that,' Cynthia said. 'What a pity. Still, if you've seen one you've seen them all, and we've never seen Sardinia.'

They had never seen Meredith Whitelaw opening the local garden fête either, Gilbert suddenly realized, but had the sense not to say it aloud.

★   ★   ★

The first episode of Helen's serial had been returned, to her dismay, with several pages of notes. A long phone conversation with the magazine's fiction editor followed.

'Don't worry about a thing,' the woman had assured her. 'You passed the worst hurdle when you won the competition; now you're only just starting to learn how to write your very first ever serial, hopefully the first of many. You're on a learning curve, and it's my job to guide you. So let's start by going through my notes one by one.'

The phone conversation had been helpful, and so were the earlier editions of the magazine sent to her so that she could study the layout of previous serials by different writers. To her delight, the first episode rewrite had been accepted, and she was now halfway through her second, and totally immersed in the storyline, when the doorbell rang, interrupting a difficult scene.

'Oh – sugar!' She was tempted to ignore it, but then it rang again and she had no option but to hurry downstairs to find out who was to blame for the interruption.

A large man with curly greying hair beamed at her as she opened the door. 'Mrs Campbell? I'm Malcolm Finlay. I recently moved into Thatcher's Cottage.' He held out a hand. 'How do you do?'

'Oh – yes. How do you do?' Her hand disappeared into his to be shaken firmly but gently, then released, while she tried hurriedly to recall where she had heard his name before, quite recently.

'Miss Hesslet, the librarian, may have mentioned to you that I was looking for a typist?'

'Ah!' Now she remembered. 'Yes, she did. As a matter of fact, Dr Finlay, I've got quite a lot of work on at the moment—'

'Please let me throw myself on your mercy, young lady,' her visitor said, then gave her a smile so warm and so amazingly charming that the refusal froze in her throat. 'Give me just two minutes of your time to plead my case.'

Helen found herself taking a step back and opening the door wide. 'Would you like to come in?'

'Thank you.' He followed her into the living room, where she hurriedly began to sweep discarded toys off the couch.

'Don't go to any trouble on my account, dear lady. I'll sit here.' He perched on the edge of an upright chair. 'And I promise not to take up too much of your time. My subject is philosophy, and since I retired a few years ago I've been kept remarkably busy writing articles on a regular basis for academic publications. To be honest, I've enjoyed the work because it helps to keep the mind active. I hand-write my articles because I'm terrified of computers.' He gave her another of his amazing smiles. 'To me, they're the spawn of the devil. A very capable woman near to where I used to live typed them out for me on her computer, and we had agreed that when I moved, I would post my work to her, and she would make it all readable and post the results back. But now she's got a wrist complaint and I'm told that she won't be able to do any typing for some considerable time. I have a contract for more articles, and if you could only help me until she recovers I would be eternally grateful.'

He looked so like a cuddly bear, harmless but helpless, that Helen found herself wanting to assist him. 'My problem is that I've recently been given the chance to write a magazine serial, and I write the village column for our local weekly newspaper as well; and then there's my husband and the children to look after—' she began apologetically. There was, of course, the other task, but she couldn't tell him that once every two weeks, having seen Duncan off to work and the children off to school, she stopped being Helen Campbell, wife, mother and hoped-to-be writer, and turned into Lucinda Keen, the *Dumfries News* agony aunt.

If Malcolm Finlay had tried more persuasion she might have managed to refuse him, but instead he said, 'My goodness, Mrs Campbell, you're a very busy lady, and I can quite understand that you don't have any free time. I'll perhaps find an agency in Kirkcudbright, or Dumfries. Thank you for being so courteous, I appreciate it.'

He was getting to his feet when she heard herself say, 'What length are the articles?'

'I've brought one with me – if you have time to look at it.' He delved into the pocket of his tweed jacket and produced an envelope. 'I'm not sure that you'll be able to make out my writing, and there are some words that may not be familiar to you.' He took about half a dozen sheets of paper from the envelope and sat down again while Helen unfolded them.

Years of typing for university lecturers and students had introduced her to all sorts of academic words and phrases, while reading the agony aunt letters, sometimes with the scrawled writing smudged by tears, or possibly, she thought at times, by spilled tea, had sharpened her eyes.

Surprisingly, it turned out that Malcolm Finlay's handwriting was large and almost childish, which not only made it easy to read, but also meant that the article was shorter than expected. There were a few words Helen didn't understand, but she was used to working with a dictionary.

'How much work would you need typed in a week?'

'I've got four articles at the moment; they've just been returned by my usual typist. After that, it's usually one a week, much the same length as that one.'

'I think I could manage that.' It would mean having to work over the weekend, when Duncan and the children were around, but now that Gregor and Gemma were both in secondary school, they could be relied on to provide some help with their two younger siblings. Gemma, bless her, was very like Helen, and enjoyed cooking and even the occasional bout of housework.

'I could start by typing the four articles for you, just to see if I can fit them in,' she offered.

'That would be much appreciated, it really would, Mrs Campbell. I'll drop the others in later today.' He started to get up again. 'I forgot to ask how much you charge per article,' he said, and when she told him, added: 'That's far too reasonable. I insist on paying double.'

'But—'

'My dear young lady, you have just lifted a load off my shoulders, and you've been so kind that I wouldn't dream of offering a penny less. Bless you!' he said, and once again, her hand disappeared into his surprisingly gentle grip.

As he went off down the garden path she closed the front door, then glanced in the hall mirror and saw that she was beaming from ear to ear. Four articles at double the money, plus the payments she had discovered that she would get as each episode of the serial was accepted – she was going to be rich! Not what most people would call rich, but certainly richer than she would have dared to hope only two months earlier.

She rushed upstairs to settle before her precious, elderly computer, her fingers flying over the keys as she set down the words suddenly tumbling into her mind.

Eleven

Jinty had been right when she told Fliss that the Women's Rural members would be happy to help with the preparations for the after-fête dinner. A few days before the event, Alma Parr led an army of women up the drive to the Hall, each lugging a bag of household necessities and eager to have their first look inside the house.

Suddenly the residential rooms, having been neglected for a good thirty years or more, became a hive of activity. Curtains covering the long, wide windows were thrown open, followed by bouts of collective coughing as the women found themselves showered by years of dust from the heavy material. The curtains were then taken down and hauled outside to have the dust shaken from them. Windows were cleaned until they sparkled, floors vacuumed, furniture polished, picture frames, ornaments and statuettes washed or dusted.

The top floor was invaded by an army of women eager to locate the beautiful vases, china and silverware that had once graced the long dining-room table. While some of them found time to help in the kitchen with baking for the fête, others flocked into the garden and drove Duncan crazy with demands for flowers and greenery with which to decorate the entrance hall, dining room and drawing room.

When they were at last allowed to have a look at the results of two days of hard labour the Ralston-Halls were stunned. The big gloomy rooms that frankly terrified them were bright, with sunlight flooding through the huge, crystal-clear windows that provided wonderful views of the lawns and flower beds nearest to the house. Vacuumed carpets and well-beaten curtains displayed brilliant colours that had gone unnoticed for so long; floor surrounds, furniture, crystal glassware and silver on the dining-room table caught and reflected the sunlight, and the rooms were filled with vases of flowers. Most of the magnificent old chamber pots once needed for long-ago house-parties had been auctioned off in the past few years, but some had been retained, and now, thanks to the nimble fingers of some of the Rural members, they were so filled with blossoms that no casual observer would have guessed as to their original use.

Each big fireplace boasted carefully arranged floral displays. In the hall, an old wooden cradle someone had discovered in the big nursery Hector had played in as a child was also massed with colour, while two large vases on stands had been placed on either side of the wide staircase.

'I had no idea that this old house could look so good,' Fliss gasped.

'I remember . . .' Hector's eyes were suddenly damp. 'When I was a child I remember seeing it like this when my grand-parents lived here. But I'd forgotten, until now.'

'How can we ever thank you?' Fliss asked the smiling group of women.

'You don't have to bother,' Alma Parr told her. 'We've had the best time ever.'

'And we can't wait to do more during the fête,' another woman chimed in. 'Some of us will run stalls, as usual, and the rest can help in the kitchen. We'll all help to serve dinner to you and your guests afterwards. It will be such fun to work in such a lovely big house instead of what we're used to.'

On the big day the sun smiled down on the Linn Hall estate, which was packed with visitors. Many of them came from further afield than usual, tempted by the well-broadcast news that Meredith Whitelaw was to be the guest of honour.

An hour before the fête opened, the villagers setting up stalls on the lawns stopped to gape as two limousines swept up the drive, carrying Meredith and her fellow actors.

Meredith herself, dressed to the nines and wearing a hat that wouldn't have been out of place on Ladies Day at Ascot, emerged from the first car and paused to wave graciously to her public and sign some autographs. She received a round of applause as she led her fellow actors into the house, where Jinty had had the foresight to organize coffee in the drawing room for them.

When the grounds were filled with visitors and the time came for the fête to be opened, she reappeared through the French windows opening on to the terrace, where a sound system had been set up, and delivered a long but magnificent speech in a ringing voice, ending with, 'My hosts have been kind enough to set up a small tent where, later in the afternoon, my friends and I will be very happy to meet our public and sign autographs. And now I am delighted to declare this year's Linn Hall fête open. Have a wonderful day, everyone, and be sure to spend, spend, spend!'

'You've got to hand it to your mother, Ginny,' Lewis's good friend Cam Gordon murmured under cover of enthusiastic applause. 'She certainly knows how to wow a crowd. I bet she was great at narrating nursery rhymes when you were little.'

'When she was there, which wasn't often, and if you fancy Little Bo Peep thundered at you as if it had been written by William Shakespeare,' Ginny retorted as her mother set out to tour the various stalls, accompanied, to the Ralston-Kerr family's relief, by Alma Parr and the Women's Rural Institute committee.

Fliss, Hector and Lewis, each with a built-in hatred of being in the public eye, had claimed that they were needed elsewhere; Hector in the improvised car park, Fliss, who had a rarely-used artistic streak, helping Anja Jacobsen and Maggie Cameron with face-painting and Lewis showing people round the grounds with assistance from some of the summer workers – and, of course, Rowena Chloe, sporting a magnificently painted lion-face.

Alma and her committee were only too pleased to look after Meredith – apart from anything else, it had provided them all with the perfect excuse to splash out on new outfits.

The guest of honour played her part to perfection, smilingly pausing at each stall to buy some small item which was then handed over to a member of her entourage. At the end of the day, she suggested to Alma that they be used for prizes in WRI competitions.

'I travel so much,' she said, 'that ornaments can be rather a nuisance at times – other than those given to me on very special occasions or by very special people.'

'How kind,' Alma said, knowing full well that everything would have to be given to charity shops, since almost all the items on the stalls had been donated locally, and the donors, many watching Meredith closely and looking forward to bragging that she had bought something of theirs, would not appreciate getting their item back as, for instance, a prize for a WRI best flower arrangement in a shoe.

At the tombola stall, run by Steph McDonald and Cam Gordon, Meredith halted to buy a ticket and discovered that she had won a little china pig. 'How very sweet,' she said, then, about to hand it to one of her attendants, she paused and looked again at Steph. 'Don't I know you, dear?'

'I'm Stephanie McDonald, Ms Whitelaw. When you were staying here a few years ago you were kind enough to give me some acting lessons.'

'Of course! A talented little actress, as I recall.'

'I'm looking forward to seeing your play in Dumfries – a whole lot of us have hired a bus to take us to the theatre, and I myself can hardly wait!'

'Thank you, my dear. What are you doing now?'

'Playing the part of Cecily Cardew in *The Importance of Being Earnest*.'

'Well done! I must try to see your performance. Which theatre are you appearing in?'

Steph blushed. 'It's – er – in the village hall. The local drama group, next month.'

Meredith was shocked. 'You didn't go to drama school as I suggested?'

'It's expensive, you see. I'm training to be a nursery nurse, but I'm planning on studying drama when I can afford the fees.'

'But in the meantime – such a waste of a young talent. Don't lose the passion, my dear – never lose the passion! Here—' Meredith held out the small china pig. 'Let this be my gift to you – a lucky charm, I hope, and a reminder to keep sight of your proper goal in life!' Then, as they moved towards the next stall, 'Who is that lady behind the counter? Her face is familiar.'

'That's Elinor Pearce,' Alma told her. 'Her husband Kevin was the drama club director before his – his death last year.'

'Of course – poor Kevin, a man of such talent, to be cut down in his prime! And poor Elinor, I must go and speak to her!' And Meredith was off, with her attendants hot on her heels.

'Poor Elinor indeed,' Cam said, noticing the look of apprehension flitting across Elinor's face as the actress bore down on her. 'What are you going to do with that quite ugly little ornament, Steph – put it back on the table for someone else?'

'Of course not! It was given to me by Ms Whitelaw. I'm keeping it for ever. It might bring me luck.'

'You never told me that she'd given you acting lessons.'

'That was long before we started going out together. I was at school then.'

'I didn't even know that you wanted to be a proper actress.'

'It's what I've always wanted.' Steph stroked the pig's head with the tip of a finger. 'And it's going to happen – one day.'

'Look,' Kay McGregor whispered, 'Meredith Whitelaw's coming our way!'

'Oh dear . . .' Elinor had thought of staying away from the fête once she heard who was opening it, and then told herself not to be a coward. Now, watching Meredith bear down on her, she quailed slightly before taking a deep breath and stiffening her back.

'Elinor, my dear, I was hoping to see you – how are you? So brave, helping the community after the terrible tragedy! I can't *tell* you how shocked I was to hear of poor Kevin's murder!'

'Thank you, Ms Whitelaw.'

'A man of many talents, and such a loss to the world! How have you been able to bear it?'

'I've had no option but to bear it.' Elinor did her best to sound civil.

'I know a very good therapist – I could send you his name and address if it would help; he's guided me through many a moment of black despair. Acting is a very stressful career.'

'My friends and neighbours have been extremely supportive and helpful,' Elinor was saying when someone came panting up to announce that some press photographers had just arrived.

'Must dash – perhaps we'll find the time to chat later,' Meredith said and hurried off.

'I didn't realize that you actually know her,' Kay said.

'She was involved in the local drama group when she lived here for a while, just after leaving that television soap. My husband ran the drama group, and they became quite friendly.'

'*That's* why she was so upset about your loss. Isn't she wonderful? So very caring. I met her when she came to the Hall – I'd no idea until then that Ginny was her daughter. My mum and me never missed an episode of *Bridlington Close.* I remember the two of us crying buckets during her death scene. It was so *real!* We went through an entire box of tissues – man-sized, they were. Even my dad got a bit damp-eyed. I'll never forget it.'

'Mmmm,' Elinor said absently, making a mental note to ask Fliss if she could be seated at some distance from the guest of honour at dinner.

Malcolm Finlay and Stella Hesslet came face to face while wandering around the stalls. 'Miss Hesslet, isn't it? The book lady!'

'Good afternoon, Dr Finlay.'

'I have to thank you from the bottom of my heart for telling me about Mrs Campbell. She's taken on the task of typing articles for me, and I cannot tell you what a relief it is.'

'I'm so glad to hear it.'

Malcolm glanced around at the busy stalls. 'Is there a tea tent here?'

'Refreshments are being served in the kitchen, round at the back of the Hall.'

'Then would you be kind enough to come and share a pot of tea with me? As a thank you for your help?'

'You really don't have to, Dr Finlay.'

'But I would like to – if you're agreeable.' He offered his arm and, flushing with excitement, Stella took it and guided him towards the house.

As the last of the visitors wandered down the drive after a very successful day, the summer estate-workers sprang into action and began to clear stalls and pick up litter while the Women's Rural split into three groups: one going to the kitchen to prepare a meal for the young workers, another putting last-minute touches to the dining room and the third heading in cars to the Neurotic Cuckoo to collect the official dinner.

It fell to Alma and two of her committee to take Meredith and her friends to a quiet corner of the terrace for a drink while their hosts changed for the evening event.

Ginny, anxious to keep well out of her mother's way as much as possible, had arranged to work in the busy stable shop all day; she had also tried to get out of attending the dinner to be held in the Hall's formal dining room after the fête was over, but all three Ralston-Kerrs insisted on her presence.

'Can I possibly borrow that outfit you loaned me last year, when Lewis took me to the pub for a birthday dinner?' she had asked her best friend, Lynn Stacey, the week before.

'Of course. Why not collect the clothes this evening and have supper with me? You can help me to choose something to wear for the occasion,' suggested Lynn, who, as headmistress of the primary school, was an invited guest. 'I'm really looking forward to dining at Linn Hall!'

Twelve

Once she got back to her camper van, Ginny changed as quickly as she could into the blouse and skirt borrowed from Lynn, gave her hair a quick brush and then hurried back to her mother.

'I thought you might like to see what I've been working

on while I've been here – the pond we've restored in the rose garden, and the lake beyond that.'

'Please excuse me,' Meredith said sweetly to the others. 'My daughter and I are going to share some family time.'

'We've been concentrating on certain parts of the grounds for the past year,' Ginny began as they crossed the lawns, 'and I'm so pleased that we got them finished in time for this summer's visitors.'

'I think I handled today quite well, don't you?'

'You were very professional, Mother – as always.'

'It's all a matter of playing a part. You have to be trained for that sort of thing. Where did you get that nice blouse and skirt, darling? They really do manage to make you look quite stylish.'

'I borrowed them from a friend,' Ginny admitted, and her mother sighed.

'I might have known. I'd hoped that you had started to take an interest in your appearance. While I'm here we should try to get to Edinburgh together – have a lovely shopping day out, with lunch somewhere special. I can't wait to choose some really nice outfits for you.'

Ginny, too, sighed, but inwardly. 'There's no point in wasting money on new clothes for me when I never have occasion to wear them.'

'But you should *find* occasions to wear nice clothes. You look almost pretty when you make the effort, like this evening. You've got quite a good figure, and you shouldn't keep hiding it away under woollies and jeans. It's such a waste!'

'I feel more comfortable in woollies and jeans. You wear what suits your lifestyle – why can't I wear what suits my lifestyle?'

'How are you ever going to find a husband when you insist on dressing like a workman?'

'I'm not looking for a husband,' Ginny said stubbornly.

'Don't be ridiculous! You've just had your twenty-fifth birthday.'

'Thirtieth, actually.'

'*What?*' Meredith almost shrieked, a hand flying to her bosom. 'Don't be ridiculous. You're twenty-five.'

'Thirty, Mother. I'm thirty.'

'But I'm only – not old enough to have a thirty-year-old daughter!'

'I know how old I am,' Ginny told her relentlessly. 'I keep count.'

'The important thing is, Genevieve, that whatever age you may *think* you are, you're old enough to be preparing to make a good marriage. You're practically on the shelf.'

Ginny suddenly saw herself perched on a potting-shed shelf – it would, of course, have to be a potting-shed shelf – among the trays of seedlings, and had to turn a giggle into a cough. Fortunately Meredith, absorbed in her argument, didn't notice.

'Every young woman wants to marry. You don't *have* to have children, you know. Women have the right now to choose how they want to live their lives; it's not the way it was when I was younger, thank God. In those days everyone expected married women to ruin their figures by producing families, then devote the best years of their lives to raising them.' She gave a theatrical shudder at the prospect. It didn't bother Ginny, as she had known all her life that her mother didn't have a maternal bone in her pampered body.

'Who was that good-looking young man – the one with the long brown hair and the lovely smile?' Meredith wanted to know as she and her daughter left the lawns and began to follow the path leading to the rose garden.

'I don't know.'

'You must know him; everyone else seemed to. He was casually dressed, but looking quite stylish at the same time – he has the figure to pull it off – and he was being very attentive to his mother,' Meredith went on as Ginny looked puzzled. 'He never once left her side.'

'Oh – you must mean Alastair Marshall. He's an artist, and he used to live in the village, but now he's working in an art gallery in Glasgow.'

'An artist? Is he successful?'

'Possibly – I don't know him all that well. We have some of his paintings for sale in the stable shop.'

'Is he married?'

'No, and he wasn't with his mother, he was with his partner,

Clarissa Ramsay. She lives in the village, and Alastair comes back regularly to see her.'

'His partner in the art gallery, you mean?'

'No, Mother, his partner in life.'

Meredith gave a small scream. 'That woman with the hair badly in need of a colour rinse and no idea of how important it is to use really good make-up? Surely not!'

'She's a very nice woman, and Alastair's a very nice man, and they're happy together.'

'For goodness sake, Ginny, you make far too much use of that word "nice". Even as a child you thought that everyone you met was nice!'

Ginny gave up on conversation for a moment, being too busy fighting the temptation to howl like a dog. Perhaps, when she described the people she now knew as 'nice', what she really meant was 'normal'. She had never felt right as part of her mother's theatrical world; had never, in fact, felt as though she fitted in anywhere until she came to Prior's Ford, and in particular to Linn Hall. Yes, she decided as she led Meredith along the path to the rose garden, the people she really liked and felt at home with were normal. And what was wrong with that?

'Isn't this an oasis of peace?' she asked as she and her mother reached the rose garden. 'Visitors love it.'

Crazy-paving paths wound between and around raised beds filled with blossoms ranging in size from miniatures to climbers and cascading blooms. Under the August sun the place was a riot of colour, from pure white, then through creamy to shades of salmon, pink and red, and on into scarlet, yellow, apricot and blue. The early-evening air was filled with their scent, and with the sound of a constant stream of crystal-clear water pouring from the urn held by a little nymph standing on a pedestal in the centre of the ornamental pool. Pots of miniature roses in all colours clustered around her slender bare feet.

Meredith cast an eye over the garden. 'This place would make a wonderful background for a modelling session. The Ralston-Kerrs could make a lot of money out of that sort of thing. What's their son's name again?'

'Lewis.'

'*He's* not married, is he?'

'No. There's a path at the other side of the rose garden that leads through trees to the lake. You must see the lake – I've spent hours clearing the banks and installing water-loving plants. I'm really excited about it.'

'Who does that little red-haired girl belong to?' Meredith wanted to know as they headed for the woodland path linking the rose garden and the lake. 'He seems very fond of her.'

'That's Rowena Chloe, his daughter. She's adorable.'

'He has a daughter? Where's her mother?'

'She and Lewis were engaged, but she's got another partner now. Rowena Chloe spends the Easter and summer holidays here with the Ralston-Kerrs, and she stays with her mother's family the rest of the time. She's as bright as a button, and we all enjoy having her around. Look, Mother . . .' Ginny bent to touch an attractive green plant arching elegantly from the surrounding ferns. 'This is Solomon's Seal; I remember reading about it in the Sam Pig books when I was little, and I always wanted to see it in real life. A month or so ago it was covered with hanging white bells. The visitors love it.'

Meredith glanced down and drew her skirt out of the plant's way. 'So he's unattached – this Lewis?'

'Yes, he's like me,' Ginny said grimly. 'Unattached, and that's the way we both like it.' And then, with relief, 'Here's the lake; isn't it delightful?'

Despite the Ralston-Kerrs' original misgivings, the dinner was a complete success. The food was delicious, and Meredith revelled in her position as the guest of honour. She and her fellow actors clearly relished the admiration they received from all the villagers, and by the time they led their guests across the flower-decked entrance hall to the dusted, vacuumed and polished drawing room for coffee and brandies, Fliss and Hector had begun to relax – until Meredith, breaking away from a group of fans, pinned them both into a corner and asked, indicating the drawing room with an elegant sweep of one arm, 'Are you aware of just how much money this place could make for you?'

'We've been thinking of opening the ground floor to visitors

in a year or so, but there's so much to do first, and it's a matter
of waiting until we can get another bank loan,' Fliss began.

'Oh, I'm sure there are other ways of getting things smartened
up! Think of all the makeover programmes people love to watch
on television nowadays – I'm sure a good film director would
love to make a programme about this lovely old house being
restored. You should give it some serious thought.'

'We'll – think about it, of course. Won't we, Hector?'

'What? Oh yes – indeed,' Hector was stammering when
Ginny came to tell her mother that the limousines had arrived
to take the thespians back to their Dumfries hotel.

Everyone spilled out on to the front steps and the gravelled
sweep to wave them off and then, as the cars disappeared
down the driveway, the villagers began to take their leave,
Alma and the other WRI members assuring their hosts that
they would be back in the morning to clear everything away.

'I'd best get home,' Jinty said. 'It's been a big success, hasn't
it? Something to remember. I'll be back in the morning to
help put everything to rights.'

'And Ginny and Lynn and I are going down to the gatehouses – there's a celebration party being held there,' Lewis
told his parents. 'You're welcome to come with us.'

'I think we'll just get to bed, thanks,' his mother said, and
his father nodded agreement.

'OK, we'll leave you to enjoy some peace and quiet – and
don't do any clearing up, it'll all be tackled in the morning.
I've checked on Rowena Chloe, and she's out cold, which
isn't surprising. She was asleep by the time I carried her upstairs
so I just put her to bed with her clothes on. There's face paint
smeared all over her pillow but I expect it'll come out in the
wash.' Lewis looked around the half-moon sweep of gravel
before the big door. 'It feels strange, leaving by the front door
for once.'

'I almost enjoyed today,' Hector said in wonderment when he
and his wife were back in the butler's pantry, finishing off what
was left of the after-dinner port.

'So did I, once I realized that it was going well,' Fliss admitted.
'It struck me halfway through the evening that that's only the

third time I've eaten in the dining room. The first was our wedding breakfast, then Lewis's christening. He looked so sweet, didn't he, in that satin gown and the little hat trimmed with white fur?'

'Mmm. The next time will probably be his wedding.'

'If he ever gets over Molly. Poor Lewis, I hope he finds someone else.'

'I expect he will, one day.'

'If he doesn't, what's going to happen to this place?'

'Let's not worry about that tonight. Listen, Fliss—' Hector held up a hand.

'I can't hear anything – it's not Rowena Chloe, is it?' Fliss began to rise.

'No, sit down. I meant, isn't it nice and quiet now that everyone's gone?'

'Mmm. I suppose we really should do something about the first-floor rooms, Hector, now that the place is watertight and the grounds almost finished. Several people mentioned today that they would have enjoyed seeing round the house as part of the attractions. From their enthusiasm, it sounds as though we could make more money by opening the place to the public.'

'I suppose it's time to consider it,' her husband admitted. 'It seems unfair to expect people to visit the gardens and deny them the house – as long as you're not thinking of taking up that actress woman's idea of doing whatever it was she called it to the place.'

'Of course not. I just meant letting people see the downstairs rooms as well as the gardens. They looked quite nice once they were dusted and the curtains opened and lots of flowers brought in. That might be enough. We'll talk to Lewis about it – some time.'

'Yes, some time. You wouldn't actually want to live there, would you? Eat in the dining room, sit in the drawing room, that sort of thing?'

'Good gracious, no; I'd feel like a pea rolling around inside a drum. In any case, if we started using those huge rooms I'd have to buy some decent clothes. We both would.'

'Not worth the cost at our age,' Hector agreed. Then, as

his wife stifled a yawn, 'Let's get up to bed, dear, it's been a busy day – and a most successful one too. But thank goodness it's over for another year.'

They were making their way across the kitchen to the door that opened into the front of the house when Muffin, who slept in the kitchen, gave a sleepy little yap and lifted his head. Then he jumped out of his basket and hurried anxiously to the door, whining.

Fliss halted and clutched at Hector's arm. 'It's not burglars, is it? We locked the front door after everyone left, didn't we?'

'Yes, we did, and if it was a burglar, Muffin would bark instead of that snuffling and whining,' Hector assured her. Even so, he made sure that his wife was slightly behind him as he went to the door and opened it.

A small, red-headed figure stumbled in, rubbing at her eyes. Her clothes were creased, and when she blinked up at them, her face was like a rainbow that had met with an accident.

'Is it time to get up yet?' Rowena Chloe asked. 'I'm thirsty, and I'm hungry too. I'm ready for my breakfuss.'

Thirteen

'Who *is* that girl?' Sam Brennan asked his partner as their latest customer left the village store. 'I feel as if I should know her, but I can't think of her name.'

'That's Kay McGregor, one of the youngsters working at the Hall this summer.'

'Why did I think she was a local lassie?'

'I assume that it's because she's in here so often,' Marcy said. 'She works in the kitchen with Jinty McDonald, and she does most of the shopping. And she's a friendly soul.'

'She certainly likes to talk.' Kay had been their only customer, and after packing everything into two shopping bags she had lingered to talk about the fête, and how exciting it had been to see Meredith Whitelaw and to be a waitress at the dinner in Meredith's honour.

'I love it here,' she said. 'My two best friends have gone off to explore France this summer, and I almost went with them, but I decided to see a bit of my own country instead, and I think I made the right decision. It's a lovely village in a lovely area. D'you know something? I think I've been having a better summer than they are – I've really enjoyed working in that big old house, and when I meet up with my pals again I can tell everyone that I've met a famous actress. I bet they'll be green with envy when we compare notes!'

'What do you do in your normal life?' Sam asked.

'I wasn't clever enough to make university, so I took a college course in bookkeeping and office work – shorthand and computing. The course has just finished, so I'll have to find a job when I finish here.' Kay gave a gusty sigh. 'It'll probably be dead boring after being in Prior's Ford, so I'm going to stay on for as long as I can – putting off the evil hour.' Then, as the door opened to admit several people, she gathered up her bags. 'I'll leave you in peace. Bye.'

All too soon August was into its last two weeks. Lynn Stacey opened the primary school for the autumn term, and Val and Tony Ewing drove down from Inverness to collect Rowena Chloe.

'I don't want to go to my other home,' the little girl told Ginny on her last morning as the two of them sat on top of the grotto, looking down over the Hall to the village below. 'I like it here with you and Daddy and Muffin and you.'

'You said me twice.'

'That's because I really, really like you, Ginny.' Rowena Chloe gave Ginny such an enthusiastic hug that for a moment the two of them were in danger of toppling over the edge.

'But you like your other home too, don't you?' Ginny said when order had been restored. 'And you'll be able to see all your friends at the nursery school when you get back.'

'Yes. I wish I had wings like this . . .' Rowena Chloe stretched her arms out and flapped them vigorously. 'Then I could just fly here to see Granfizz and Grandpa and have my dinner with all of you! Then I could just flap my wings . . .' This time she flapped her arms so vigorously that her round little bottom started to bounce across the stone roof and Ginny caught at the back of her shirt, afraid that she might work her way to the edge. '. . . and go back to my other house to play with my friend Amy.'

'If you had wings you would be a bird instead of a girl and you would live in a nest at the top of a tree.'

'That would be nice too,' Rowena Chloe decided. 'I could fly and fly all day and then go to sleep in my nest, like this.' She tried to push her head underneath her arm.

'And eat worms all the time instead of cake.'

'I wouldn't be that sort of bird. I'd be a cake-bird. What would you do if you were a bird and you could fly all over the whole sky wherever you wanted to go?'

'I'd stay right here, in this garden,' Ginny said as Lewis arrived.

'Time to come down,' he called up to them from where he stood below, hands on hips. 'It's almost lunchtime.'

'I'm a bird, daddy,' Rowena Chloe shouted back. 'Catch me!' She jumped to her feet and headed for the edge of the roof, flapping her arms.

'No!' Ginny shouted, reaching out. But the little girl was too quick for her, and the tips of her fingers just managed to brush against the back of her checked shirt before Rowena Chloe stepped confidently off the grotto roof, calling again, 'Catch me!'

'Lewis . . .!' Ginny got to the edge just in time to see his arms swing up, and the child fall straight into them. She landed with enough force to make him take a step or two back as his arms closed tightly around her.

'Don't ever do that again,' Ginny heard him say as she scrambled down to join them.

'But you catched me, Daddy, like I knew you would. Now put me down,' his daughter ordered, and when he did as he was told, she skipped ahead of them, going down the steep hill with practised ease.

'She doesn't know the meaning of the word fear, does she?' Ginny said as the two of them, still shaken, followed.

'No, but I do,' Lewis answered. 'I don't know what I would do if anything ever happened to her!'

*   *   *

By the time the Ewings arrived, both well bronzed from a sun far warmer than the British variety, Rowena Chloe was ready for the journey back to Inverness. As her other grandparents got out of the car, she ran to greet them, and Tony swept her up into his arms and carried her into the kitchen.

'Have you had a good holiday, Princess?' he asked.

'Ab-sol-*lute*-ly,' she told him cheerfully.

'Your mummy sends you lots of hugs and kisses,' Val said. 'And there's a big new dolly from her as well, waiting for you at home.'

'How is Molly?' Fliss asked.

'Loving Portugal. She and Bob are coming home in October for Bob's sister's wedding, so she'll be able to spend time with Weena then. Did you hear that, Weena? Your mummy's coming to see you soon. That'll be exciting, won't it?'

'Mmmm,' said Rowena Chloe, astride her rocking horse. 'Look at me galloping across the fields, Papa!'

When the time came for her to leave, she insisted on hugging everyone, including the rocking horse and Muffin.

'Why don't we take Muffin with us?' she suggested to her grandparents. 'He needs a holiday.'

Val shuddered at the prospect of a large hairy dog rampaging over her smart home. 'No, petal, I don't think so.'

'OK. P'raps another time.' The little girl hugged Ginny tightly. 'Look after my garden for me till I get back,' she whispered, her lips tickling the lobe of Ginny's ear. 'And look after my daddy, and Muffin.'

'I will.' Ginny set her down and rubbed at her ear.

Finally, the farewells over, Rowena picked up the big fancy doll from Portugal that had spent the past two months sitting in a chair in her bedroom, and looked up at Lewis.

'We need a carry to the car, Daddy,' she said, and he gathered her and the doll into his arms.

When the car left, with Rowena Chloe blowing extravagant kisses through the rear window, there was a sudden silence before everyone began to disperse. Lewis was the first to disappear, without a word to anyone.

'There's one good thing, Mrs F,' Ginny heard Jinty say as the two women and Hector returned to the kitchen, 'that little girl is well-loved, by the Ewings as well as us. And she knows it. That's why she can move from one set of grandparents to the other without a tear or a wobble. With so much loving, she doesn't really need her mother.'

That, Ginny thought as she walked down to the rose garden, was a blessing. She herself had never had a proper mother, and it had hurt through all the years until she arrived at Linn Hall and realized that life had its compensations.

'I'm lucky,' she told Muffin, who for some reason had opted to follow her.

To her surprise, Lewis was sitting on one of the benches, watching the water pour from the nymph's urn. She would have retreated silently, but Muffin hurried over to put his head on Lewis's knee as though trying to provide comfort, or seeking it. As he fondled the dog's ears he looked up and saw Ginny hesitating.

'Come and sit down.'

'You don't want to be alone?'

'I did, in a way, but you're different. Surprising, how empty a place can suddenly seem when one little girl leaves,' he went on as she sat down beside him.

'One little girl with one big personality.'

'She's pretty fantastic, isn't she?'

'Totally. I got the fright of my life when she walked off the edge of the grotto roof this morning.'

'Me too. Thank God I managed to catch her.'

'Just as she knew you would. I envy her in a way.' The words were out before Ginny had time to stop them.

'Why?'

'It was something that Jinty said after the Ewings had driven away. She said that although Rowena Chloe's mother isn't around, she's loved by a lot of people, including two sets of grandparents and you. I know what it's like not to have a mother who's always there for you, but my father wasn't there either, nor grandparents. Just nannies. It was – lonely.'

As though he understood what she was saying, Muffin left Lewis just then to lean his big, heavy head on Ginny's knee.

'It must have been lonely, but amazingly, you've come through it.'

'I'm not sure that I did come through it, until I started working here, in the Linn estate. I suddenly felt, almost at once, that I'd come home.'

'That's good to know. You're part of the place now, and I'd hate to lose you,' Lewis said, and her heart gave a startled jump. Then he went on, 'You're like one of the family – the kid sister I never had. This place wouldn't be the same without you. Well – back to work.'

He gave her knee a friendly pat and then got up and left, Muffin gambolling after him.

'Darn it!' Ginny said aloud when man and dog were out of earshot. 'Well done, Genevieve! Now he looks on me as his kid sister!'

A pile of scribbled papers, delivered on the previous evening by Malcolm Finlay, stood by Helen Campbell's elbow, and her fingers, darting over the computer keys, were going at top speed. She had become used to his handwriting surprisingly quickly, although she rarely understood much of what he wrote.

As always, she was working against the clock. To her relief, the school summer holidays were over, and the autumn term had just begun, which meant that she had more time to herself during the day. The beds were all made, the lunch organized, and Helen planned to do some shopping in the village in the afternoon, which gave her one hour to complete Malcolm's article. With any luck she would manage about two hours' work on her magazine serial in the afternoon.

These days, every second counted, so when the doorbell rang she muttered something unprintable under her breath before hitting the computer's 'save' button and hurrying downstairs to find Jenny on the doorstep.

'I've just picked the last of the raspberries, and there are too many for us, so I thought you might like some . . . but I've come at a bad time, haven't I? I'll leave them with you and go.'

'No, come on in and have a coffee.'

'Are you sure . . .?'

'Absolutely. I need one myself, and it's a bad day when I turn a friend away, especially when she comes bearing gorgeous gifts.' As she led the way into the kitchen, Helen lifted the bag to her nose and inhaled the almost-perfumed scent of the soft red fruits. 'Thanks, they'll be perfect for tonight's pudding.'

'You sit down, and I'll do the coffee,' ordered Jenny, who knew her way around her friend's kitchen. 'To be honest, love, we're all a bit worried about you having to work so hard. You're looking tired. You shouldn't have agreed to do typing for Dr Finlay right after you'd won that serial competition.'

Helen took the biscuit tin down from the shelf and opened it. 'I'll admit to you, but don't tell the others because Ingrid will start scolding me, that there are times when I feel like a circus juggler, trying to keep half a dozen balls in the air at the same time without dropping any; but that's what being a wife, mother, agony aunt and writer's all about.'

'I'm not so sure, and neither are the others.' Jenny spooned instant coffee into mugs. 'Doesn't Duncan notice that you're tired, and try to make you ease up?'

'I don't think he notices much at all, including me. After all those years of marriage I reckon that to him, I'm part of the furniture. To tell the truth, Jenny, Dr Finlay's very generous when it comes to payment, but I haven't told Duncan that. For the first time since we got married I've been able to open my own bank account, and it's growing nicely.'

Jenny set the mugs of coffee on the table and sat down. 'Presumably Duncan doesn't know about this account?'

'No idea,' Helen said happily.

'Good for you!'

'It's so good to know that I've got some money of my own for emergencies. Remember that Dr Finlay's got his own typist and once she's recovered from her repetitive strain injury he'll return to her. I need to make hay while the sun's shining.'

'Just be careful, and don't take anything else on until you've completed the serial. That,' Jenny pointed out, 'is the road to your future as a novelist.'

'I hope! How are the kids?'

'No worries there so far, touch wood.' Jenny tapped on the table. 'Calum loves school and Maggie's determined to make the most of her final school year. She's still talking about journalism as a career.'

★　　★　　★

There was still time after Jenny had gone for Helen to finish the article she was typing out. Feeling refreshed by her friend's visit, she hurried back upstairs and returned to work.

She had just finished the article, checked it carefully for errors and printed it out when she heard Lachlan's and Irene's voices as they came running along the road. They burst into the house, breathless and glowing from the dash between school and home, as she came down the stairs.

Exactly one noisy hour later they were fed, gone, the dishes washed and she was back in the bedroom she shared with Duncan, settling down at the long piece of wood balanced on two sets of drawers that she called her desk.

Sometimes Dr Finlay handed in only one article, sometimes two; today, it was two. As Helen gathered up the pages she had just typed, tapped them on the desk to coax them into a tidy set and slipped them into a cardboard folder she glanced up at the wall clock. She had half an hour to herself; that should give her enough time to key in most of the next set of notes, and if the work went well she might even manage to fit in some more work on the next episode of her serial before heading down to the kitchen to start on preparations for dinner. All the free time on the following day would have to be given to the newspaper's fortnightly agony aunt page.

She brought up a fresh page on the computer screen, lifted the first sheet of lined paper – Dr Finlay always used lined paper – and began to read swiftly. Then she gave a puzzled frown and went back to the first line, this time reading slowly and carefully. Half an hour later she had read to the end of the pile without having typed a single word.

She went downstairs to pick up the phone and dial a number. The phone at the other end of the line burred several times before the receiver was picked up.

'It's Helen – Helen Campbell,' she said. 'I wonder – could I come and have a word with you tomorrow morning, around nine o'clock?'

Fourteen

'I need help with a problem.'

'You're Jamie Greenlees, aren't you?' Naomi Hennessey asked the child standing on the manse doorstep.

'That's right. I live in the Neurotic Cuckoo across the village green with my mum and my gran and grandad. I see you in church on Sundays, and sometimes when you visit the school.'

'Yes, of course. Well, you'd better come in. I was in the middle of filling up the washing machine,' Naomi went on as Jamie followed her broad back through the cluttered hall and into the cluttered kitchen, 'so I'll just get that finished first if you don't mind.'

'Oh, you've got a cat.' He squatted to stroke the large marmalade cat.

'That's Caspar.'

'We can't have a pet because fur makes my gran sneeze, but I've got a rabbit called Tommy that lives at the farm. Aunt Jess and Ewan gave him to me for my last birthday.'

Naomi shut the machine's door and pressed the start button. 'Does your mother know you're here?'

'Not exactly – she said I could go to play with Faith and Frankie McDonald, and I'm going there as soon as I leave here.'

'We'd better make it quick, then. Do you like lemonade?'

'Yes, please. I heard Aunt Jess at the farm saying that she always goes to you when she needs advice, so that's why I'm here now,' Jamie explained as the lemonade was being poured.

'It's part of my job as a minister. Keeping things secret is part of my job too,' Naomi assured him. 'So what's your problem?'

On open days at Linn Hall, Hector Ralston-Kerr's task was to exchange money paid at the gate for tickets, direct cars along a short side drive leading to a cleared parking area, and welcome all comers. Although a painfully shy man, he had come to enjoy the task and was proud of himself for managing to be useful.

But he recoiled on the Saturday when the near passenger window of the car drawn up before him was rolled down to reveal Meredith Whitelaw.

'Hector, sweetie, how nice to see you again. I've brought two very clever friends who are going to help you and Fliss with your lovely home, as promised. Straight up the drive, Fergus, then park in front of the house,' she instructed the driver and rolled the window up again.

'Wasn't that Ginny's mother?' asked Kay McGregor, who had just brought him a flask of hot coffee and some sandwiches.

'Good Lord . . .' The food and drink went flying as Hector tried to scramble out of his chair. 'I have to warn Fliss—'

'I'll go, you stay.' Kay dug into her pocket and brought out her mobile phone. 'I'll phone Ginny on my way,' she added, and she sped up the driveway, skimming past cars and talking into the phone as she went, while Hector's refreshments disappeared under the wheels of a car turning in at the gate.

Ginny was helping Lewis to arrange trays of winter bedding plants in the stable shop when her phone rang.

'What? Are you sure? No, you go on round to the kitchen and warn them to set up some refreshments while I go to the front door – and get someone to open it when I ring the bell, will you – no, hold on, it'd be better for me to get to the door from inside so I'll go in through the back door.' She snapped the phone shut. 'That was Kay; my mother's arrived with some people – they're coming up the drive right now.'

'On an open day? My parents'll go into a panic!'

'Your father's already in one – he was the first to see them. I'll go through the kitchen, it's faster. You'll have to stay here,' she added as some visitors appeared.

'I'll try to find someone to take over from me,' he called after her.

As she ran across the courtyard Kay appeared round the corner and they burst into the kitchen together, Kay making for Jinty while Ginny sped through the baize door leading to the main hall. She opened the door to see her mother standing on the gravel sweep, arms gesticulating as she talked to the man and woman with her.

Meredith turned as her daughter came down the steps. 'Genevieve, darling, what perfect timing! Come and meet my friends. My daughter is one of the gardeners here,' she told her companions in a voice trained to hit the back wall of any large theatre, 'which explains her rather strange appearance.'

'I think we worked that out for ourselves, Meredith,' the man said, striding forward and extending a hand to Ginny. 'Fergus Matheson – you're looking a bit startled, if you don't mind me saying so. Did you not get advance warning?' He himself was dressed casually in faded jeans tucked into high boots, an open-necked shirt and a broad-brimmed safari hat. His voice was deep, his accent pleasantly Scottish, his eyes amused and his hand large, with a firm grip.

'I'm afraid not – this is one of our open days, so everyone's quite busy.'

'Meredith, you've landed us on our hosts without warning.'

'Are you sure? I thought I'd phoned you the other day, Genevieve – but theatre life's so hectic now that the play's started its run that I may have forgotten. Is Fliss in the kitchen?'

'She's probably on her way here now.'

'Good, because Angela's longing to see inside the house, aren't you, darling?'

'Indeed. How do you do? I'm Angela Steele.' She was quite tall and well-built, with a great mass of scarlet hair that couldn't possibly be her natural colour swirling around a pretty, beautifully made-up face dominated by eyes the colour of emeralds. She wore a loose, ankle-length patterned silk dress under a lacy shawl, and her handshake was firm and brief.

'This isn't the first time you and I have seen each other,' she went on, giving Ginny a warm smile. 'The last time was years ago, when your mother held a party and your nanny brought you downstairs to meet the guests. But you won't remember that. You cried, and I don't blame you. Do you really like being called Genevieve?'

'I prefer Ginny.'

'Much more sensible. My mother christened me Angelica but when I started to bite her every time she said it, she soon changed it to Angela – I should perhaps say that I was only four at the time and I haven't bitten anyone since then.'

The more Fliss saw of Meredith Whitelaw the more the woman terrified her, and if Jinty hadn't offered to accompany her she would probably not have been able to leave the kitchen's safe familiarity and venture to the entrance hall, where she was immediately hailed by Meredith.

'And here at last is our hostess! Fliss, I've brought my dear friend Angela to save your lovely home. She's the best interior designer in the country, and she's going to work wonders with this magnificent home of yours. Aren't you, Angela?'

'That,' said Angela Steele, 'remains to be seen. How do you do, Mrs Ralston-Kerr? Forgive us for bursting in on you unexpectedly. I've just found out that this is a really busy day for you, but I'd love to have a quick look around the ground floor, if you can spare the time.'

'Not a problem, Mrs F,' Jinty told her employer cheerfully, 'we'll keep things going in the kitchen – that's where we do teas for the visitors,' she informed the newcomers, 'so if you'd like to start with the study and library and dining room that'll give me time to arrange for refreshments to be served to you later, in the drawing room. Ginny, you'll help Mrs F, won't you?'

'Of course.' Ginny gave Fliss a reassuring smile as Jinty hurried off. 'Shall we begin with the study?'

Angela Steele dipped into her shoulder bag, large enough to be used for weekend luggage, and took out a notebook and pen. 'I'd prefer to begin here, in the hall, if I may. It's most impressive – have your husband's family always lived here, Mrs Ralston-Kerr?'

'Yes, indeed. As I understand it, one of my husband's ancestors built it so that he could live close to his slate quarry, just outside the village. The house was built in the early nineteenth century – I'm not quite sure of the exact year.'

'It was built in eighteen hundred and nine,' Ginny offered, 'to a design by a Dumfries architect – Walter Newall, I think his name was. I've spent time studying family papers, trying to work out what the gardens looked like in their heyday.'

'Well recalled,' Fergus Matheson said, and she blushed at the compliment.

'Yes, indeed,' Angela agreed. 'The staircase is very fine. What do you plan for the upper floors?'

'Nothing for the time being. My husband and son and I have our bedrooms on the next floor, but the other rooms there and on the top floor are used for storage. We only recently managed, thanks to an unexpected and very generous donation, to get the roof and windows repaired. We've been thinking of doing something about the ground floor rooms, though, because several visitors have said that they would like to be able to see something of the house as well as the grounds.'

'I've told Fliss and her husband that they'd be mad not to do it as soon as possible,' Meredith interrupted.

'It would certainly be worth your while financially, in the long run,' Angela commented. Her green eyes noted every piece of furniture and every portrait and painting, and she scribbled copious notes as Fliss led her visitors around the ground floor, with Ginny hurrying before them to pull the curtains back to let as much light into the place as possible.

Angela Steele took her time in each room, and to his mother's open relief Lewis arrived just as they reached the drawing room, apologizing for his absence as he shook hands.

'Things can be hectic on an open day – I'm responsible for the stable shop today, and I had to find someone who was free to take over.'

Angela's bright eyes swept over him, clearly liking what they saw. 'Our fault, we should have made sure that you knew we were coming. So what exactly is the stable shop?'

'It's set up in the old stable block, to sell bedding plants, fruit and vegetables, photographs of the gardens and the house, and whatever else we can think of to separate our visitors from their money. It was Ginny's idea – she found a whole lot of items in the rooms upstairs when she first arrived here and came up with the idea of starting up the shop in order to sell the smaller things off to raise money for the place. The more important finds went to auction.'

'A young woman with many talents,' Fergus Matheson commented.

'We think so,' Lewis responded as Jinty, who had managed to cover a small table by one of the windows with a crisp damask cloth and a selection of scones and cakes, bustled in with a teapot, followed by Kay with coffee.

'You have a wonderful view,' Fergus said as they settled at the table. 'The grounds must take a lot of looking after.'

'When I was a child and my grandparents lived in the Hall there was a fleet of gardeners, but those times are long past,' Lewis told him wryly. 'Up until a few years ago we could only afford one full-time gardener to help me, plus hiring young students who spend their summer breaks working in places like this. They live in the two gatehouses and eat in the kitchen in return for working in the gardens and the kitchen.'

'Is that how you come to be here?' Angela asked Ginny.

'No – my mother rented one of the houses in Prior's Ford a few years ago after she was—'

'—overworked and advised to take a rest,' Meredith broke in swiftly. 'Genevieve came along to nurse me back to health.'

'You're a nurse?' Fergus's well-shaped eyebrows arched.

'No, just a daughter. I was working in a garden centre at the time. When Lewis offered to show me round the estate I fell in love with the place. I've been installed here ever since.'

'We couldn't manage without her now,' Fliss broke in. 'Ginny's done wonders in the gardens; she even discovered a whole lot of foreign plants that one of my husband's great-uncles brought back from abroad. They'd been forgotten about, but thanks to Ginny and the publicity the surviving plants have given us we've had more visitors this year.'

'And the open days have enabled the Ralston-Kerrs to bring in an assistant gardener, a lad who lives in the village,' Ginny contributed.

'I'd like to see those foreign plants,' Fergus said.

'Unfortunately,' Meredith cut in, 'I have to get back to Dumfries for a photocall before tonight's performance. When one is involved in a television series one tends to forget how exhausting live theatre can be. You've seen all you need to see for the moment, haven't you, Angela?'

'Yes, I think I have. You have a charming home, Mrs Ralston-Kerr, thank you for showing us around it. I'll send you a written report on what can be done to help you open it to the public.'

'How long do the grounds stay open to the public?' Fergus asked Ginny as they followed the others out to the car.

'Until the end of September.'

'Good. I'll be back before then for a tour of the gardens,' he promised.

'I'm really sorry about this,' Ginny said as the three visitors drove off. 'My mother had no right to bring people to look round the house without warning – and without asking Mr Ralston-Kerr's permission.'

'It's not your fault, dear,' Fliss assured her. 'We always enjoy seeing your mother. What's bothering me is that we can't really afford to spend more money on the house at the moment – can we, Lewis?'

'That's something we'll worry about when it happens,' her son said firmly. 'You heard the designer say that she'd send written recommendations on what needs to be done; they could be interesting, I suppose, but we don't have to act on them unless we want to – and until we can afford it.'

'I suppose you're right, dear. I think I'll walk down the drive to have a word with Hector; he'll be wondering what's going on.'

'You do that, Mum. I tell you what, why don't I take you and Dad to the Cuckoo for a meal tonight?'

Fliss looked uncertain. 'Can you afford that?'

'I can afford the occasional decent meal and a glass of wine – plus some brandy with the coffee. It's my treat, and it would do you both good.'

'I suppose I could put on my opening-the-garden-fête dress – and Hector could give his suit an airing.' Enthusiasm began to creep into Fliss's voice. 'It would be nice to get out for a little while. I'll ask your father.'

'And make sure he says yes,' Lewis called after her as she left.

'You go back through the hall, Ginny, so that you can shut the front door. I'm going to look for Duncan. Why don't you join us for dinner?' he added as she began to mount the steps.

'I think it should just be you and your parents. After all, you're taking them out to make amends for the fright my mother gave them, landing her friends on them as she did without warning.'

'You're not responsible for your mother, Ginny.'

'I wish I could believe that,' she said wryly. 'In any case, tonight should be a family occasion.'

'It still will be – as I've said before, you're family as far as we're concerned.'

'As you said before – your younger sister?' Ginny couldn't quite keep the dry note from her voice.

He gave her a puzzled look before saying, 'If you want to put it that way. Or, in other words, I would like you to have dinner with us.'

She made one last try. 'I've got nothing decent to wear . . .'

'Have you got a clean shirt and pair of jeans?' he asked, then when she nodded 'Perfect – that's what I'll be wearing. No need to borrow anything from Lynn Stacey this time.'

'*What?*' Her face suddenly felt hot.

'I've seen you both with the same outfit on – and you both look good in it.' He grinned up at her from where he stood on the gravel sweep. 'I'll book a table for the four of us at seven o'clock,' he added as he set off towards the corner of the house.

'I'm going to have to buy a decent outfit,' Ginny told herself as she went inside and shut the door.

Fifteen

'We'd given up on you,' Ingrid said as she opened the door to a breathless Helen. 'The others have been here for half an hour.'

'Sorry.' Helen followed her into the immaculate living room. 'Apologies, everyone. Marcy not here today?'

'Been and gone.'

'That's too bad.' Helen sank into a chair, running her hands through tousled hair. 'When I finally managed to get the kids off to school I thought I'd get some work done on the computer, then clean forgot to keep an eye on the clock. When I realized what time it was I ran all the way.'

'We know; you're puffing like a grampus, whatever that is,' Jenny said.

'The old name for a killer whale,' Ingrid told her. 'Ella found that out once during a school lesson and it was her favourite word for weeks. I'll bring fresh coffee.'

'Were you working on your serial?' Jenny wanted to know.

'I should have been, but I was finishing off something for Dr Finlay. I handed it in to him before I came here.'

'Hence the breathless rush. Are you sure you can keep helping him out like this? The magazine serial's important – you don't want to let them down after winning the competition.'

'They're happy with the first episode now, and I'm well into the second. I'm determined to keep both projects going while I can – with the children growing so fast I need the money. I Googled Dr Finlay,' Helen said, 'and it turns out that he's published two books that are used in universities and colleges, and he's a regular contributor to about half a dozen academic publications.' Then, as Ingrid arrived, bearing a steaming pot of coffee, 'I'm ready for this!'

'Prior's Ford feels like one of those villages in a horror film tonight,' Robert Kavanagh said as Joe Fisher poured his drink.

'What d'you mean?'

'Look about you, man – there's not a woman in this bar, is there?'

'That's not all that unusual – though I'll agree that there are usually a few.'

'And I'd be willing to bet that there's nobody in for a meal tonight.'

'True.'

'And all the men in here tonight are middle-aged. It's the *Village of the Damned*.' Robert picked up his drink and took a hefty swallow.

'What are you talking about?'

'Where,' Robert asked in a low voice, leaning over the counter, 'is your Gracie?'

'She's gone to . . . ahhh . . .!' It suddenly dawned on Joe. 'To Dumfries to see that play Meredith Whitelaw's in. That's what you're going on about.'

'Exactly. So's my Cissie and just about every woman in the village. And the men in here tonight are all around my age, and yours, because the younger married ones are at home, minding the youngsters. You're probably minding young Jamie, aren't you?'

Joe nodded. 'I can't deny it.'

Robert drained his glass. 'I'll have another. We'd best make the most of the peace and quiet because it's not going to last. They'll be talking about that play for weeks to come.'

In the MacBain household at around the same time, Cynthia was telling Gilbert, 'Tomorrow evening we'll have to be a little late for rehearsal – I'd say about twenty minutes.'

'Why?'

'Because almost everyone else in the drama group is off tonight to see *Blithe Spirit*, that's why. As soon as they get into the hall for rehearsal tomorrow, they're going to start going on about it, and I for one am not interested. Kevin would never allow idle chit-chat at a rehearsal; but sadly, Lynn Stacey's a little lax in that direction.'

'We've only got two more weeks before our own show – perhaps she'll be firm and insist on starting right away.'

'I doubt it, since she's off with the rest of them to see the play. Twenty minutes exactly, Gilbert – we'll spend the time here, working on our lines.'

'If you insist, dear,' said Gilbert, who would have been interested in going with the others to Dumfries, to see how a professional cast and director tackled a play.

If only Meredith Whitelaw hadn't been among the cast, he and Cynthia could have been in the audience, he thought as he began to work on the newspaper crossword.

'In fact,' Cynthia said, 'we should be having a run-through of the lines right now.'

'We're both word perfect.'

'I know, but it's important that we, at least, maintain the standards set by poor dear Kevin.'

'Indeed,' Gilbert said, putting the newspaper down.

The first thing Neil White did when he returned from his training course at Tulliallan Police College was to drive up the farm lane to his allotment, where he found everything in order and his mother-in-law so hard at work that she didn't notice his arrival until he tapped her on the shoulder.

'Neil!' She plunged the spade she had been using into the vegetable bed and hugged him before holding him back at arm's-length. 'You've changed in the past four weeks.'

'You think?'

'Definitely. There's a new confidence in your eyes, and darn it, you're even better looking than you were before.' Then, with swift concern, 'You've not met another woman, have you?'

'As if I'd had the time!'

'That's good, because Gloria's missed you.'

'Does that mean that she's really missed me, or she's missed me in the way that a boxer might miss the punch bag he uses for his training sessions after he's managed to burst it?'

'Don't be such a pessimist. She has missed you in the way that a woman misses the man she loves.'

'Did she say so?' He was still wary.

'A mother can tell,' Rosemary said enigmatically. 'Let's go to the pub for a drink and you can tell me all about what's been happening.'

'I'll need to put that on hold because there's a drama rehearsal tonight, and I must spend some time with my script before then. There's not much time left, and right now the play has to come before Gloria.'

He dropped a kiss on her cheek then headed for the gate, turning with his hand on the latch. 'Sorry – forgot to say thanks for taking care of the allotment. It looks great – and so do you.'

'I've loved working here – I've even put my name down on the waiting list. Good luck.'

'With what?'

'The job, and your wife – and with the drama rehearsals.'
She blew him a kiss.

Despite the MacBains' unexpected holiday and Neil White's
unexpected month-long training course, Lynn had somehow
managed to keep the drama club's rehearsals going by breaking
the play up into scenes. That night, knowing that Neil, who
held one of the principal parts, would be back from his training
course, she was aiming for a complete run-through.

Rehearsals began at seven thirty, and on this occasion she
arrived fifteen minutes early, aware that all those who had
been on the previous evening's theatre visit to Dumfries
would be anxious to talk about the event, and planning to
forestall them.

Fortunately, Kevin Pearce had instilled good timekeeping
into all members of the group, and as the minute hand of the
big clock set above the stage reached twenty-eight minutes
past the hour the first arrivals came in, already discussing the
previous evening. By thirty-three minutes past, the entire cast
was there, other than Cynthia and Gilbert MacBain.

Lynn clapped her hands. 'Attention, everyone! I know we
all had a wonderful time last night – the play was most
enjoyable, and Meredith Whitelaw and the rest of the cast
were superb, but yesterday was yesterday and today is today.
You've been given the chance to see a group of professional
actors in action, and I hope that as well as enjoying yourselves, you paid close attention, as I suggested on our way
there, to the individual performances. We go onstage in two
weeks' time for only three nights, and now that we've seen
the role models, I want you to do just as well as they did.
We've got Neil back with us – and we're delighted to see
you, Neil – and so we're going to forget about last night
and concentrate on tonight instead. I want to see the play
run through from start to finish, with a quick tea-break
between acts, during which I will give you my notes. So
– places, everyone, please.'

'Cynthia and Gilbert aren't here yet,' Alison Greenlees
pointed out.

'Knowing the MacBains, I'm willing to guess that Cynthia will be here with Gilbert in time for Lady Bracknell's entrance,' said Lynn, who, after years of teaching experience, had become very good at judging what was going on in adult's heads as well as in children's. 'Places, please!'

Five minutes before her entrance was due, Cynthia arrived with her husband, ready to switch personalities and step on to the stage as Lady Bracknell the moment she heard her cue.

'I'm impressed,' Lynn told her cast two hours later. 'We've got two weeks to go, and you're all ready to appear before your audiences.'

'That's thanks to dear Kevin,' Cynthia MacBain said at once. 'He was a professional to his fingertips, and he trained us all to follow in his footsteps.'

Cam grinned. 'That depends on how far we have to follow him.'

'Excuse me?'

'Poor old Kevin was murdered – I don't know that I want to follow too closely in his footsteps.'

'That's an offensive remark!' Gilbert snapped.

'And also typical,' his wife added. 'I'm just glad that Elinor isn't here this evening.'

'We do owe a lot to Kevin,' Charlie Crandall broke in swiftly, 'and to Lynn, who stepped in to continue his work at a time when we all felt so demoralized. She's done a wonderful job of pulling us back together.'

'Hear, hear!' Pete McDermott began to clap, and the others joined in slowly, the MacBains glaring at Cam, who smiled back, unruffled.

'Thank you, all of you,' Lynn said. 'I'm happy to announce that the costumes should be available on Monday, which should give us time to try them out before opening night. So – prompt arrivals then, please!'

Anja had been smiling warmly at Neil whenever their eyes met throughout the rehearsal. Knowing that she would expect him to walk her home as he usually did, he had been trying hard to think of a way to gently end their relationship. Having come up with new ideas as to how and when to tackle his estranged wife, he could no longer afford to be seen with Anja. Nor was it fair to let the girl continue to think that they had a future together.

So he let her slip her hand through his arm as usual as she left.

'Did you enjoy the police course?'

'It was terrific.'

'And you won?'

'I passed the exams; that means that I'm a detective constable now.'

'Congratulations – shall we get to your home and celebrate?' She snuggled closer as they stepped out of the community hall gates.

The moment had come. 'Actually, Anja . . .'

'This means that you walk me home – again – instead of me walking you home. You've found another woman, yes?'

'Not exactly found, but – how did you know?'

'Men are like the books, and women are like the readers. Your eyes were guilty every time you looked at me tonight. Is she beautiful?'

'I think so.'

'And does she appreciate you for the nice man you are?'

'I hope so. Anja, you're a very nice girl and I like you – a lot.'

'Never as much, I've thought, as *I* would have enjoyed liking *you*. British men are very shy, and I don't know why that's so. Perhaps it's because of the way they're treated by the British women.'

They walked the rest of the way to her aunt's house in silence while Neil tried to make sense of what she had just said. When they reached the gate, he said, 'You're a very sweet girl, Anja, and I'm sorry if you feel that I haven't appreciated you in the way you wanted me to.'

To his astonishment, she beamed up at him. 'Never be sorry, Neil. You have someone else in your life, just as I always have someone else in mine. There are plenty more fish in the sea, huh? It's been fun, you and me, but we call it a day now, though we will always be good friends.'

She pulled his head down, locked her soft mouth on his for a long, passionate kiss, then she was off up the path, turning at the door to give him a wave and a warm smile.

Sixteen

The wheeled ladder went one way, and Sam Brennan, who was on the top step, reaching up and to the side to fetch a box of soap powder from a high shelf, went the other. Inevitably, they parted company and the few customers in the village store scattered as Sam landed heavily on the floor.

'What's – Sam!' Marcy deserted the till, where she was totalling the goods in Cissie Kavanagh's basket, and raced to the back of the shop. 'Are you all right?'

'Of course I'm not all right!' Sam covered his head with his arms as he was deluged by packets falling from the shelf. 'Blasted steps!'

'How often have I told you that we need a new ladder? That old thing's an accident on wheels. I've said the same thing to him time and again but he never listens to me,' Marcy appealed to the shoppers who had gathered around, clucking sympathy.

'Never mind that. Just get me up, will you?'

'You take that arm, Marcy, and I'll take this one,' Alma Parr said. 'Someone fetch a chair from the back shop. OK, Sam, easy does it.'

She and Marcy had almost got him on to his feet when Sam gave a scream and crumpled, nearly pulling the two of them down on top of him. 'My ankle!' he yelped.

'Sit him on the floor till the chair arrives,' Alma directed, and then as someone brought one from the back shop: 'Which ankle hurts?'

'The right one. I think I felt something go when I landed on the ground.' His face was tight with pain.

'Let's have two people on each arm and someone ready to slide the chair in beneath him. Put your weight on the left ankle, Sam.'

When they had managed to get him on to the chair, Alma knelt and felt gently round his bad ankle. Sam yelped.

'I'll phone the doctor,' Cissie offered.

Alma shook her head. 'I think a doctor would recommend a visit to the Accident and Emergency department for X-rays. You might as well take him there yourself, Marcy.'

'I'll bring the van round to the door.'

'And what about the shop?' Sam wanted to know as Marcy made for the door.

'We'll close it, of course.'

'You will not! You stay here and I'll get a taxi to the hospital.'

'I am *not* going to let you go on your own. For goodness sake, man, stop being so silly!'

'Then I'll wait until six o'clock and you can drive me to A and E when the shop's closed.'

'Sam Brennan, you are the most . . .' Marcy began as Kay McGregor stepped forward from the small, gaping crowd.

'You take Sam to the hospital, Marcy, and I'll look after the shop until you get back. My parents used to have a shop like this, and I helped in it frequently,' she added as Marcy began to protest.

'The till—'

'I've used a till like that before. I'll phone Linn Hall and let them know where I am. I'm sure they'll understand. Go on now, poor Sam's in a lot of pain. The sooner you get there the sooner you'll be back.'

It was true that Sam's face was drawn and quite grey, so Marcy went to fetch the van and then, with help from some of the others, managed to get Sam into the passenger seat. Then she hurried back inside to where Kay was putting the ladder away in the back shop.

'You won't be able to manage the post office counter too.'

'I'll explain about that to the customers.'

'I don't know how long we might be. If we still haven't returned by six, close the shop and keep the keys until we get back. They're in the drawer below the till, together with a list of prices.'

'OK. Drive carefully, and good luck!' As the van left, Kay went behind the counter and said cheerfully, 'Right, everyone, form an orderly queue, please, and treat me gently because I'm probably going to be slower than Marcy and Sam are until I get into the way of it.'

★   ★   ★

Kay was about to close the shop when Marcy finally arrived, to report that Sam had ruptured his Achilles tendon.

'It sounds nasty.'

'It is.' Marcy looked tired. 'They're planning to operate as soon as possible, so I had to leave him behind. If they do manage to get him to theatre today I should be able to collect him around lunchtime tomorrow.'

'That's good news.'

'In one way, yes. In another perhaps not because Sam's a terrible patient and I'm going to have problems keeping him from getting back to work before he's able. Apparently an operation can help to speed up the recovery, but he'll still have to spend at least six weeks in plaster. So how did you get on?'

'It was fun. I was slow because it's been a while since I last worked in my parents' shop during school holidays but everyone was very kind and patient. I think you'll find everything in order. I phoned Linn Hall to explain what had happened, and Mrs Ralston-Kerr was very understanding. She says that I can keep on helping you while you need it, so I'll be here tomorrow to hold the fort while you go to collect Sam.'

'That's kind of her, and you.' Marcy ran her hands through her short dark hair. 'I'm going to have to take you both up on that offer until I know just what life's going to be like. D'you have to go back to the Hall right now?'

'No, the day's work will be finished and they'll be having dinner now.'

'D'you fancy a meal at the Cuckoo? I'll have to go back to the hospital for evening visiting, and to find out if they've managed to fit Sam's surgery in today. With all that's happened, I can't be bothered cooking and you'll have missed dinner at the Hall.'

Kay's face lit up. 'That would be great, thanks. It'll give us a chance to get to know each other properly.'

Because Neil was only just back from Tulliallan and was waiting to go into CID, and Gloria was working shifts, they hadn't seen each other in the twenty-four hours since his return.

The tough and intensive four-week training course had forced him to stop thinking as a husband and start thinking as an individual. He had learned a lot about himself and his capabilities, and once back in Prior's Ford he discovered the time spent on the course helped him to look at their situation in a new light. For one thing, he had to decide whether or not he still wanted to be married to her, and to spend the rest of his life with her.

The answer, clear and simple, was that he did want both these things, and that he had to do something about it instead of just hanging around and hoping that somehow everything would work out eventually.

The day after he finished with Anja he returned home before Gloria and watched for her car passing on the way to her own house. Then he waited for ten minutes before walking to her front door. He kept a finger on the doorbell, listening to its continuous ring and knowing that it must be driving her mad.

The door suddenly flew open. 'What the—' Gloria began to storm, and then she jumped back out of the way as he surged in.

'I'm back and I passed the course.' He kicked the door shut behind him.

'That is no reason to—'

'Gloria, I've had enough – more than enough. It's time we got divorced.'

Her eyes widened 'Divorce? But—'

'I want to be married, and before you ask, yes, you do know her. It's the beautiful uniformed sergeant at the station. She's been driving me crazy and I know that she fancies me like mad, so let's get things sorted out between us here and now. Oh – wait a minute, she's you, isn't she? And we're already married, which is very useful since we don't have to go through all the palaver of courtship and a wedding. Let's just make up for lost time.'

She gave an astonished squeak as he swept her up in his arms and began to carry her up the stairs. 'Neil, what d'you think you're doing! Put me down!'

'It's make-up-your-mind time, Gloria. What do you want – divorce or marriage?' He kicked open the closed master bedroom door, saying as he carried her into the room, 'Sorry about the lock, I'll get it repaired tomorrow.' Then, holding her over the bed. 'This, Gloria White née Frost, is your last chance.'

'I'm – Neil – for goodness sake—!'

'It's now or never, yes or no. I mean it!'

'Look here, I—'

'So it's a yes – good choice, you won't regret it,' Neil said as the two of them landed in a heap on the bed.

Ewan McNair strolled round the side of the farmhouse, following the sound of a familiar voice. 'Hi, Jamie.'

'Hello.' Jamie Greenlees looked up from where he lay on his stomach in his rabbit's large wire-netting run, his head propped in his hands and an open book between his elbows.

'What are you up to?'

'I'm reading Tommy a story.'

Ewan looked at the rabbit, intent on nibbling grass.

'I didn't know that rabbits like stories.'

'Tommy does. What are you doing?'

'I'm going up to the top field; I thought you might like to come along.'

'Can I just finish the story first? It won't take long.'

'Can't Tommy read the rest of it for himself?'

'Don't be daft,' Jamie said scathingly. 'Rabbits don't go to school and that means they never learn to read. That's why they've got big ears – good for listening.'

'I never knew that. And since he's got strong teeth too, I suppose that if you left him to read the book for himself he might start nibbling it.'

'There's that too,' Jamie acknowledged.

'In that case I'll wait, if it isn't going to take long.'

'I'm almost finished.'

Ewan opened the door of the run and ducked inside. The space was large enough for him to stretch out on the grass, watching the little boy's index finger move from word to word as he read the story aloud.

Now that the farm was easier to run and the bank balance looked healthier than it had been for years, Ewan sometimes found himself with free moments, and he always enjoyed spending them with Jamie.

If only, he thought as he laced his fingers behind his curly brown hair, he could spend some of that free time with Alison as well as her son. But his firm belief that it was a man's place to fend for his family had made that dream impossible. It had been hard for him to accept the business plan she had put together to save the farm, and deep down he knew that if his mother and Victor hadn't forced him into seeing sense, Tarbethill might well have been lost by now.

Sadly, knowing that it was thanks to Alison that they still owned the land and lived in the farmhouse made it even harder for him to swallow his pride and admit that he still loved her, and always would.

He didn't know that he had groaned aloud until Jamie said accusingly, 'You've gone to sleep!'

'I haven't.'

'Why did you just snore, then?'

'I didn't snore.'

'It sounded like a snore. Or have you got a pain in your tummy?'

'Hurry up and finish the story.'

'I have finished it – didn't you hear me saying "the end"? That proves you were sleeping.' Jamie unlatched the door of the run. 'Stay, Tommy,' he ordered the rabbit, who took no notice. 'I'm off to help Ewan in the top field. I'll be back.'

Together they crossed the farmyard, passing the almost-empty barn. It had originally been earmarked as the new deep-litter hen house, but the fact that Bert McNair had killed himself there made it difficult for his widow and sons to consider making use of it. Nor could they bear to raze it to the ground. Again, it was Alison who suggested letting it out, and she was now advertising it.

Jamie, running ahead of Ewan, unlatched the gate into the first field, jumping on to it as it slowly swung open and then jumping off.

'You come through and I'll close it,' he instructed, and when Ewan was in the field the little boy hauled the gate shut and latched it again.

'I used to do that for my dad when I was your age,' Ewan

said as they walked across the field together, watched by the sheep he had brought in to replace the dairy herd.

'Why haven't *you* got a boy to do it for you?'

'I've been too busy to get married and have a boy of my own.'

'There's always me – I can do it for you any time you want.'

'Thanks.'

'You're welcome,' Jamie said graciously, adding, 'but you should probably get your own boy just case I have to go away.'

'Who said anything about you going away?'

'Nobody has, yet, but I don't think my mum likes living here any more.' Jamie, who had been practising his speech since he and Naomi Hennessey worked it out together, shot a side-long glance up at Ewan. 'If she goes away I'll need to go too. But I'm hoping that we stay here because I want to learn to be a farmer, like you.'

They walked in silence for a few moments before Ewan said cautiously, 'What makes you think that . . .?'

'Look,' Jamie said. 'A butterfly!' And he took off across the field, leaving Ewan on his own.

Seventeen

'Marcy, you look exhausted.'

'That's because I *am* exhausted. Can I have my coffee in the largest mug you have, Jenny? Or an empty vase would do. I need the equivalent of at least two cups, and I have to get back to the shop as soon as I can. I was just desperate for a break, no matter how brief.'

'So Sam's being a difficult patient?' Ingrid raised an elegant eyebrow.

'You could say that. If he'd only stay in the house and watch television, or take up reading, life would be so much easier; but he's more like the captain determined to go down with his sinking ship. At this moment he's wedged in behind the post office counter – goodness knows how we're going to free that plaster cast at the end of the day. Thank you, Jenny, and bless you!' Marcy seized the proffered mug with both hands and took a long drink. 'Oh, that hit the spot! I don't know how I'd cope without Kay McGregor, she's been wonderful, and so have the Ralston-Kerrs, freeing her from her work at Linn Hall. Sam's quite taken with her, which is a blessing.' Then, glancing round the room, 'Where's Helen?'

'I phoned to ask just that ten minutes ago. She's working on some more papers from Dr Finlay when she should be getting on with her serial. He seems to be giving her more and more to do, but according to her he pays so well that she can't say no. Such a pity,' Jenny said, 'that he came along with all that work to offer just when she landed first prize in that magazine competition.'

Helen, pounding busily on her faithful old computer at that moment, would not have agreed with Jenny. The money from Dr Finlay, tucked away in a bank account that Duncan knew nothing about, was growing into quite a nice little nest-egg, and the serial was also coming along well, with ideas filling her head in a way that had never happened before.

She had never been busier, happier, or so full of energy. It was as though she had a new lease of life.

Two weeks after Meredith had brought him to Linn Hall, Fergus Matheson phoned Ginny.

'I happen to have a free day, so I thought I'd make the most of it. Any chance of you getting time off? I'd like you to give me a personal tour round the gardens, and if there's enough time I'd like to be shown round the village as well.'

It was mid-morning. The sky was overcast, and drizzly rain came and went. Not many visitors were about, and it didn't look as though the weather was going to get much better.

'I could probably take time off,' she said cautiously. 'I'll check with Lewis.'

'Would you prefer it if I waited for your next official free day?'

'I don't usually take days off.'

'Really? Then your boss can't really complain if you decide to disappear for just one day, would he? I'm leaving now, and if necessary, I'll kidnap you,' he said cheerfully, and hung up.

'You only needed to ask if you wanted days off,' Lewis said when she spoke to him about the phone call.

'That's what I'm doing now,' Ginny pointed out. 'Fergus is interested in having a look round the entire estate, and the village as well. We're not likely to be swamped by visitors on a day like this, so you don't really need me, do you?'

'I suppose not,' he said reluctantly.

When Fergus arrived Ginny was in the kitchen garden polytunnel.

'Lewis told me where I could find you.' He inhaled deeply through his nose, eyes closed. 'This place smells great – all greenery and moist warmth. It takes me back to the childhood holidays we used to spend in an old gypsy caravan. It belonged to my grandparents, and they kept it in a field by the sea. The caravan site was near a market garden, and we kids were always sent there to buy tomatoes from the vine. I loved going into the greenhouses because they smelled just like this place. Funny how a smell can mean so much, isn't it? Especially when it belongs to the days when life was nothing more than a matter of enjoying ourselves.'

Ginny nodded. 'This is one of my favourite places, especially on a drizzly day like this. I have a soft spot for the entire kitchen garden, because this is where I started when I came to work with the Ralston-Kerrs.'

'Tell me all about it.'

'It's not a very interesting tale. I'm sure that your life is much more interesting than mine.'

'I'd still like to hear the whole story.' He reached into a pocket and produced a small, neat camera. 'I've brought my video cam – would it be all right if I used it? I never feel right about anything if I'm not recording it – it's become a way of life with me.'

'I don't mind, and I don't think anyone else would; visitors take pictures all the time.'

'Then let's retrace your steps, starting with this place and finishing with whatever project's on the go at the moment.'

He switched on the video cam. 'Just talk me through the entire time you've been here.'

'Well – the kitchen garden had been neglected for years, and it was completely overgrown, but as soon as I set eyes on it I could see its possibilities. It took an entire year of very hard work to get it going again, and it would have taken longer if Lewis hadn't asked Jinty's son Jimmy to help. He was a schoolboy then, but now he's the estate's assistant gardener, and in charge of this area. We grow enough fruit, vegetables and herbs to keep the kitchen and the stable shop going,' Ginny said proudly.

Fergus was a good listener, quick to grasp everything he was told, and not shy about asking for explanations when necessary. From the kitchen garden they moved round the house and started across the smooth lawns that had been more like fields when Ginny first saw them.

'This is what I call a real haven of peace, even on a day like today,' he said when they reached the rose garden.

She nodded. 'It's one of my favourite places. I love the sound of the water running into the pond. So soothing. When Lewis first showed it to me the pond had been turned into a flower bed and the small lake near the village end of the estate was dry. I felt so sorry for the pretty little nymph, standing there, holding her empty water-carrier. I longed to help her.'

'Where had the water gone?' Fergus asked.

'That's what I wanted to know. It turned out that Lewis and his friend Cam had dammed up the water supply at the top of the hill when they were teenagers. It was supposed to run down the hill in a series of waterfalls, to serve the pond and lake. It took a while to persuade Lewis to let me do something about it. You'll see the lake in a few minutes – that was last year's main project, and this year I've been concentrating on the hilltop behind the house, where the water supply was dammed. That's where we discovered a collection of exotic plants that one of Mr Ralston-Kerr's great-uncles brought back from trips abroad. Once we knew that they were there, I discovered that they had been listed and dated in an old account book. All the house account books were in a cupboard on the top floor of the house. Some of the plants were lost by then, but we managed to save most.'

'That would be well worth a look.'

'Come back when the weather's better; it doesn't look its best on a day like this.'

'Never mind the weather; I want to do the entire tour today.'

'If you're sure, we'll visit the lake first, and then head for the hill.'

Recalling all her hard work and showing off the result was a pleasure for Ginny, and she forgot about the recording almost as soon as the tour began. Leaving the lake, they walked back through the estate, only meeting a few people, and climbed the hill to admire and film the rare plants. Despite getting soaked, Fergus's interest didn't flag; he even insisted on climbing to the grotto roof to record the view. It wasn't until Ginny's stomach began to complain that she glanced at her watch and realized that the morning was over.

'Would you like to come to the house and have something to eat?'

'I was planning to buy you lunch at the local pub.'

'Best to eat here – then I don't have to change from my gardening clothes. The young workers will have finished their lunch by now, but I'm sure Jinty could rustle up some soup and sandwiches. The old kitchen's worth seeing,' she went on as they descended the hill. 'It's the heart of the house and has been for years.'

They arrived in the kitchen to find Fliss and Kay washing the lunch dishes while Jinty had already started making preparations for the evening meal.

'We have soup on the go all the time,' she told Fergus cheerfully, 'like the old days, when housewives kept the stockpot on day and night and tossed in whatever they could get hold of at regular intervals. Sit yourselves down and try some. We've still got enough chilli for two as well if you'd like it.'

'Sounds great.' He took his broad-brimmed hat off and put it near the big stove, ruffling his curly hair with his free hand. 'I remember hearing about that continuous stockpot idea when I was working on a programme about old-fashioned cooking years ago. It didn't seem to do anyone any harm. This is a terrific kitchen!'

'I keep telling Mrs F that whatever's done to the rest of the house, she must leave the kitchen alone – we need a big space like this with all those youngsters living here in the summer months.' Jinty put two steaming bowls of soup before them. 'I'll cut some bread for you. It's home-made.'

The rain had eased off and a watery sun was appearing by the time they finished lunch and crossed the courtyard to visit Lewis in the stable shop.

'You've done wonders with this estate,' Fergus told him. 'Ginny's filled me in on all the hard work it's taken, and I'm impressed. You must feel good about the way you've managed to put everything back to the way it once was.'

'A lot of it's down to Ginny. She was the one who insisted on restoring the water course down the hill and setting up this shop.'

Fergus wandered around. 'I like the before and after pictures on that wall – good idea.'

'Lewis's friend Cam in the village is a good photographer.'

'And you've got jars of honey on sale as well – I didn't see any beehives.'

'Gilbert MacBain in the village keeps bees,' Lewis said. 'It sells well here and in the village store.'

Fergus produced his wallet. 'I'll have four jars of that and some photographs of the place. Feeling up to a wander round the village before I leave, Ginny? I'd like to visit that bee-keeper.'

Ginny looked questioningly at Lewis, who shrugged and said, 'It's a quiet day. Take as long as you like.'

'In that case, we'll make a proper day of it and finish off with a visit to the local pub,' Fergus decided. 'Thanks, Lewis – keep the change.'

'Thanks.' Lewis dropped the coins into the collecting box on the counter and watched Fergus drape a casual arm around Ginny's shoulders as they left the shop.

'Smart-ass,' he muttered under his breath.

When he had put his purchases into the boot of the blue sports car parked on the gravel sweep in front of Linn Hall, Fergus suggested that they take a walk down to the village.

'Give me fifteen minutes to change out of my work clothes. I'll meet you back at the car,' she suggested and rushed off to the camper van, where she tore her jeans and heavy jersey off, kicking them into a corner, then washed her face, pulled on a pair of clean trousers, a warm jumper and a waterproof jacket and dragged a brush through her short hair.

When she returned to the car Fergus was leaning back against it, studying the house. 'This is a really attractive building,' he said when she joined him. 'I hate to see lovely old homes like this one pulled down and replaced with blocks of flats, or supermarkets. Shall we go? Let's start with this bee-keeper, if he's at home,' he went on as they walked down the drive.

Gilbert MacBain was home and only too happy to show off his beehives and explain the intricacies of bee-keeping. Fergus Matheson, Ginny noted now that his attention was focused on Gilbert, was a very good listener who asked sensible questions and didn't miss a thing.

When they left Gilbert they visited the church and had a chat with Naomi, who was in the vestry, then after a wander round the rest of the village they walked along to the old priory ruins that gave the village its name. By the time they left the priory they were both ready for some refreshment.

'This,' Fergus said over a drink and some sandwiches in the Neurotic Cuckoo, 'is an utterly delightful village.'

'I think so. I love being here.'

'Have the Linn Hall family heard from Angela yet?'

'Not as far as I know.'

'She was impressed – I think she's really keen to work on those rooms on the ground floor, and I can guarantee that she'd make a good job of it. We first met when I was commissioned to do a documentary on her restoration of a place not unlike Linn Hall. She did an amazingly good job of it. We did the filming once the work had been done – she's camera shy and refused to be in the film.'

'It's a case of raising the money as far as the family are concerned. That could take some time.'

'Understandable, but I hope that they manage it.'

'What they want more than anything, all three of them, is to keep the house and estate in the family.'

He studied her face for a moment before asking, 'And what do *you* want, Ginny Whitelaw?'

'I'd like to stay on here if I can find enough to do. I've come to love the place, although my mother hates the thought of having a gardening daughter.'

'What's it like, having a mother who's a famous actress?'

The question took her aback and for a moment she blinked in confusion, then laughed. 'Nobody's ever asked me that before! Everyone here seems to think I'm so lucky to be Meredith Whitelaw's daughter, but the truth is that I've always longed for an ordinary domesticated mum who didn't expect me to be glamorous and sophisticated like her. Sadly, we tend to irritate each other. Have you known her for long?'

'Not really – Angela's the link between us. I've seen the play in Dumfries, and your mother's a very good actress.'

'Yes, she's great at what she does, but I just wish she could see that I'm quite good at what *I* do.'

'You never fancied treading the boards yourself?'

'The very thought horrifies me! I couldn't even join the local amateur group.'

'What about your father?'

'He's an actor too – Jerome Whitelaw. They split up when I was small, and he moved to Australia. He's still there, married and with a family. Still acting, and I've visited him a couple of times, but we don't really keep in touch other than Christmas cards.'

'I'd really intended to drive you somewhere special for dinner as a thank-you for giving up so much of your time, but the day flew by,' Fergus said as they left the pub. 'May I take you out for dinner properly on another occasion?'

'You don't need to!'

'I know that,' he said, 'but I want to.'

Eighteen

'Have you seen Helen lately?' Jenny asked Marcy when they met in the village.

'She was in the shop yesterday, in a hurry as usual, but she was all right, as far as I could see.'

'She just doesn't seem to be around much. I normally bump into her every day, but that seems to have become a thing of the past. I thought I might—'

'Talk of the devil,' Marcy interrupted, glancing over Jenny's shoulder.

Turning, Jenny saw Helen alight from Ginny Whitelaw's camper van and then reach in to collect a variety of shopping bags before stepping back to wave the van off as it headed past the pub on its way back to Linn Hall.

'Helen?'

She glanced over, and then hurried towards them.

'You've had your hair done!' Marcy said, and Helen beamed and put a hand up to touch her brown hair, normally shoulder-length and somewhat wispy; now feather-cut to follow the shape of her head.

'I got it this morning. What d'you think?'

'It's gorgeous, Helen,' Jenny told her. 'Have you had it done for a special occasion?'

'No, I just needed cheering up. Fancy a quick coffee in the Cuckoo? I've got half an hour before the kids get home from school.'

Jenny nodded, but Marcy hesitated, glancing back at the village store. 'I should be – oh, why not! Kay can hold the fort for another fifteen minutes.'

'How's Sam coming along?' Helen asked as they headed for the pub.

'Being difficult as usual. Men never make good invalids, and I swear that Sam's worse than most. Mind you, it can't be easy, having to lug that heavy plaster around.'

'Is Kay coping well in the shop?' Jenny wanted to know when they'd ordered their coffees.

'She's an absolute godsend, and miracle of miracles, she and Sam get on like a house on fire. She's got this quite amazing knack of sensing when he's getting stressed and teasing him out of it even before he becomes aware of it himself. I don't know what we would have done without her.'

'How long can she stay? Isn't this the time of year that the Hall's backpackers start to disperse?' Helen settled her shopping bags in a corner by her seat.

'Yes, but she's not in a hurry to leave, so the Ralston-Kerrs kindly said that she could stay on in the gatehouse while we needed her; then Elinor Pearce offered her the use of her spare room, so she's just moved in there.'

'Which is more suitable than the girl staying on her own at the end of that long driveway, and I imagine Elinor will be glad of the company,' Jenny said. 'She must be lonely without Kevin to look after.' Then, as the coffees arrived, 'Thanks, Gracie.'

'Why did you need cheering up, Helen?' Marcy wanted to know.

Helen sighed. 'I got a bit of a downer this morning – a phone call from the editor to say that the episode they've just received is too spicy.'

'Spicy?' Jenny's eyebrows rose. 'You're a lovely person, Helen, but I have to admit that I've never thought of you as spicy.'

'Neither have I,' Marcy said. 'You're a dark horse. What exactly does the editor mean?'

'To be blunt, the episode's too sexy. She said that some of their older readers might not like it.'

'Are you going to have to make many changes?'

'Not all that many, thank goodness. I should be working on them now, but the phone call depressed me so much that I caught the bus to Kirkcudbright and hit the shops.' Helen nodded at the bags in the corner. 'After I left the hairdresser's I had quite a lot of fun buying a few things for the kids and a wee treat for myself. Look at this!'

She delved into one of the bags and produced a tailored navy jacket. 'It was in a sale and I couldn't resist it. What d'you think?'

'It's very smart.' Jenny reached out to touch the jacket. 'Beautiful material, too.'

'Isn't it? All I need now is an opportunity to wear it. Until then it'll have to be hidden away, otherwise Duncan's going to ask me where I got the money to pay for it. When he does, I'll tell him that I found it in a charity shop – it's amazing how many women can afford to give really good clothes to charity shops.'

Helen folded the jacket carefully and replaced it in the bag. 'I met Ginny Whitelaw in the dress shop – she said that she's getting tired of living in jeans, jerseys and shirts, and thought it was time she bought something decent to wear just in case. We had a really good time helping each other, and then she gave me a lift back to the village. She got a nice outfit too.' She beamed at her friends. 'It was such a terrific feeling, getting something nice for myself. That doesn't usually happen to mums with growing kids. It helped me to forget about the rejected episode for a while. Once Lachlan and Irene are fed and on their way back to school I'll get started on the rewrite. I've got a pile of work to do for Dr Finlay as well. Whoever said that a woman's work is never done is spot on.'

'Although you've taken on so much work, you're looking a lot better than you were a few weeks ago,' Jenny said, puzzled. 'Surely typing dreary academic articles can't be much fun.'

'You'd be surprised, Jenny.' Helen giggled, then as they both looked at her with raised eyebrows she went on swiftly, 'What I mean is, it's not the articles, it's the payment. It was great to be able to spend some money this morning. Dr Finlay is very generous.'

'I still can't get my head round you being a sexy writer,' Marcy confessed. 'Unless Duncan . . .?'

'No, he isn't,' Helen told her. 'Don't even think that.'

'Then have you been getting some really interesting letters for the agony aunt page?'

'Nothing out of the ordinary – and I do mean ordinary.'

'Can it be,' Marcy asked, 'that you've been reading too many sexy books?'

Helen's face went red. 'What do you mean? When do I have time to read?'

'Didn't you borrow one of those Lilias Drew books from Ingrid a while back?'

'Oh, that – I haven't had time to open it yet.'

'Then better not, until you've finished your serial.'

'Golly, look at the time – I'll have to rush.' Helen took her purse from her bag.

'I'll have another coffee – what about you, Marcy? And put that purse away, Helen,' Jenny ordered. 'I'm getting the coffees today.'

'Thanks.' Helen scooped up her bags and left.

'I'm convinced that she's working too hard, but at the same time she looks great,' Marcy said when Helen had gone.

'You're right. Come to think of it, she has got a bit of a glow on these days, and she's wearing more make-up than she used to. You don't think—' Jenny stopped abruptly, shaking her head.

'Think what?'

'I suddenly had the most ridiculous thought – she looks as if she's just fallen in love.'

'Surely not – I mean, Duncan's quite a dour man; I can't see him suddenly becoming an ardent lover at his age.'

'You read some strange stories about the effects Viagra can have on people.'

'Can you imagine Duncan Campbell on Viagra?'

'It's stretching the imagination a little too far, isn't it?'

'It is indeed. Although Duncan could never be thought of as the most exciting man in the world, I'd say that their marriage is rock solid. Besides, Helen's so busy that she hasn't got time to have an affair, and even if she did have the time and the inclination – which doesn't sound to me like our Helen – who's she likely to meet in Prior's Ford?'

'The only new man in the village is Dr Finlay. You don't think that he . . .?'

'Absolutely not! The man's clearly a confirmed bachelor, and he's loads older than Helen. No,' Jenny said firmly, producing her purse from her bag. 'Helen's just feeling good because she's won the serial competition, and at almost the same time Dr Finlay's presented her with another source of income. She's had to work hard to make Duncan's salary stretch to feeding a growing family, and now she's even managing to treat herself to a new jacket and put some money by as well. Good luck to her, say I!'

Making her way home, Helen chastised herself for giggling at exactly the wrong time. She hated keeping secrets from her closest friends, especially the secret she was nursing at the moment, but she had made a solemn promise that must be kept.

It had happened only a few weeks earlier, when she was hurrying to get some of Malcolm Finlay's academic articles typed up and printed out before the children arrived home from school, clamouring for attention and something to eat. She had finished one article and started reading the next, only to discover that she was actually reading what appeared to be a chapter of a somewhat explicit romantic novel. The pages were covered with Dr Finlay's sprawling writing style, and they were so gripping that she found her eyes skimming greedily over the lines.

Although her brain kept telling her that he had included them with his usual work by mistake and she should stop reading them at once, she kept going until the end, when she was left longing for more.

Lachlan and Irene were due home from Prior's Ford Primary school at any minute, so she only had time when she finished reading to tuck the chapter into a folder and hurry downstairs, where she phoned Dr Finlay and asked if she could call on him the following morning.

The children burst in through the door as she put the phone down, both trying loudly to give her their day's news.

'Is something wrong?' Lachlan, who was more observant than his younger sister, asked as the two of them raided the fridge in search of a drink while Helen began to make sandwiches to keep them going until dinner time.

'No, why should there be anything wrong?'

'Your face is a bit red.'

'Have you gone and broken something?' asked Irene, herself the butterfingers of the family.

'No, I was just – working hard,' Helen lied.

'Oooh, there's still some chicken left.' Lachlan brought out the plate of slices saved from the weekend's chicken dinner. 'Can I have some on my sandwich – *pleeease!*'

'Me too, please please *please*?' Irene chimed in, and Helen, in her state of confusion had made the two chicken sandwiches before she realized that her planned chicken curry for dinner, with lots of filling rice, would now have to be tomorrow's stewed sausages with mash.

Malcolm Finlay's small living room was neat, but still managed to feel comfortable and welcoming. Helen, used to the chaos that four children could cause effortlessly, took to it as soon as she walked in through the door on the day after she had read the chapter mixed in with the articles he wanted typed out.

'Coffee?' he offered. 'Or I have Earl Grey tea if you would prefer that.'

It was too soon after breakfast for elevenses, but the aroma of perking coffee was tempting. 'Coffee would be lovely.'

While he was in the kitchen she studied the small bookcase which, as was to be expected, held mostly academic volumes, cheek by jowl with a few books on birds and gardening, and some classical novels by Anthony Trollope, Dickens and Sir Walter Scott. A former log basket by the fireplace was now home to a pile of the type of magazines he wrote for. Although he had only been in the village for about four months the place had a relaxed, lived-in feeling that to Helen's mind would have pleased Doris Thatcher, who had come to the cottage as a young bride and stayed for more than sixty years.

'I like the way you've furnished this room,' she said when he brought in the tray.

'I'm glad to hear it – I chose the furniture more by instinct than anything else, and I'm pleased with what I bought. Help yourself to sugar, milk and biscuits if you wish them.'

The business of pouring coffee and choosing from the plate of assorted biscuits over, Helen returned to her chair and picked up the first of the two cardboard folders she had brought with her. 'I've brought the two articles you gave me. Let me know if anything needs redoing.'

'Thank you, Mrs Campbell.' He laid the folder aside unopened. 'I'm sure that there will be no errors; your work is always perfect, and done so swiftly too. I really appreciate you taking on the extra work when I know you're such a busy young lady.'

'That's all right, really.' She swallowed hard, and then, with a hand that shook slightly, she picked up the second folder. 'I brought this as well. I think it must have got mixed up with the articles.'

'Really?' He looked puzzled, then as he opened the folder and glanced at the written pages within his eyes widened. He gave a sort of gasp and the hand holding the folder jerked, knocking the plate on the arm of his chair to the floor. A half-eaten biscuit bounced on to the carpet as he started to choke.

'Dr Finlay? Oh, my goodness!' Helen, who had studied advice on how to relieve choking when her children were small, jumped to her feet and began to thump his broad back hard with the heel of one hand. He whooped for air, fumbling into his pocket for a handkerchief, which he clapped over his mouth. His face turned red, then purple, and she was just wondering if she had the strength to heave this large man to his feet and get behind him in order to perform the Heimlich manoeuvre when he gave a gasp and started breathing properly again.

'Crumb – went down wrong way,' he said huskily as she stepped back. 'So sorry.'

'No, not at all. I'm just glad that you managed to dislodge it. I'll fetch a glass of water . . .' She fled to the kitchen, which was as tidy as the living room, found a glass on the draining board and turned the tap on.

By the time she returned to the living room he had retrieved the biscuit from the carpet and was back in his chair, wiping his face with his handkerchief. He took the glass and drained it.

'Thank you, Mrs Campbell, that was so rude of me.'

'You weren't rude – you were choking and it was probably my fault for handing that thing to you instead of explaining it first.' She picked up the folder from the floor.

'Ah – yes.' He took it from her and put it beside the other on the small table by the side of his chair. His face, she was glad to note, had returned to its usual colour. 'I've been very clumsy – you should never have received those pages. I hope they didn't shock you.'

'On the contrary, I found them very readable.'

His eyes widened in horror. 'You read the whole chapter?'

Now it was Helen's turn to go red. 'One page led to the next and I couldn't help myself. I'm the one who should be apologizing.'

'No, it's always good to receive a compliment; I know that the books have been selling well, but even so . . .'

'Books? You've actually published romantic novels?'

'They're my main source of income,' Dr Finlay said apologetically. 'Not under my own name, of course. I use a nom de plume – Lilias Drew.' Then, as Helen gaped at him, 'I think we both need another cup of coffee.'

Nineteen

Helen had intended to spend all day working on the agony aunt column, but it was totally forgotten as Malcolm Finlay told her about his amazingly unusual background.

'You wouldn't think it to look at me, but my parents were very open-minded – I'd say they were almost Bohemian. They adored each other, but they both had a series of affairs – our house was always full of their friends. I was the youngest, and my three sisters adopted my parents' lifestyle enthusiastically. Daphne still lives in England; she's married to a man she adores, who managed to talk her into settling down and having children and a normal life. Now she's a grandmother and throws her energy into running various local groups, breeding Labradors and bossing me about. The other two live abroad, each with a series of lovers. Have you ever seen that play that was made into a film – *Shirley Valentine*? I sometimes wonder if the writer knew Rose, my middle sister. She lives in Spain.'

Malcolm – the two of them were now on first name terms – paused to top up their coffee cups. 'I expect you're now wondering if I was like the rest of my family – to be honest, I was more like a fish out of water. I always used to wonder if I'd got mixed up with another baby in the hospital where I was born. It wasn't until I got into university that I began to feel like the other students. It was a surprise and a relief to discover that their families were totally unlike mine. I liked my parents and I like my sisters, of course I do, but I just never felt as though we shared the same genes.'

He sighed and shook his head. 'Anyway, university turned out to be a huge relief when I got there – everyone seemed to be more like me than my family were, and I thrived within those hallowed walls, as a student and then as a lecturer. I never married – I think there was a fear deep in my mind that falling in love might trigger off some family gene lying dormant in the depths of me, and I enjoyed academic life too much to take the chance of losing it.'

Helen glanced at the clock and realized that she should have left long ago. 'But Lilias Drew . . .' she prompted.

'That came as a bit of a surprise, to be honest. A few years ago, not long before I retired, I was thinking about the sort of things that used to go on at home, and the sort of conversations my sisters used to have when they thought I was reading and therefore oblivious, and I started to put some of the thoughts down on paper. It started as some form of release – write it down, throw it away and it's gone and forgotten – but then it became a bit of an obsession, like keeping a diary. Before I knew it I had written thousands of words. I showed the writings one day to a close friend who taught literature and to my astonishment she then showed it to an editor she knew – and I was being offered a two-book contract. Obviously, I couldn't use my own name, so I came up with Lilias Drew. I've published four of the books now – in fact, they paid for this cottage – and I've got a contract for another two.'

'Are you going to have enough material for more books?'

'Oh yes – one memory seems to lead to another. My family lived what's called life in the fast lane – all except me. My parents were still going strong in their eighties. I'd say "rest their souls" but I don't think that would please them.'

'I must go,' Helen said reluctantly, putting down her coffee cup.

'Of course. I apologize profusely for putting those pages in with the articles by mistake – and I hope that you will keep my rather shameful secret.'

'I can promise you that I'm good at keeping other people's secrets, though I don't know about it being shameful – do you know how many women here in Prior's Ford love the Lilias Drew books?'

'I've heard people in the mobile library ask for them several times – that never ceases to surprise me.'

On her way to the front door a thought struck Helen. 'Who's typing the Drew books for you just now?'

'It was the lady who did all my typing before – like you, she's good at keeping secrets.'

'So your current manuscript is still waiting to be typed?'

'My editor's agreed to wait for it.' He opened the door for her.

'I could do it for you – if you want.'

'But I can't take advantage of your good nature like that. You've got your own work to do, and your family to look after.'

'I could give it a try and let you know if it's too much.'

His relief showed. 'That would be wonderful – and I insist on paying you double again for the novel. I'll bring the opening chapters to you in a day or two, if that's all right?'

It wasn't until she was hurrying home that Helen suddenly pictured herself thumping Dr Finlay's back in an effort to dislodge the biscuit crumb that was choking him, and about to try the Heimlich manoeuvre. Even if she had managed to get him upright and move behind him, her arms wrapped as far around his midriff as they could reach, he could well have fallen backwards, pinning her to the chair beneath him. She giggled at the mind-picture, and then had to turn the laugh into a cough as a close neighbour came towards her.

Perhaps she would find a way to introduce the word-picture

into her serial or into a short story, just as Dr Finlay had managed to turn his amazing family's activities into lucrative novels.

Having read one chapter, she could scarcely wait to start reading more of his novel – while at the same time being paid for the pleasure.

'I was wondering, Marcy,' Kay McGregor said, 'if we could meet up for a chat tonight?'

'I don't see why not. Come to our place for a drink, if you like. Sam and I aren't doing anything else – we like to relax after a busy day in the shop.'

'I wasn't thinking about the three of us – just you and me, Marcy, if you don't mind.'

'Of course I don't mind. Want to meet in the pub?'

'Elinor's going to visit her sister this evening, and she says she'll probably stay the night and come back tomorrow. Could you come to her house round about nine?'

'Yes, if that suits you better. There's not anything wrong, is there?'

'No,' Kay said swiftly, then, 'not really, I'd just like to have a word with you in private.'

Then, as Sam, who with his plaster cast was jammed in behind the post office grille, yelled, 'Shop – now!' she added:

'You go and attend to the customers, and I'll see to the coffees.'

'Why just you?' Sam wanted to know that evening when Marcy had finished washing the dishes and was getting ready to walk along Kilmartin Crescent to the house Elinor and Kevin Pearce had shared until Kevin's death.

'I haven't the faintest idea. Perhaps she's decided that it's time for her to leave Prior's Ford.'

'I thought she enjoyed working in the shop.'

'Me too.' Marcy scuffled through her handbag. 'Now where's my lipstick gone? I wish someone would come up with some way of making tiny helium balloons that could be attached to everything in a woman's handbag, so that they all rose to the surface instead of hiding in the depths. I'd miss her if she left now.'

'Me too. She's a nice girl.'

Marcy located the elusive lipstick and took it to the wall mirror. 'You've not been grumpy with her about something, have you?'

'I have not.'

She blotted her lips with a tissue. 'Or made any improper overtures?'

He gave a scornful laugh and thumped a fist against his plaster cast. 'Even if I wanted to, which I don't, this anchor would make it impossible. Pass me the telly remote before you go, there's a football match coming on soon.'

'In that case, I'll not hurry back.' Marcy located the remote and handed it over, then tipped his chin up so that she could give him a quick kiss.

Kay must have been watching for her, because the door opened as Marcy walked up the path. 'Thanks for coming,' the younger woman said as she led the way into the front room.

'My pleasure – Sam's watching a football match, and I hate football.'

'I quite like it – my dad used to take me to matches when I was a kid. Then when I was eighteen I had a boyfriend who played in the local team, so I went to watch him every week, in all sorts of weather. Now then,' Kay went on, 'I thought we might have a drink – would gin and tonic suit you?'

'Lovely, thanks.'

'I'll put them together in the kitchen.'

Left on her own, Marcy snuggled into the deep armchair. 'This is a nice room,' she said when Kay returned with a tray. 'I've never been in this house before.'

'It's very comfortable, and Elinor's a lovely landlady.' Kay set the tray down carefully on a small table between the two armchairs. 'I've brought crisps and nuts – help yourself.' She handed over a tall glass and asked anxiously when her guest had taken a sip, 'Is it all right?'

'Perfect, thanks; lots of gin and ice, just as I like it. Elinor tells me that she's enjoying having you as a lodger. We all thought she would go to live with her sister when Kevin was – when he died – but it's good that she's still here.'

'She's still talking about moving to her sister's, but at the same time she doesn't want to leave the home she shared with her husband. She loved him very much.'

'I know she did.' Marcy took another drink and gave a contented sigh. 'I'm glad you suggested this get-together; it's great to be able to relax after a busy day in the shop. Sam and I really appreciate your help, Kay – I don't know how we would have managed to cope with his accident on our own.'

'I'm enjoying it. I never had any brothers or sisters, so I loved working in our shop at weekends and during school holidays. My parents were quiet people, and I enjoyed the hustle and bustle of folk coming in and out of the shop all day. I would have liked to keep it on when they died but I was about to go to college and I didn't want to miss out on that.'

'What happened to your parents – or don't you want to talk about it?'

'No, it's all right. They were going to the warehouse in their van when a lorry's brakes failed. The collision was head-on, and they were both killed instantly. It was quick, and at least neither of them was left to mourn the other.'

'How old were you?'

'Seventeen years and three months.'

'I wasn't much older than that when I was orphaned.'

Kay took a great gulp of her drink then said, 'That's what I wanted to talk to you about, as it happens. I'm not really orphaned because I still have a mother.'

'You do? But . . .' Marcy was confused.

'Yes, I do. And I believe that it's you.'

Marcy, who had just sipped at her drink, inhaled instead of swallowing and had to put her glass down swiftly so that she could snatch up a napkin.

'I'm sorry, that was terrible timing. Would you like a glass of water?'

'No, just – no!' Marcy got up and went to the window. As she coughed into the napkin she saw, through streaming eyes, a group of young people pass the house on their way, probably, to the nearby Neurotic Cuckoo. Cam Gordon, Steph McDonald and her twin Grant, a rising star in the world of professional football, were among them.

When the coughing eased she was able to turn back to face Kay, who was watching her anxiously.

'Typical – I've been practising for this moment for ages, but I still managed to make a complete mess of it.'

'What the hell d'you think you're talking about? How could I possibly be your mother? I'm not *anyone's* mother!'

'My mother – the woman I thought was my mother – was called Katherine Metcalf. My father was Clive Metcalf, and you worked in their corner shop in Dundee for about a year,' Kay said. Then, watching Marcy's face closely, 'You remember them, don't you?'

Marcy's legs suddenly felt as though they were no longer able to support her weight. She returned to the armchair, almost fell into it, and reached for her half-finished drink.

'You *do* remember them.' Kay pulled in a deep breath, let it out again in a sigh of relief and reached into the pocket of her jeans. 'After they died, when I was getting the house ready to be sold, I found this.' She held out a small photograph.

Marcy took it with a hand that still trembled. It showed three people, two quite elderly, but the third, Marcy, was in her early twenties, with long dark hair hanging loose about her shoulders. They were grouped at a shop doorway, smiling into the camera. She turned the photograph over and saw the words: '*Kathy and Clive Metcalf outside the shop with Marcy Copleton, March, 1988.*'

'That's a copy I made, so you can keep it if you want. I found a letter, too,' Kay was saying. 'More of a contract than a letter, really. An agreement signed by three people, the Metcalfs and you.'

'I remember,' Marcy said, and Kay's face was suddenly lit by a relieved smile.

'I'm so glad! It makes me feel – good – to know that. They never told me, you know. I always thought that they were my blood kin.'

'Your father was, I can assure you of that.' Marcy looked up at the daughter she had made herself forget. 'They were lovely people. I'd had a miserable childhood, then a bad marriage. I always seemed to be running away from something or someone, but when I met Katherine and Clive and began to work for them they were like the parents I'd always longed for. They should have had lots of children, and they'd have loved that, but Katherine was barren.'

'So you had me, for them?'

'It seemed the right thing to do at the time.'

'What's it like,' Kay asked, 'giving up your own child?'

'Not that difficult when you know that she's going to such loving and deserving parents. I was a traveller, with no wish to settle down. I moved on when you were three weeks old. But where did the name McGregor come from?'

'My real dad died when I was five, and Mum married George McGregor two years later. He adopted me. I count myself as really lucky,' Kay said, smiling. 'It turns out that I had twice as many dads and mums as most kids, and there wasn't a wicked one among them. So when I found the picture, with your name on the back, and the letter identifying you as my biological mother I just wanted to know what had happened to you, and what you were like. And now that I've found you I'm perfectly happy to leave it at that. I just needed to know.'

'I'm not sure that *I* needed to know.'

'I'm sorry about that.'

'Don't be. I just don't know whether or not I can tell Sam the truth.'

'That's up to you. I certainly won't say anything, and you needn't worry – I'm a bit of a traveller too, and I'm not ready to settle down yet. Once Sam's leg's better I'll be on my way. Now – a nice cup of tea?'

'I'd rather have another drink,' Marcy said, and Kay laughed.

'We're so alike in some ways,' she said and took the empty glasses to the kitchen.

Twenty

It was late when Marcy returned to her own home, and Sam had gone to bed, but as she began to go upstairs he called her name from the small dining-room which had been turned into a temporary bedroom.

He was propped against the pillows, a book in his hands. 'You're late back. What have the two of you been up to?'

'Just talking about this and that. I meant to be back ages ago. How did the game go?'

'A draw – scarcely worth watching, as it turned out.'

'D'you want anything before I go to bed?'

'No thanks, I was just about to switch the light off.'

'See you in the morning, then.' She kissed him then went to bed, where she lay awake most of the night, tossing and turning and glad for once that Sam's accident meant that he wasn't by her side, wanting to know why she was so restless.

Even though she and Sam genuinely cared for each other they often had their disagreements, and a few years earlier she had left him, staying away for the best part of a year. Recently, though, their situation had become more settled – and now, she thought despairingly, turning her pillow over and thumping it into a comfortable shape for the third time, another threat was looming, this time in the shape of the child she had brought into the world, given away, and tried hard to forget.

She had been happier with the Metcalfs than ever before in her life, and when, in desperation, they asked her to become a surrogate mother to the child they longed for, she had seen her agreement as a way of repaying their kindness to her.

Marcy herself had never considered having children, and throughout her pregnancy she concentrated on the thought that the child she carried belonged to the Metcalfs, not to her. Giving birth, in her mind, was akin to having her tonsils or appendix out – once the baby was born it would cease to be of any interest to her. She didn't realize until the little girl was laid in her arms following a short and trouble-free birth that bonding begins in the womb.

It was unbelievably hard to hand the baby over, but there had been no other option, so less than a month later Marcy was on her travels again, shutting out the past, as she had done several times before, and concentrating on the future.

But now the past had caught up with her, and although Kay was no longer a tiny child, but Kay McGregor, the independent young woman who had come into her life on the day of Sam's accident, Marcy was faced with a dilemma – whether or not to tell Sam what she had just discovered.

'I don't want Sam to know,' she had said firmly before leaving Elinor Pearce's house.

'He'll certainly not be told by me,' Kay had assured her. 'Nor will anyone else. And I don't intend to be a nuisance. It's just good to know that I've found my real mother at last, and that I'm not completely alone in the world.'

It was easy for Kay, Marcy thought as the church clock struck two. She had found someone she was seeking for – Marcy, on the other hand, had found someone she had, after a hard struggle, managed to forget.

'I've completed my recommendations on Linn Hall,' Angela Steele reported to Fliss over the phone, 'and I'd like to talk it through with you rather than send it by post. I could come to the Hall at around three, if that suits you.'

'Em – yes, that should be all right. Could you drive round the side of the house to the stable yard at the back? The front door's hardly ever used because we spend most of our time in the kitchen area.'

'Certainly – it'll give me the chance to have a look at the kitchen itself,' Angela said enthusiastically, and hung up, leaving Fliss in a panic.

'We don't have the money to pay for any work on the house,' she wailed to Hector and Lewis when she got them together. 'How are we going to tell the woman that she's wasting her time?'

'She's not wasting her time at all, Mum. We already know that we're going to start work on the house itself over the next year or so, and I'm looking forward to hearing what she suggests. She knows we're not in a position to raise another loan at the moment,' Lewis pointed out. 'And now that the gardens are beginning to make a small profit, work on the ground floor of the house might just be possible sooner than you think.'

'Do you really need me to be at the meeting?' Hector asked apprehensively.

'Yes, we do, Hector, I couldn't manage without you!' Fliss clutched at her husband's arm.

'We all need to be there, Dad. Linn Hall needs every one of us, and so far,' Lewis said, 'we've not let the old place down. Onward and upward!'

At three o'clock precisely a green estate car drew up in the stable yard and Angela Steele emerged, complete with her oversized bag, to meet the Ralston-Kerrs at the kitchen door.

'Good afternoon.' She shook hands with them all. 'Even the back of this place is attractive. What are those buildings?'

'It's the stable block, built in the days when the family had horses and carriages,' Lewis explained. 'Then for a long time they were used as store rooms; the carriage house still is, but the stables have been turned into a shop that does well on open days.'

'I really must find the time next year to visit the grounds. Fergus tells me that they're well worth seeing. Mind you, from the way he spoke about her, I think that his guide was the main attraction. I believe it was Meredith's daughter, that nice girl who went round the ground floor rooms with us. What was her name?'

'Ginny,' Lewis said shortly, a frown tucking his brows together.

'She's been an absolute godsend to us,' Fliss said warmly. 'I don't know what we would do without her now. Shall we go indoors?'

Their visitor was highly impressed as soon as she stepped in through the kitchen door. 'This place is amazing – so untouched! I can almost sense the servants all hurrying about, preparing the next meal for the family upstairs, fetching hot water for the bedrooms and coals for the fireplaces!'

'And now,' Jinty said wryly, 'it's only me and Mrs Ralston-Kerr and some of the young folk who work here during the summer season. There's coffee set out in the butler's pantry – that's known as the family room now.'

To their surprise, Angela also fell in love with the long, narrow pantry, with its two long walls lined with cupboards and counters. 'Do outsiders see this part of the house at all?'

'We sometimes serve teas and coffees in the kitchen, but most of the time it's needed to feed the backpackers who work here,' Lewis said. 'Nobody comes in to the pantry, though. It's Dad's bolt-hole when life gets him down, and where we spend our evenings when we're indoors, and also where we do all the paperwork.'

'Have you ever thought of turning that carriage house into a tea room?'

'We could, I suppose – when we can afford it.'

'I realize that there's a shortage of money, but I'd love to give the public the chance to see more of this beautiful home of yours. And speaking of that –' Angela dragged her gaze away from the closed cupboard doors and whatever treasures might be hidden behind them – 'the real reason I'm here is to talk you through my thoughts on the ground floor rooms. Don't even think about cost at the moment – I know that you have a lot of thinking and planning to do before anything can be started. I've printed out a copy for each of you so that you can follow what I'm talking about. Don't hesitate to ask questions. So – shall we start with the coffee?'

Once the refreshments had been organized she took a pair of spectacles from her bag and perched them on her nose. 'Now – we know already that the Hall was built in 1809, possibly by Walter Newall of Dumfries, and that it's built to the neoclassical style.'

'Which is news to me,' Hector put in.

'Neoclassical architecture is based on buildings from ancient Greece and Rome – no fuss, and good clean lines, as can be seen on the outside of this particular building and in the way your public rooms on the ground floor open off a large square reception hall, with the domestic quarters located to the rear and accessed from the hall via a corridor. When you start opening part of the house to the public, the phrase "neoclassical" looks good in advertising literature.

'Now to get down to the current state of the ground floor rooms. As is to be expected, there are signs of wear in all four rooms – the drawing room, dining room, library and study – but in general, the cheering news is that the original plasterwork and woodwork seem to be in fairly good condition. You've also got some nice pieces of antique furniture that I think may have been made by a man named William Trotter, a respected Edinburgh cabinet maker, and the collection of oil paintings and family portraits is impressive and worth holding on to if at all possible.

'The soft furnishings are appropriate to the style and period of the house, and carpets and curtains will need closer detailed attention to check for fading and moth damage. With any luck, such damage could be repaired or even camouflaged if it's not too bad. Any questions?'

'What if the soft furnishings can't be saved at all?' Lewis wanted to know.

'They can be replaced with materials that fit in with the decor, but wherever possible I'd try to retain the existing material. A few upholstered pieces of furniture belong to the nineteen twenties, clearly replacing other, original items, but I was pleased to see that they've been chosen carefully to fit in with the overall neoclassical appearance. Now then—'

Angela ran a finger down the report. 'Oh yes – the original flooring's in fair condition, which is excellent news, and in general the paintwork and colours are appropriate to the age and style of the house and can be left for the near future.' She glanced up at them, pushing her spectacles further up her nose. 'Though you have to be aware that once the rooms are opened to the public and the curtains drawn back to admit sunlight through those lovely big Georgian sash and case windows, the fabrics and paintwork will need regular attention. Hopefully, by the time that stage is reached, the house will have become financially self-supporting.'

'Have you any idea of the cost of the essential work?' Hector's brow was furrowed anxiously.

'I can't say at the moment, because we know nothing of

the current condition of the electrics, plumbing, drainage and heating. You'll need to bring in experts in those fields before any renovation starts, and it would also be wise to talk to a reliable architect. I'll try to come up with a rough figure to cover my side of the work, if you want me to do that, but it will only be an estimate at this stage.'

'We would appreciate that,' Lewis told her, and she nodded and made a note.

'So much to think about!' Fliss said.

'It's all going to take time, Mrs Ralston-Kerr. Think of it not as one huge job, but as a series of steps. This meeting is only the first step; you're going to have to consult tradesmen and, as I suggested, a reliable architect, then when you've got the whole picture you can start to work out the cost. And remember that everything has to be done in the correct order, which means that you'll be paying the money out in hopefully manageable pieces.'

'That's very true, Mum. We've already made the place weathertight, including the windows, using that system, so there's no great urgency for the interior work. It's taken us five years to sort the roof and windows, and the garden's taken the same length of time, but it's beginning to pay dividends. When we began, Duncan was our only gardener – now the gardens earn enough for us to have Ginny and young Jimmy McDonald on the payroll.'

'Exactly,' Angela said, nodding. 'Rome wasn't built in a day. May I have more coffee? There are other suggestions on my list,' she went on as Fliss topped up the coffee cups. 'The public access to the ground floor will be from that lovely front door, so you'll need to power-clean the sandstone steps and talk to the local council regarding the provision of a suitable ramp to accommodate disabled visitors. You've got a cloakroom off the hall complete with toilet and wash hand basin, and if you do decide to turn the carriage house into a tea room you'll have to have a public toilet installed there. There are some cracks in the marble flooring to the rear of the hall that will require specialist attention, but the staircase is magnificent, though the red carpet needs replacing.'

'The public won't use the stairs,' Fliss protested.

'That's true; they'll be cordoned off during viewing days, but they'll still be seen, and in any case, the carpet's frayed enough to be dangerous for anyone using the stairs now. They need new carpeting quite urgently; if you're unable to budget for that at the moment, a paint effects expert could create a marble finish to the treads and risers. I can give you some names of people I've worked with in the past. And as we've covered everything so far –' Angela glanced at her wristwatch – 'I'd better be on my way.'

'Take plenty of time to think over what I've suggested,' she added before getting into her car, 'and remember that time is on your side. From what I've gathered from yourselves and from my friend Fergus, who was most enthusiastic following his tour of the grounds, you've all done a marvellous job so far. You clearly love Linn Hall and its gardens, and although there's still a lot of work ahead, you come over to me as a very determined family team. The only thing you lack is money, and while you're waiting for it you can still keep on planning. Contact me any time you want. Good luck.'

'Is there any brandy left, Hector?' Fliss asked as the estate car disappeared round the side of the house.

'Fortunately, yes. Lewis?'

'I'd better get back to work,' Lewis said and headed for the kitchen garden in search of Ginny. Suddenly, inexplicably, he needed to talk to her more than he needed alcohol.

Ginny was nowhere to be seen, but Jimmy McDonald and Duncan Campbell were both in the polytunnel. As Lewis approached, Duncan emerged and began to walk down towards him.

'Seen Ginny anywhere?'

'Not for a while.'

'Have you any idea where she might be?'

'I'm only the head gardener, so how would I know? She goes where she pleases, that one,' Duncan grunted as he passed on his way to the wooden door leading to the stable yard.

'What's the matter with Duncan?' Lewis asked Jimmy as he went into the polytunnel.

Jimmy shrugged. 'Search me – we've both been working in

here for the best part of an hour and I've scarcely heard a word
out of him. He's been like a bear with a sore head all week.'

'Any idea where Ginny is?'

'She said something about some work needing done by the
lake – she might be there.'

Twenty-One

Ginny was on her knees beneath one of the trees lining the
path to the lake, carefully clearing the area around a small but
beautiful plant that was in constant threat from encroaching
weeds. She glanced up as she heard Lewis come down the
path. 'Hi – how did the meeting go?'

'It was promising in that she believes that it's largely a case
of using the materials we already have, but it also involves
checking out things like the electrical work to make sure that
it's up to scratch.'

'That sounds reasonable.' She got to her feet and dusted
down the knees of her jeans.

'I've got a copy of her report if you'd like to see it.'

'It's not really my business. I'm a gardener – an outdoor
person rather than indoor.'

'I know, but you've been a lot of help to us in the past and
I'd like to hear your thoughts on it. I'll buy you a drink in
the Cuckoo tonight,' he offered, 'and we can go over it then.'

'In that case, how can I refuse? Eight o'clock?'

'Fine,' Lewis said.

Over a glass of lager in the pub that evening, Ginny studied
Angela Steele's proposals, then said, 'She's certainly thorough
– and practical.'

'So you believe that we should take her ideas on board?'

'As I said earlier, Lewis, I'm a gardener. I'm at my best out
of doors, surrounded by plants.'

'But you've come up with a lot of good ideas where the
Hall's concerned – selling off unwanted items to raise money

and spending hours going over the old account books. To be honest, I sometimes think that you've got more common sense than me and my parents put together. We all value your opinions.'

Ginny felt herself blush at the compliment. 'My indoor work has been mainly trawling through old accounts to find out about plants that have been brought into the estate in the past. I like Angela Steele's suggestion about turning the carriage house into a tea room; that makes a lot of sense.'

'Yes, it does. I wish,' Lewis said, 'that you had been in on today's discussion. My parents tend to panic over the thought of more upheaval, and more money to be found, though Angela did keep emphasizing that it's all going to take time, same as the gardens.'

'That's very true. You'll be fortunate if you can get started on her plans next year.'

While Lewis and Ginny were discussing the recommendations for the Hall's ground floor rooms, Duncan Campbell came into the pub and glanced around before approaching Bill Harper, the local garage owner, who stood at the bar.

'Can I have a word, Bill? I've got a bit of a problem and I need some advice.'

'Of course you can, mate. Fire away.'

'Not here . . .' Duncan looked at the tables; as usual of an evening in the Neurotic Cuckoo, most were occupied – one of them, he saw, by Lewis and Ginny, both seemingly interested in reading something. Then he spotted an empty table in a corner, where there was less danger of being overheard.

'Over there.' He nodded at it. 'You grab it before anyone else does and I'll get the drinks in. Another pint?'

'Great.' Bill drained the glass already before him and set it down, his eyebrows rising as he threaded his way between busy tables to reach the corner. It wasn't like Duncan Campbell to offer to buy a man a drink – whatever he wanted to talk about, it must be important.

'So fire away,' he invited when the fresh drinks were on the table and Duncan was sitting opposite.

'It's – a bit embarrassin'.'

'Oh?'

'I need to know that you'll never breathe a word of it to anyone else – not even to your wife or any of your mates.'

'You're not in trouble with the law or anythin' like that?'

'Of course I'm not! What d'you take me for? It's just . . .' Duncan cast a look around to make sure that nobody at the nearby tables could hear him, and then leaned forward, almost into Bill's drink. 'It's very personal.'

'Oh.' Bill, now on fire with curiosity, took a firm grip on his glass and used one finger of his free hand to draw a plus sign across his broad chest. 'Cross my heart, Duncan, an' I can't say any more than that, can I?'

'As long as you mean it.'

Bill's patience began to wear thin. 'Look, I'm not goin' to cut my finger an' swear a blood bond – that's the sort of daft thing we did when we were kids. Either get on with it or forget it!' He took a long swallow of beer just in case Duncan took him at his word and withdrew the free drink.

'OK! It's just – difficult.'

'You said that already. Are you sure you'd rather not write whatever it is down and send it to that agony aunt that has a page in the local rag? My wife swears by her; it's always the first page she reads.'

'That's the last thing I'd want to do – write about my personal life to some woman who's goin' to print what I say in the local paper,' snarled Duncan.

'So spit it out, will you?'

'It's Helen – the wife.'

'I know who Helen is.'

'She's changed, and I don't know what to do about it.'

'Changed in what way?'

'She's – *demandin*'.' Duncan had to force the word out. He wasn't a natural talker, and it was hard for him to make such an embarrassing statement, even to a close friend.

'Demandin' what – more of your wages? Never keep your wife short of money, Duncan; it always ends in grief – the man's grief, I mean – never the wife's.'

'It wouldn't be a problem if she wanted more money because I haven't got it to give and that would be the end of it.' Duncan took a gulp of his drink, untouched until then, then hissed across the table, 'Demandin' more of *me* – in the *bedroom!*'

'Ah!' Bill almost heard the 'ching!' as a penny dropped within his head. His first impulse was to laugh out loud, but he managed to stop himself by taking another drink, which also gave him time to think. Unlike Duncan, Bill had a somewhat wicked sense of humour – the only people who were aware of it were his long-suffering wife and daughter, and the occasional caller at the garage. It bubbled to the surface now and would not be stopped.

'D'you mean,' he said slowly, setting his glass down, 'that Helen's goin' on at you to decorate the bedroom? Women – what are they like? At times I feel as if my house is like the Forth Road Bridge – I've no sooner finished freshenin' up one of the rooms than my Margie's on at me to start all over again.'

'God save us!' Duncan's frustration was building up fast. 'I'm talkin' about when we're on our own, together, in bed! When we should be gettin' a decent night's *sleep!*'

'Oh, you mean sex!'

'Will ye keep yer voice down,' Duncan hissed, colour rushing into his already weather-beaten face.

'Sorry, pal.' Bill, who was enjoying himself, looked around, and then said in a stage whisper, 'I don't think anyone overheard me sayin' – you know, that word.'

'I hope not! I don't know what to do, Bill! When a man's put in a hard day's work out in the fresh air no matter what the weather's like, is a man no' entitled tae enjoy a good sleep instead of bein' pestered?'

'When did this start?'

'About a month ago.'

'Can you think of anythin' that changed in your lives about a month ago that might have triggered this off?' Bill asked. 'For instance, did she have a birthday?'

'What would a birthday have to do with it?'

'Gettin' older sometimes upsets women. Makes them feel that they've lost their attraction where men are concerned.'

'Helen was thirty-six last March, but it didn't seem to bother her. And as far as her bein' attractive's concerned, I married her, didn't I? Surely she must know that I wouldn't have done that if I thought she wasn't attractive – to me, at any rate.'

'That was a while ago, though. When did you last tell her she looked nice?'

'For heaven's sake, Bill, we've got four kids – there's so much noise in the house when they're all there that even if we did get the time to say nice things to each other they'd not be heard.'

'Except in bed, when there's just the two of you an' no kids around tae hear ye or interrupt ye.'

'Have you not listened to what I'm tryin' tae tell you? It's not conversation the woman wants then – it's somethin' I havenae got the energy tae give her. In any case, like I said, we've already got four kids – we can't afford any more!'

'I see what you mean.' Bill stroked his bristly chin thoughtfully to indicate that he was deep in thought. 'Are you sure nothin' out of the ordinary's happened recently? She's not found another man, has she?'

'I doubt that – why would she be so keen on kissin' an' cuddlin' with me if she'd another man tae do it with? All I want's a decent sleep before I have tae get up in the mornin'. Right now I almost wish she *did* have another man in her life.'

'Since she seems tae be the only person who knows why she's behavin' the way she is, mebbe ye should just ask her what she's up tae.'

'I can't do that!' Duncan was aghast at the thought. 'It's no' the sort of thing a man can discuss with his wife. Not after fifteen years of steady marriage and four children!'

'Well, Duncan, I'm sorry for your problem, but I can't for the life of me think of what tae say tae help ye.' Bill emptied his pint glass and wiped the back of one hand across his mouth. 'Except one thing – give in tae the woman.'

'Dear heavens, has it come to that?' Duncan groaned.

'If ye can't solve a problem one way, try another. Ye might even discover that ye enjoy some kissin' an' cuddlin', and if ye don't, ye'll have tae endure until she decides tae let ye off. It's worth a try.' Bill stood up and gave his friend a sympathetic pat on the shoulder. 'I have tae go now. Thanks for the drink – an' the best of luck!'

He couldn't wait to get back home to tell his wife what he had just heard. Margie, who was a bit of an invalid and didn't get out and about much, loved an interesting tale and a good laugh.

'What do you do,' Jamie Greenlees asked, 'when you have a really big, really difficult problem?'

'I deal with it,' his mother said, 'or if I can't deal with it, I ask someone for advice.'

'I've already done that but it hasn't helped yet.'

Alison, intrigued, left the washing-up and went to sit opposite her son, who was supposed to be doing his homework at the kitchen table. 'So what's your problem?'

He opened his mouth to speak and then hesitated, his fair, curly head slightly bent over the exercise book so that he was looking up at her from beneath his eyebrows. At that moment he was so like his blonde, hazel-eyed father that Alison felt her heart turn over. Finally he said, 'I don't think it's the sort of thing I can talk to you about.'

'Surely you can talk to your mother about anything in the world?'

'But it's *about* you – sort of.'

'Now you've got me worried. Have I done something wrong?'

'Of course not.'

'Let's start at the beginning, shall we? Who did you ask for advice?'

He hesitated before saying, 'The minister.'

'Naomi Hennessey?'

'Mmmm.'

'And what did you ask her about?'

'If you must know, it was about Ewan.'

'*Ewan?*'

'The thing is, I want to be a farmer like Ewan when I grow up. I love going to the farm, and you love going to the farm too, and Auntie Jess is great. She always likes to see the two of us, I know she does.'

'And Ewan's kind to you as well, isn't he? He bought Tommy just for you, and made him a lovely hutch with a run big enough for you to go into it and sit with your rabbit. And you know that he doesn't mind you going to the farm as often as you want.'

'Mmm, but he's not so nice to *you* now.'

'Of course he is,' Alison said swiftly.

Jamie shook his head. 'He used to come and have supper here, and he always looked happy whenever he saw you, but now he just looks as if he doesn't like you as much as he did—'

'Jamie . . .'

'—and Auntie Jess used to say that you and me might be able to live on the farm one day,' he hurried on as though anxious to spill it all out now that he had started, 'so that Ewan could teach me to be a farmer. But then he stopped smiling at you, and I think that means we're never going to live there now.'

'Jamie, listen to me.' Alison reached a hand out to cover her son's. 'Ewan's had a very difficult time. His brother Victor used to help him and their dad on the farm, but then Victor decided to get married and live somewhere else, which meant that Ewan had to work harder. Then Ewan's and Victor's father died, and Ewan was left to run the farm on his own with only Wilf to help.'

'And Victor helps sometimes too.'

'Yes, but he's got another job in Kirkcudbright, and he's married now, so Ewan's doing most of the farm work, which means that he doesn't have time to be friends the way he was before.'

'But don't you see – that's all the more reason for you and me to go and live with him and Auntie Jess!' her son argued. 'If we lived there I could learn to help him and you could help Auntie Jess. And even if we didn't go to live there, why is he angry with you when all those things that happened weren't your fault?' He stabbed so hard at the exercise book with the pencil he had been holding that the lead point cut a groove along the page before breaking off with a crack.

'Sometimes,' Jamie shouted, 'I think that grown-ups are the most stupid people in the whole of the world!'

'Jamie!'

'Sometimes I just hate all of you,' he bellowed, then slid from his chair and ran out of the room. The kitchen door thudded into its frame, and she heard his sandalled feet pounding up the stairs. Then the door of the box room where he slept slammed shut.

Twenty-Two

Jamie's angry exit hadn't gone unnoticed in the pub, where both his grandparents were working. As Alison went out of the kitchen she met her mother coming from the bar.

'What's going on?'

'It's Jamie – he's upset because he thinks that Ewan doesn't like me any more. I was trying to explain that Ewan's been through a bad time, but he suddenly slammed out of the room and went thundering off upstairs.'

'You can't blame him for getting upset – Joe and I aren't happy about the way Ewan's treating you either. It's not fair, after you working so hard on that business plan. He must be able to see by now that it's working, and yet he's still keeping you at arm's-length. It's as much as I can do to be civil to him when he delivers the eggs.'

'His pride's hurting, Mum – we have to give him time to get over everything that's gone wrong in his life.'

'Stuff his pride,' Gracie said shortly. 'You've not had a good time either, what with your Robbie being murdered and you being left to raise Jamie without a dad. I don't like to see you hurting, Alison, and neither does Joe. You deserve better, and if Ewan's going to start upsetting Jamie as well as you, we'll not stand for it.'

'Mum!' Alison, suddenly aware that Jamie could easily have crept back out of his room and be standing on the upper landing listening to them both, drew her mother into the kitchen and closed the door. 'You have to leave things to me – please!'

'Jamie worships Ewan – it's bad enough my daughter being hurt without my fatherless little grandson suffering as well.'

'I'm Jamie's mother, and it's up to me to find an answer.'

'And I'm *your* mother—'

'Yes, you are, and I can remember you standing up for me when I was Jamie's age. What about the time Johnny Williams pushed me into a muddy puddle and you doused him with the garden hose to teach him a lesson?'

'That was one of the highlights of my life. He never put a finger on you again.'

'I appreciated that then, and I still do. You looked out for me because I was your child. Now it's my turn to look out for my own child. And I promise you that I will.'

'But when? So far you've let Ewan behave as he pleases.'

'I've left him to work through the pain of his father's death and what he sees as Victor's desertion. He's a proud man with old-fashioned ideas about a man having to be able to support his wife and family.'

'His own mother's a farmer's wife, and he's seen *her* working alongside his father.'

'He's taken Jess's contribution for granted because he grew up in a world where the women work as hard as the men, perhaps even harder at times. I'm sure that if I had come from farming stock he'd have married me before this.'

'If only!'

'I agree. But I know he still cares for me, and I know that we're going to end up together, Mum. I was willing to wait, but now that I've been made aware that Jamie's hurting I'm going to have to do something about it. Jamie and I,' Alison said, 'are going to have to do something about it, together. Trust me when I say that Ewan won't be able to resist us if we work as a team.'

'You're sure about this?'

'I'm sure. Just let me sort things out with Jamie first. Then we'll deal with Ewan.'

'Mmm,' Gracie said, and then, as her husband was heard calling for her, she added, 'but I'm still going to keep that garden hose in mind, in case it turns out that I need it!'

Alison went upstairs and tapped on the door with the sheet of paper taped to it, saying in shaky, dark blue crayon letters: 'JAMIES ROOM KNOCK'.

When she heard a muffled grunt she went into the small room to find her son sitting on the bed, hugging the teddy bear he still slept with every night. He glared up at her, his lower lip sticking out.

'Jamie, I can understand why Ewan's annoyed with me.'

'Well, tell me, because *I* can't!'

She sat down on the bed. 'After Mr McNair died I could see that Ewan and Auntie Jess found it very difficult to run the farm on their own, with only Wilf to help. And I could see that most of the hard work was because of the dairy herd. You know by now about looking after cows, don't you? They need to be kept safe in barns during the winter, and properly fed, and they have to be milked early every morning then again in the afternoon. When they're in the fields they have to be brought in to the milking shed then taken back to the fields, and that takes a lot of time and hard work.'

'I like cows.'

'So does Ewan. He loved the herd the way his dad loved them, but it was all getting to be too difficult for Auntie Jess, what with the hens to see to as well as the housework and cooking and baking.'

Jamie nodded. 'She's not getting any younger either.'

None of us are, Alison thought. If only Ewan would stop being so obstinate! Aloud, she said, 'When I told Ewan that his life, and Auntie Jess's life too, would be a lot easier if he sold the cows and got more sheep and hens instead, he got angry with me, and neither of us can blame him. It was like me telling you that you should sell Tommy. You wouldn't want to do that, would you?'

'But the cows are gone now and he's *still* angry with you. If he didn't want to sell the cows, why did he listen to you? Why didn't he just tell you to get lost?'

'He tried to, but Auntie Jess and Victor both knew that Ewan couldn't keep on working so hard, so they talked him into selling the herd. He's still angry because he misses the cows, but nobody can stay angry for ever, can they?'

'I suppose,' Jamie muttered into the top of the bear's head. 'But I don't like the way he's making you sad.'

'I'm not sad, honestly.'

'You *are*. I want to stay here, but I don't think you do. That's why I talked to the minister about it. Ministers are supposed to be good at helping people, aren't they? She was nice, but she didn't help much.'

'What exactly did she say when you told how you felt?'

'She said that she knew Ewan really liked you, deep down, and us all living on the farm together sounded like a very good idea because it would make everyone happy.'

Alison was taken aback to realize how much interest and approval her fairly brief romance with Ewan had attracted. 'And what advice did she give you?'

'She said that if someone like me who knows you very well told Ewan that you were unhappy and that you were thinking of going away, he would probably try to stop you. She knew that you weren't really thinking of going away, but sometimes it's all right to tell a white lie if it makes something that's wrong be put right – she said.'

'Ah.'

'So I told him that, and I said that if you went away I'd have to go with you and then I'd never be able to help him or learn how to be a farmer.'

'What did he say to that?'

'Nothing,' Jamie said sadly. 'D'you think I should speak to the minister again, or maybe to Auntie Jess? She's Ewan's mum. Boys have to listen to their mums, don't they?'

He was speaking into the bear's stomach, so Alison was able to smile without him noticing. 'Ewan's not a boy now, he's a man.'

Jamie glanced up at her with sudden interest. 'Does that mean that I don't always have to do what you tell me when *I'm* a man?'

Alison dared to ruffle his hair. 'Don't push it, kid, you're not going to be a man for a while yet, so you still have to listen to me. And my advice is – say nothing to anyone, even Auntie Jess. Give me time to think up a plan.'

'Not *another* plan – the last one was bad enough!' Jamie threw the bear up in the air and then drop-kicked it so that it slammed hard against the chest of drawers before falling to the floor.

Alison picked it up, smoothing its fur. 'I'll think of a better one this time,' she said, but her son just glared at her and turned over on to his stomach, burying his face in the pillow.

As happened at the beginning of every school autumn term, Lynn Stacey and her staff brought the primary school children to Linn Hall estate for a half-day of exploring the gardens, a game of hide and seek in the wooded area, juice and biscuits in the kitchen and ending with a tour round the kitchen garden, where Ginny, Lewis, Duncan and Jimmy handed out a potted herb to each child, with advice on how to look after it.

This year, the children had the added fun of seeing the pond in the rose garden with its water-nymph fountain, and the neglected lake, now filled with clean water and edged with plants.

'As always, a wonderful visit,' Lynn told Ginny and Lewis before shepherding the children back to school, each clutching a small plant pot. 'Young Jimmy's doing well, and he was great with the children.'

'Probably because he's got so many brothers and sisters,' Lewis suggested.

'Probably. But Duncan Campbell's the big surprise – this is the first time he's been involved, and he's been really good with the children too,' Lynn marvelled. 'Usually if we see him at all on a school trip, it's from a glowering distance. He actually answered questions civilly and smiled once or twice!'

'He's mellowed over the past couple of weeks – we've noticed it,' Ginny agreed.

'I think his wife's putting tranquillizers in his food,' Lewis added with a grin. 'Whatever it is, long may it last!'

'Of course we're all going to see Neil in the local play,' Rosemary Frost said firmly. 'He needs our support, don't you, Neil?'

'I don't mind, really. From what I hear, the drama club's well supported by the local people.' The last thing Neil wanted was to have to go onstage knowing that his wife and her parents were sitting in the audience.

'In that case, let's just leave it,' Gloria said at once. 'Don't you agree, Dad?'

'I can't say that I've ever been a playgoer,' Gordon Frost declared. 'Not since an aunt dragged me along to see one of the Shakespeare plays as a treat for my thirteenth birthday.'

'This isn't Shakespeare, it's a light comedy by Oscar Wilde, and you got over being thirteen many years ago, Gordon. Besides, now that Gloria and Neil are back together again you and I need to show family solidarity. Neil, get three tickets for the first night,' Rosemary ordered, and it was decided.

'Is it going to be a success or a mess?' Gloria wanted to know as Neil drove them both back to Clover Park from her parents' house, where they had been invited to dinner.

'A success, definitely. Lynn Stacey's a terrific director, and there's quite a lot of talent in that club.'

'Including you, Detective Constable White?'

'I think I can say that I tread the boards as gracefully as any other member of the cast.'

'Is your pretty little Swedish friend in the play as well?'

'Anja is Norwegian,' Neil said for the umpteenth time. 'And she's part of the make-up team.'

'Mmm. I hope she's stopped making up to you.'

'For your information, I believe that she's going out now with Grant McDonald, a professional football-player who makes more money than I do and is closer to her own age than I am.'

'So she's lost interest in you?'

'I wouldn't know about that, but I'm certainly not interested in her. Not now that I'm a sort-of married man again. Which reminds me – when are we going to stop being sort-of?'

'Actually, I rather like being sort-of.' Gloria snuggled closer to him. 'With us each having our own house, it means that we don't have to start wondering about selling off one of them. And being sort-of makes life more interesting, don't you think?'

'You could be right,' Neil admitted. Being back together in a sort-of way meant that they had to respect each other's wishes, whereas during their shared-home marriage, Neil had found himself giving in to Gloria more than he should have. His new-found confidence had been further strength-ened on a few occasions when he and his wife had attended a crime scene together and he, as a detective constable, had been able to outrank Gloria, a uniformed sergeant. On the first occasion she had scarcely been able to contain her frustration, but now she seemed quite proud of his new-found authority.

'Do you really want a family appearance at this play?' she asked as the car approached Clover Park.

'The thought of your parents seeing me onstage is a bit frightening.'

'Not my mother, surely – you know that she adores you.'

'Your father doesn't. *He* adores *you*, and quite frankly, he terrifies me.'

'So now's your chance to show off before his very eyes. You heard him say how much he hates stage plays. Prove him wrong!'

'And what about you? Do you really want to come and see me poncing about on the stage of the village hall?'

'I've been wondering why you didn't ask me to come to see you, instead of leaving it to my mother to think of it.'

'I didn't think it was your thing.'

'It's not – but I'd like to see what you look like as an actor. You're going to be kissing someone else, I presume?'

'Absolutely. I get to make love to Gwendolen Fairfax, played by Alison Greenlees – she's the daughter of the couple who run the Neurotic Cuckoo.'

'Do you enjoy it?'

'Absolutely,' Neil said again as the car turned in through the Clover Park gateposts. 'What red-blooded man wouldn't? Especially one who was being denied the chance to kiss his legally married wife and sergeant.'

'You'll only be able to kiss her for another two weeks.'

'Sadly, yes, but life does have its compensations. Your place or mine tonight – or each to our own?'

'Yours is closer.'

'Good thinking.'

Twenty-Three

Ewan and Wilf had just had their afternoon break and Jess was washing the dishes when she heard the car drive into the farmyard. She dried her hands and went to the open door to see Naomi Hennessey squeezing out from behind the steering wheel.

'Naomi, come in and have a cup of tea.'

'I'd love one, but I want a word with Ewan first. Any idea where he is?'

'You've just missed him, but I think he might be in the tractor shed.' Jess nodded at the wooden building opposite the farmhouse.

'I'll have a look.'

'And I'll make a fresh pot of tea,' Jess called as the minister set off across the yard, her long multicoloured skirt swaying about her ankles.

Ewan and Wilf were working on the tractor's engine, but Ewan left the farmhand to get on with the job while he followed Naomi into the sunny yard.

'I think I might have found a tenant for you. I've had a phone call from a friend in Nottingham. He knows a Polish glass-blower who's setting up on his own and interested in relocating; he's looking for somewhere quiet, but with the potential for good business, and my friend thought that Dumfries and Galloway could be the ideal answer – villages, countryside, and lots of craft shops and summer visitors within reach. I immediately thought of your milking shed. It's still empty, isn't it?'

'Yes, but would it be suitable for a glass-blower?'

'My friend thinks that a spacious weathertight building like that could be ideal. It stands on its own, and it has electric lights. Can I have a look at it? It could be just what the man's searching for,' Naomi said when the two of them were inside the building. 'He'd have to come and see it for himself, of course, if you're willing to let him.'

'There'd be no harm in that, I suppose.'

'It would mean more income for you and Jess. And I was wondering about the cottage on the lane – how are the summer lets going?'

'We've had a few folk staying there over the summer, but now that the fields to both sides of the lane have been turned into allotments the lane's quite busy – the cottage has lost some of its attraction without an open field behind it.'

'The glass-blower might be interested in that as well. You never know. So can I tell my friend that you're willing to let –' she took a piece of paper from her pocket and consulted it – 'this Stefan Krechevsky have a look at the milking shed?'

'If he wants to, I don't see why not.'

'If he does decide to view it for himself you'll have the chance to meet him; then it will be up to you as to whether or not you'd want him on the farm. From what I hear, he's a decent fellow. And now I'm going to have a cup of tea and a good gossip with your mother. How is the farm coming along?' Naomi asked as they emerged back into the sunlight.

'It's doing well enough.'

'So Alison Greenlees's business plan is working out?'

'It's not what I wanted for Tarbethill, or what my father would have liked, but yes, you could say that it's working.'

'Your mother looks better on it – not as tired and worried as she's been for the past year. And Ewan – I think that Bert would be proud of the way you've kept Tarbethill going against all the odds. So many farmers are selling off their land these days, to be turned into building sites, but not you. And thanks to your allotments, the church is going to be filled with beautiful local produce at Harvest Thanksgiving.'

He nodded, staring down at the ground, where the toe of one boot was making circles in the dust, then said, 'Naomi, have you heard a rumour about Alison Greenlees leaving Prior's Ford?'

'Now that you mention it, yes, I did hear something of the sort.' Naomi mentally crossed her fingers. She wasn't exactly telling a lie, since Jamie Greenlees had said that his mother was unhappy.

'So is it only a rumour, then?'

Clearly, not-quite-a-lie wasn't going to be enough. 'I'd say it's more than that. Joe and Gracie are content with the village, but they're running the pub and that keeps them busy, whereas Alison's still a young woman with most of her life before her and a son to think of. I know that she's got this morning job in a Kirkcudbright office, but how long is living with her parents going to suit her? I think she's lonely, and there's no doubt that Jamie needs a father. Time will tell whether it's just a rumour, won't it?'

She paused, and then, as Ewan kept silence, said, 'Well now – Jess will be wondering where I've got to, and you've got plenty to do. I'll let you know if I hear any more about the glass-blower – it would be interesting to have a talent like that in the village.'

'So how are you?' Jess said as she set a filled mug before her friend and pushed a plate of freshly-buttered scones across the table.

'I'm very well, apart from my conscience. But sometimes, Jess,' Naomi said vigorously, 'even a minister has to tell lies – and surely as long as they're not malicious, and just might do some good to some people who deserve good things, ministers can be forgiven?'

'I don't know what you're talking about.'

'Perhaps one day,' Naomi said, before biting into a scone, 'I'll be able to tell you. By the way, I've got some tickets for the drama club's play at the end of the week. Why don't the two of us go to see it together?'

'I've just had the most wonderful idea,' Meredith's voice trilled down the telephone line.

'What sort of idea, Mother?' Ginny asked cautiously. Whatever it was it couldn't be good for anyone but Meredith herself.

'It's to do with Angela's makeover on Linn Hall.'

'The Ralston-Kerrs haven't made any decisions on that yet – they haven't even heard how much it will cost, so—'

'I think I've solved that little problem for them. Wouldn't it be great if we got Fergus to turn it into a television programme, with me as the presenter?'

'*What?*'

'Don't you see the sense behind my idea, Genevieve? If the makeover was televised, the television people would pay for it. That would be very good news for the Ralston-Kerrs, and it would also mean that it could be done soon, between my play finishing its run and me going back to Spain to do the next sitcom series. Two birds with one stone. We could even hold a mock Christmas party as a celebration when the work's finished, and then the show could go out over Christmas. Of course, you'll be at the party, so we'd have to think of a makeover for you as well, darling, but that will just add to the fun. Isn't it exciting?'

'But you're talking about your friend Angela's project. Surely *she* would be the presenter if it was to be televised.'

'Angela doesn't have the sort of skills required for a presenter, whereas I've done a lot of television. I'm a trained actress and very photogenic. Angela and Fergus will write the script between them, of course. Makeovers in the home are all the rage just now – the public can't get enough of them, and my name would help to publicize the programme. Suggest it to the Ralston-Kerrs, darling, I'm sure they'll jump at the idea.'

'I wouldn't know what to say, and I don't think Mr and Mrs Ralston-Kerr would be very happy about your idea, Mother. They're very private people.'

'That's not a problem – they don't need to be in the programme at all, unless Fergus wants to go ahead with the Christmas party idea. Don't be tiresome, Genevieve, you can surely see that the sort of programme I'm thinking of would attract lots of visitors to Linn Hall next summer – everyone's going to benefit.'

Ginny had been thinking hard while her mother chattered on. Now she said, 'I think the best thing would be for Fergus to talk to the Ralston-Kerrs. Lewis and his parents are more likely to agree with a televised makeover if it's suggested by a television producer.'

'You could be right. I'll have a word with him. In the meantime, perhaps it would be best to say nothing to the Ralston-Kerrs; we don't want to get their hopes too high, do we? Must dash, darling.'

The line went dead, and Ginny switched off her mobile and went looking for Lewis. She found him clearing out the poly-tunnel that had been chosen as a winter shelter for the more fragile of the garden plants.

He groaned when she told him about Meredith's phone call. 'What's your mother trying to do – frighten my parents to death? Can you see them agreeing to fill the ground floor with television cameras?'

'I know. My mother's so focused on herself that she never stops to think about how other people might feel.'

'I will never understand,' Lewis said, 'how you've managed to grow up to be such a terrific person, with a mother like that.'

'I suppose I must have had some sort of built-in sense of preservation,' Ginny started to say, then, when the words 'such a terrific person' hit her: 'What did you say?'

He shook his head. 'I shouldn't have been so blunt. After all, she is your mother. I'm sorry.'

'No, I meant – what exactly did you say just now?'

'Surely Fergus Matheson would refuse to have anything to do with such a mad scheme? She did say that she was going to contact him, didn't she?'

'Yes, but . . .'

'Do you have his phone number?'

'Yes, I do.'

'Then let's not panic until there's good reason,' Lewis said. 'Give it a few hours, and then try phoning him this evening. If he hasn't heard from your mother by then you could tell him what she's planning. Are you busy with something right now?'

'Nothing that can't wait.'

'Since we're nearly into October and the opening season's almost finished I thought we could make a start now on potting up some of the plants that need to overwinter in here. OK?'

'OK,' Ginny said. It was too late now to remind him that he had just called her a terrific person. He probably wouldn't even remember saying it now.

But he had, and that was of some comfort.

★   ★   ★

Fergus phoned Ginny a few hours later.

'I've just been speaking to your mother . . .'

'She phoned me earlier today.'

'About a televised makeover programme with her as—?'

'—the celebrity presenter, that's right. She wanted me to get the Ralston-Kerrs' agreement, but I suggested that she phone you first. I doubt if Mr and Mrs Ralston-Kerr would be happy about the idea. They don't court publicity.'

'The important thing is that this makeover has nothing at all to do with Meredith. It's between them and Angela . . .'

'Exactly.'

'. . . and Angela happens to be a good and valued friend of mine.'

'I know.'

'I'm going to have to speak to her before any decisions can be made, but she's away at the moment, something to do with work. I'm not sure when she'll be back. This isn't something I want to tell her over the phone when she's working, so I've put Meredith on hold until I can get the chance to break the news to Angela – gently. I don't want her to hear it from Meredith.'

'I can understand that. I'm sorry you've been dragged into this, Fergus.'

'Don't worry about it – I was already involved, as the producer of said televised makeover. I'll try to sort it all out as soon as I can talk to Angela. It's perhaps a good thing that she's not available at the moment – it gives things a chance to settle down a bit, and me the chance to think about what I'm going to say. She can be quite a fiery lady when she's roused. Obviously that red hair isn't a natural colour – I've never known what her natural colour is, but I do know that she's got a red-haired temper.'

'Oh dear!'

'Don't worry about it, just leave things to me.'

'Thank you for phoning.'

'My pleasure. I was planning to call you soon in any case. I'd like to meet up with you again. Are you terribly busy at the moment?'

'The open days are about to end, and the backpackers have

already begun to disperse. We've started on the task of settling the grounds down for the winter.'

'Are you staying on or are you a seasonal worker too?'

'I stayed on last year, and I'm hoping to do the same this winter. The estate isn't totally finished as yet, and there are always plans to be made for the future.'

'Let me know if your plans change. See you soon,' Fergus promised.

The village hall was fully booked for the three-night run of *The Importance of Being Earnest*. The dress rehearsal went well, which, as Cynthia MacBain made a point of reminding Lynn Stacey when it was over, was a bad omen.

'A good dress rehearsal tends to mean a bad first night – every actor knows that.'

'Don't worry, Cynthia, those daft superstitions probably apply only to professional actors, not village amateurs like us,' Cam Gordon assured her, knowing full well that Cynthia hated to be referred to as an amateur. 'Professionals are very touchy about bad luck, such as not mentioning the word Macbeth in a theatre. Oops!' he added when both Cynthia and Gilbert gave horrified cries. 'I wouldn't worry about that slip of the tongue because this is a village hall, not a theatre.'

'This week,' Cynthia almost screeched at him, 'It's a *theatre!*'

'In that case I hope we're not going to be haunted by late members of the WRI or the aerobics class.'

'You shouldn't tease poor Cynthia like that,' Steph MacDonald scolded Cam as they left the hall to walk arm in arm to the pub.

'I know, but she's so gullible that I can't resist it. And she was talking rubbish in any case – we've all worked hard, Lynn's done a fantastic job, and our public is going to love us,' Cam promised her.

Twenty-Four

Cam's forecast came true. The first night of the play was perfect, with no unexpected ghosts, no forgotten lines and no noticeable nerves. Lynn, who had run rehearsals quietly and calmly with none of Kevin Pearce's fussing, had done an excellent job as director, and the cast rewarded her with strong, competent performances.

Almost every seat in the hall was taken, and when Ewan McNair, unable to stay away as he had planned, came in quietly during the final scene, in which the two young couples in the play were discovering that at last the path of true love was running smoothly, there was nowhere to sit. Instead, he leaned against the back wall, his eyes fixed on Alison.

Following several curtain calls, during which the audience kept applauding, Lynn was brought onstage to receive her own applause, then Cynthia, undoubtedly one of the best Lady Bracknells to tread the amateur stage, gave a short but glowing tribute to Kevin Pearce, 'the man behind the decision to stage this wonderful play in our own small village of Prior's Ford. Kevin, we dedicate this week's performances to you!' followed by a brief thanks to Lynn for taking over the play 'when Kevin was torn from us before his time'.

'Why on earth,' Ginny, who attended the first night, asked Lynn the next day, 'did you let her do that?'

'I had no choice. It even made poor Elinor feel uncomfortable, but believe me, it's easier to control a primary school filled with children than to say no to Cynthia and the parrot on her shoulder.'

'The what?'

'I'm referring to Gilbert; everything she says, he echoes, and everything she wants, he makes sure she gets. And if you ever repeat that,' Lynn threatened as Ginny began to laugh, 'I'll never speak to you again. Unfortunately she's going to pay the same tribute every night so we're all glad that there are only another two to go.'

As the final curtain fell and the audience began to leave via the main exit, the cast rushed backstage to change into their own clothes and remove the stage make-up while the stage-crew set the scenery up for the following night's opening scene.

'Alison?' Jinty McDonald glanced into the female dressing-room. 'Someone wants to see you at the side entrance.'

'The side entrance? Who is it?' Alison was make-up-free and halfway out of her elaborate stage gown.

'I don't know. I'm just passing on the message. The side door, not the main doors,' Jinty said and went on her way.

Alison hung up her dress carefully, donned her own clothes, and then hurried out, stopping here and there for an excited word with a member of the group. Everyone, actors and back-stage crew alike, glowed with delight over the first-night success.

Along the passage she went, then opened the side door and stepped out, blinking at the sudden change from lit corridor to dark night – straight into Ewan's waiting arms.

'I've been such a damned *fool*!' he said before he kissed her.

'Don't you think we should take Kay to the pub for a meal after the shop closes?' Sam suggested the following day.

'What's brought that on?'

'I don't how we could have managed without her. She's been wonderful, and I think we should show our appreciation.'

'I'd have managed – somehow. I always do.' Guilt made Marcy's voice sharper than it should have been, and Sam looked at her, puzzled.

'What's wrong with you these days? It's almost as though you resent Kay being in the shop when you should be grateful to her.'

'Why would I resent her?'

'That's what I'm beginning to wonder.'

Marcy sighed. 'Of course I'm grateful, but it's not as if we had to ask her for help – she was the one who offered.'

'Which is why we should show our appreciation. If you don't want to come to the pub, that's OK – I'll take her, since it was my idea.'

'Of course I'll come. After all,' Marcy said, 'it's not often that you come up with an invitation like that.'

As soon as she had said it she wished that she hadn't. It was true that Sam had never been the sort of man who bought flowers or suggested eating out. Like him, she appreciated Kay's cheerful assistance at this difficult time, but guilt over the secret she was keeping from him plagued her day and night.

Kay's face lit up when Sam suggested the meal that evening. 'That would be lovely – but you don't have to, you know. I'm having the time of my life in this shop, and being paid for it's an added bonus.'

'We just want you to know how much we appreciate your offer of help, don't we, Marcy?'

'Yes of course.'

Sam picked up the phone. 'I'll phone the Cuckoo and book a table for eight o'clock.'

'Great,' Kay said. 'We'll have a terrific evening!'

The three of them met at the pub door as the church clock chimed eight times, and went inside together, to the sound of laughter and applause from the public bar. The door opened, and Jamie Greenlees emerged, dressed in his pyjamas and closely followed by his grandfather.

'We're getting married!' the little boy told the new arrivals, grinning from ear to ear.

'Jamie, you know that you're not allowed to go into the bar,' Joe scolded. 'You're too young, and if the police found out I could be in a lot of trouble.'

'But I just wanted everyone to know!'

'Right – now they know, and it's bedtime. Your table's ready, and the menus are on it,' Joe welcomed the newcomers. 'Gracie will come and take your orders as soon as we get this handful to bed.' He gathered up the little boy and began to carry him upstairs.

'We're getting married!' Jamie called over his grandfather's shoulder. 'Me and my mummy are going to marry Ewan and I'm going to learn to be a farmer . . .!'

'I love this village!' Kay enthused as the three of them went into the small restaurant. 'There's always so much going on!'

★　★　★

Ewan McNair and Gloria Frost were both in the audience for
the final evening of the drama club's performance. Ewan
couldn't take his eyes off Alison when she was on the stage;
he was glowing with pride, while at the same time wishing
that he had been able to take part. It was during the run of
one of the plays directed by Kevin Pearce that he and Alison,
onstage together, had fallen in love.

Gordon Frost had managed to avoid having to go to the
play, but Rosemary, determined that Gloria should see for
herself how talented Neil could be, insisted on her company.

Gloria didn't mind ballet and opera, but plays and musicals
had never interested her. She fully expected not to enjoy
herself, then was astonished to discover that from his first
entry onstage, Neil captured her attention. He suited the male
fashion of the time, and she had to admit to herself that he
looked particularly handsome in a three-piece suit and floppy
bow tie. Not only did he look good, he also actually managed
to make her fall in love with John Worthing, the character
he played.

As it happened, Neil and Alison had been cast opposite each
other, which meant that at least two members of the audience
experienced jealousy each time they gazed into each other's
eyes, held hands and, worst of all, kissed.

'I didn't realize that you could act,' was all that Gloria could
permit herself to say when Neil found mother and daughter
in the hall after the final curtain.

'If you ask me, there's a lot you haven't as yet realized about
your husband, my dear,' Rosemary told her daughter before
throwing her arms around Neil and bestowing the sort of kiss
not normally granted by mothers-in-law on his lips. 'Darling,
you were wonderful – and you look good enough to eat in
that Edwardian outfit. So much more attractive than the clothes
men wear nowadays!'

'Thanks,' he said awkwardly when she released him. 'So you
enjoyed the play, Gloria?'

He was still in costume, and Gloria, to her annoyance,
suddenly recalled what it had felt like to have a schoolgirl crush
on a favourite film star.

'It was quite enjoyable,' she said primly.

'You're coming to the after-show party, aren't you? It's at the MacBains' house.'

'Of course she is,' Rosemary said. 'You'd better go and get changed. I'll wait with Gloria until you come back, then I'll head for home – my car's parked outside Gloria's house.'

'I'm not looking forward to this party,' Gloria said when he had gone. 'I won't know anyone there.'

'Don't be such a muffin,' her mother ordered. 'They're your neighbours, and if you haven't met them yet you can make up for it at this party. You and Neil are back together, aren't you?'

'I don't know if I'd agree with—'

'Gloria, I'm your mother and we both know that you almost swooned just now when you saw how delicious he looked in that outfit. It's your duty to support him in his hour of triumph. If Gordon looked as gorgeous as your husband did on the stage tonight, I'd certainly not allow him to go to a party without me there to ward off the predators!'

'I hadn't thought of it like that.'

'I know you hadn't.' Her mother reached out to stroke her face. 'Sweetie, you absolutely must start separating the police sergeant from the married woman, because the two of them don't work well together. Walk into that party hand in hand with Neil tonight and try very hard not to arrest anyone – please?'

'You really liked the play?' Neil asked eagerly as the two of them walked to the MacBains' house later.

'Yes, I did. I was proud of you,' Gloria admitted.

'Really?'

She nodded, and took his hand.

He ran his thumb over her fingers, then did it again before stopping in his tracks. 'You're wearing your wedding ring! You didn't have it on earlier.'

'I happened to have it with me,' lied Gloria, who had kept the ring close throughout their separation. 'I just thought that since we're getting back together, and going to meet a lot of the local people tonight, I should get used to wearing it again.'

'Wow!' Neil said, his cup of happiness running over. 'Oh, wow!'

*   *   *

As the MacBains were both taking part in the play they had hired caterers for the party and gone straight home after the final curtain in order to make sure that everything was in order, which meant that they were still in costume and make-up when their guests arrived.

Everyone was admiring Alison's new engagement ring when Neil and Gloria arrived; Anja was there too, her eyes widening as she saw the two of them come in hand in hand.

'That stuck-up sergeant?' she managed to say to him during the evening. 'That is the other woman in your life?' Then, when he nodded, 'Neil, you are a man filled with surprises.'

'I've got one more surprise for you,' said Neil. 'That stuck-up sergeant's my wife.'

Fergus Matheson phoned Ginny to report, 'Angela's back. I've told her about Meredith's idea and she's not at all happy.'

'I was about to call you – my mother's just phoned Mrs Ralston-Kerr to say that she's coming here tomorrow afternoon to see them. She says that she's got some wonderful news.'

'It sounds as though she's hoping to get them on her side before she speaks to Angela and me. Your mother is beginning to come over as a devious woman – sorry, Ginny, I shouldn't have said that.'

'No, you're quite right; she does like to have her own way.'

'So does Angela – and so do I, if it comes to it. I'm going to make a point of being there tomorrow, and I have a feeling that once Angela knows what's going on she'll find the time to come with me.'

'I don't know whether to tell Mr and Mrs Ralston-Kerr about your arrival or not,' Ginny panicked. 'They're already in a flap about my mother coming, but if they think that there might be trouble . . .'

'Say nothing,' Fergus advised. 'I'll make sure that there's no blood shed in front of them. See you tomorrow.'

As soon as she could, Ginny sought out Lewis and told him about Fergus's phone call. 'He thinks it's best not to tell your parents that he and Angela will probably turn up as well, but I thought you should know.'

He groaned, then nodded. 'You're right, they'd probably flee the village rather than face what might be on its way tomorrow. I'm glad you had the sense to tell me, though.'

'None of this would have happened if I wasn't working here,' she agonized.

'Don't be daft! For one thing, it was your mother who decided to come to Prior's Ford when she was between contracts, while you only came to the village to keep her company. For another, if I hadn't had the sense to offer you a job here Duncan and I would still be struggling along on our own, the gardens would only be half finished, the lake and pond would both be dry and I would never have found out what a natural gardener young Jimmy is. You're one of the best things that's ever happened to me – I mean, to all of us, and to Linn Hall,' he corrected himself a little too swiftly. 'Come to think of it, perhaps I should be grateful to your mother!' Then he laughed and shook his head. 'No, I can't make myself go that far.'

'So we just keep quiet and see what happens tomorrow?'

'We can't do much else. One thing's for sure; I'm not going to let my parents be pushed into making any decisions on makeovers,' he said firmly. 'Not until we know what we're letting ourselves in for, and whether or not we can afford it. So – back to work in the meantime.'

Ginny nodded, but after they parted company she found herself recalling the words: 'You're one of the best things that has ever happened to me . . .' It must have been a slip of the tongue, because he'd swiftly corrected himself.

But even so, she would remember it, as she remembered every nice thing he had ever said to her.

Twenty-Five

Early on the following afternoon the Ralston-Kerrs assembled in the drawing room to await their visitor. Ginny was also there, at their insistence.

'You're like part of the family now, dear,' Fliss had told her, 'and you've got such a practical mind as well. We would never have managed all the improvements to the estate without you.'

Jinty had seen to it that the furniture was dusted, vases of flowers set in the large fireplace and the curtains drawn back to let daylight pour into the room. A table in one of the window bays was set for afternoon coffee.

'And when you're ready for the coffee, Mrs F, don't come running to the kitchen for it; use the bell pull and I'll bring it in to you.'

Fliss eyed the tapestry bell-pull by the fireplace nervously. 'I don't think I could. It looks as though it will come away in my hand.'

'Of course you can pull it.' Jinty grabbed the material and gave it a hefty tug. 'See? It's as strong as it ever was. Try it for yourself. Harder than that,' she added, as Fliss pulled timidly. 'I reckon I could swing on it like Tarzan without doing any damage, and you're not nearly as heavy as I am.'

'There's not that much difference between us, Jinty.'

'I'm big boned and you're not. Go on, give it a good hard pull. That's better,' Jinty added as Fliss yanked on the pull.

'Is it still working, though?'

'There's no reason why it shouldn't be.'

'We've probably got mice in this house – they could have nibbled through the wiring or whatever it is that makes the thing work,' Hector suggested.

Jinty stifled a sigh. 'I tell you what. Give me time to get to the kitchen and then give the rope a good tug and I'll come back and let you know if it works.'

'Mother, you're going to have to stop being so scared of this house,' Lewis said as they waited. 'I remember seeing my grandmother use that bell pull when I was very small. I recall wanting to do it too, but she wouldn't let me. You must have seen her use it.'

'But Hector's mother wasn't at all like me, dear. She was – think of a way to put it, Hector; I don't like to criticize your mother in front of you.'

'Big and bossy,' he said promptly.

'Exactly, dear. Thank you.'

'Not at all like you, Fliss – thank goodness.'

'Mrs Whitelaw could be arriving any minute, Mum, and I think Jinty must have reached the kitchen by now. Pull the cord.'

'Ginny, would you . . .?'

Ginny wouldn't. 'I think it's your place rather than mine, Mrs Ralston-Kerr.'

'A good hard pull – give it a jerk,' Lewis suggested as his mother nervously took hold of the cord. She closed her eyes tightly, jerked the bell pull, then let go and stepped back with a gasp of relief.

'Well done, Fliss.' Her husband patted her on the shoulder.

Jinty arrived a few minutes later, slightly breathless. 'It works,' she said, 'but even though I was expecting it, it made me jump. I'm really sorry for the poor servants who had to keep running back and forth, answering bells all the time. Up and down stairs too, some of them would have had to run, goodness knows how many times a day.'

'You need never worry on our account, Jinty dear,' Fliss assured her. 'Even if we do get the ground floor rooms fit for viewing, I could never bring myself to actually live in them!'

'Nor me,' Hector agreed. He loved the security of the butler's pantry.

Ginny had been keeping watch at the window. 'Here comes the limousine,' she reported. 'And as expected, the chauffeur's been told to draw up in front of the big door.'

'Just in nice time for me to let her in.' Jinty patted her hair into place and smoothed her floral wraparound apron. 'Sit down, Mrs F, and don't worry, everything will be fine.'

The doorbell rang, and she went to answer it while Fliss and Hector seated themselves primly on the edge of a long sofa by the fireplace. Lewis, grinning at Ginny, took up a 'son of the house' pose with one elbow resting on the mantelshelf. Ginny herself retired to one of the windows, where she could cover her amusement by pretending to look out at the lawns.

A murmur of voices came from the hall, and then the door opened, Jinty announced, 'Mrs Whitelaw,' and Meredith swept into the room, arms outstretched as she bore down on Fliss and Hector.

'How lovely to see you again, and what a beautiful day for a drive into the country! Fliss – Hector—' As the Ralston-Kerrs rose to greet her, she put her hands on Fliss's shoulders and kissed the air inches from each ear, then, to Hector's horror, did the same to him.

'How well you both look. The country air suits you. Lewis . . .'

'Mrs Whitelaw, it's a pleasure to see you again!' He left the fireplace and forestalled her attempt to air-kiss him by grabbing her hand and shaking it vigorously.

'My dear boy, surely we know each other well enough by now for you to call me Meredith. And – Ginny—?' Meredith raised her eyebrows. 'I thought you would be pottering about in the gardens, dear.'

'I'm allowed indoors twice a day for a non-pottering break, Mother.' Ginny gave Meredith a daughterly kiss on the cheek while Lewis managed to turn a sudden laugh into a bout of coughing.

'It's just such a pity that your dress sense is so out of place in a lovely old room like this,' Meredith chided her daughter, and Lewis's fit of coughing stopped as suddenly as it had started.

'Coffee, Mrs F?' Jinty said loudly as he opened his mouth to speak.

'Are you ready for some coffee, Mrs – er – Meredith?'

'Thank you, Fliss, that would be most welcome. This –' as Jinty left them, Meredith turned away to look round the room, hands outstretched – 'is such a magnificent room! I can so easily imagine it as it will be soon, restored to its original majesty, its former life breathed back in to it, filled with sunlight and colour, ringing with the chatter of voices – and with you, my dear Fliss and Hector, holding court where you belong!'

As she spoke she moved about the room, arms wide, while the three Ralston-Kerrs gaped at her. Only Ginny, well used to her mother's ways, knew that Meredith was now using the room as a stage and delivering a performance before her rapt audience.

She paused, held a pose with one arm outstretched for a

few seconds, and then swung round on them all, beaming. 'Won't it be *wonderful* when your lovely home is restored?'

Fliss gave her husband an imploring look, and Hector cleared his throat. 'If you're referring to your friend's kind assistance, we've received a very interesting report from her, but at the moment we have no way of raising the necessary funds – have we, Lewis?'

'We hope to eventually, but it won't be for a while.'

'But, my very dear friends, that needn't be! I have a wonderful solution that should make it possible for the work to be done almost immediately, without costing you a penny!'

She waited for a response, but none came. If this really was a stage play, Ginny thought, there would have been a prompt hidden behind the long window curtains, ready to feed Hector the proper response – which her mother probably expected to be a cry of gratitude. But nothing happened, and so Meredith, trouper that she was, soldiered on with a ringing cry.

'Television!'

'Television?' Hector quavered, totally confused.

'Television,' Meredith confirmed. 'I was thinking about your financial problems, and it suddenly came to me that Angela's friend Fergus is a television producer, and that people adore makeover programmes on television. Why don't you ask him to do an hour-long documentary showing these lovely rooms being brought back to life, step by step? The television company will almost certainly be willing to pay for the makeover, and as I said, it won't cost you a penny.'

'Are you sure?' Fliss wanted to know.

'Of course. You might even be paid for the use of your lovely home, and think of the publicity you'll get, especially if the programme's presented by a famous personality. I myself would be more than willing to help out, provided that the filming can be fitted around my sitcom commitments in Spain,' Meredith was saying when a kick at the door indicated Jinty's arrival.

'I don't know how the servants managed to carry trays and open doors at the same time,' she said when Ginny let her in. 'A small table outside the door, perhaps, to put the tray on? There's a nice little table upstairs that might do the trick,' she went on as she carried the tray across to the window. Then, setting it down, 'Oops, here comes another car. Are you expecting more visitors, Mrs F?'

'No, not at all.'

'It's that red-haired lady that came to look at the house,' Jinty reported from the window, 'and the nice young man who brought her here before. I'll open the door to them and then run to the kitchen for more cups. I'll start more coffee too,' she said over her shoulder as she hurried back to the door.

'I didn't know that Angela was intending to call on you today.' Meredith, her daughter was pleased to see, looked slightly ruffled.

'We had no idea,' Hector said as voices were once again heard in the hall. 'This is turning out to be a very busy day.'

The door opened. 'Miss Steele and Mr Matheson,' Jinty reported, 'and I'm off to fetch more cups. Won't be a mo.'

'Angela! And Fergus, what a surprise!' Meredith took on the role of hostess, going to air-kiss the newcomers. 'I thought you were away on business, Angela.'

Angela Steele gave her a cool smile. 'I was, but I'm back now. Just in time –' she paused for just one second, then went on smoothly – 'to meet you here, Meredith. What a coincidence.'

As his parents seemed to be dumbstruck, Lewis spoke for them. 'Meredith dropped in to discuss the makeover.'

'*Make*over?' Ginny, who had recently seen the local drama group's performance, thought that Angela Steele boomed the word out in a manner very similar to Cynthia MacBain's magnificent rendering of the famous line, 'In a *hand*bag?'

'Hasn't Meredith mentioned it to you?' Lewis raised his eyebrows.

'No, because I'd only just thought of it, and as I said, you were away, Angela. It's a wonderful idea – I think you'll like it.' Meredith was beginning to get over the surprise arrival. 'These lovely people have had to spend so much money so far on restoring the house and the grounds that they can't afford your fee at the moment . . .'

'I haven't named a fee. That's one of the many things still to be discussed.'

'Whatever it's going to be, they can't afford it at the moment, and then it occurred to me that if Fergus agreed to use Linn Hall for a television makeover documentary, it would save the Ralston-Kerrs all that money.'

Angela gave her friend a long, steady look, then pointed out, 'I'm an interior designer, Meredith. I have never worked in front of television cameras, and I don't ever intend to.'

'Of course not! Nobody would expect you to go before the cameras. That takes a certain skill, not to mention the need to be photogenic, with good bone structure. Nobody could or would expect *you* to appear before the cameras, darling. I, on the other hand, am as comfortable before cameras as I am on the stage. I've been trained for it. And I'm superb when it comes to learning lines. All *you* need to do is write the script – with Fergus's help – and I shall be your front-of-camera presenter.'

'Sadly for you, I don't work that way either, Meredith.'

'It won't be all that difficult. You only need to tell Fergus exactly what the viewers need to know, and he'll organize the script – won't you, Fergus?'

Fergus, too, gave her a cool look. 'I'm not sure that that would work, Meredith.'

'Of course it would work. There are loads of documentaries on television nowadays – how to cook, how to garden, how to build houses, how to auction rubbish found in attics – how to do all sorts of things.'

'Yes, there are, but they're all presented by people who actually know how to do these things. Angela, for instance, knows everything about interior design – but, sadly, you don't.'

'As I said, darling, I would work with a script.'

'But I prefer to work with a genuine expert on-screen,' Fergus was saying when another kick at the door announced Jinty's arrival with more cups, more biscuits and more coffee.

A definite chill had come into the air. When the coffee had been poured, Angela took her cup on a tour of the room, ignoring everyone else, while Meredith managed to ease Fergus into a corner, where, Ginny noticed, she talked earnestly while he said very little.

When offered more coffee, Meredith announced shortly that

she had to get back to the theatre, and Lewis escorted her to her car. While he was away, Angela continued with her examination of the room while Fliss and Hector huddled together on the sofa.

Fergus wandered over to Ginny, grinning. 'At least there was no blood shed, although I suspect that Angela longed to haul your mother's hair out by the roots. I had quite a job calming her down on the way here.'

'You don't intend to direct a television makeover, then?'

'Even if I wanted to, I couldn't because I promised Angela that it was never going to happen – at least, not as far as I'm concerned. It wouldn't have worked in any case – these two are clearly surface friends only and I'd be a fool to try to work with both of them.'

'I'm glad to hear that, and the Ralston-Kerrs will be, too.'

'So – when does Meredith leave for Spain?'

'At the end of this month, I think.'

'Which will please Angela, I'm sure. Are you planning to visit her there? It'll be warmer than a Scottish winter.'

'I doubt it. I'm happy to stay here if it's all right with the Ralston-Kerrs.'

'Can you spare me a day some time over the next few weeks? I'm looking for some gardening advice.'

'You have a garden?'

'Not exactly. It's to do with another estate. I'd like you to have a look at it.'

Ginny was intrigued. 'That sounds interesting – just let me know when.'

'I certainly will.'

Twenty-Six

Fliss and Hector Ralston-Kerr were probably the most abstemious people who had ever lived in Linn Hall. While the old quarry was active, providing work for many local people and making money for the Ralston-Kerr family, the Hall's wine cellar was filled with the best wines and the large, handsome oak sideboard still standing in the dining room held a selection of expensive spirits, but once the quarry closed and the wealth dwindled, the beautiful decanters and crystal glasses fell into disuse.

The only drink Hector and Fliss could afford now was a bottle of good brandy at Christmas, and even that had to be eked out as much as possible over the following year. They had become used to drinking tea instead of alcohol, but there were times, such as the day they had just had, with Angela and Meredith facing up to each other across the shabby drawing-room, when nothing would do except a good stiff drink.

'Is there any brandy left from that dinner we had after the fête?' Hector wondered when they found themselves alone in the pantry that evening. Dinner was over and the dishes cleared away, Jinty had long since gone home to her family and Lewis and Ginny were both taking part in a darts competition in the pub.

'Almost an entire bottle. I put it away,' Fliss said, 'because I felt we should keep it for a special occasion.'

'To hell with a special occasion, woman,' her husband told her with feeling. 'After what we went through this afternoon we need a drink now!'

'What a lovely idea,' she said warmly and went to fetch glasses from one of the cupboards lining the walls.

They sat for a while in silence, savouring the brandy, then Fliss said, 'I think I'm right in saying that Mrs Whitelaw isn't going to be allowed to turn our drawing room into a television programme?'

'I would say that Miss Steele definitely won the match.'

'That's such a relief because I'm in no hurry for those rooms to be made over or whatever it is they call it.'

'I think Lewis quite likes the idea because of the money we could charge for viewing.'

'It would be useful, but—'

'What is it, Fliss? Why don't you want the rooms to be restored?'

'We wouldn't be expected to actually live in them if they're improved, would we, Hector?'

'Not if we don't want to. After all, it is our house, and we should be able to say who lives where in it.'

'I'm so relieved to hear you say that!' Fliss exclaimed. 'I've been worrying about it ever since Ms Steele's first visit.' Then, as Hector poised the bottle over her glass, eyebrows raised, 'Should we?'

'I think we deserve it. Another thing,' Hector said thoughtfully as he poured fresh drinks, 'those big rooms would be absolute bastards to heat. We couldn't possibly afford to live in them.'

'Good!' Fliss lifted her refilled glass in a toast. 'I'll drink to that.'

'I wish,' Lewis said as he and Ginny made their way back to Linn Hall at the end of the darts match, 'that your mother would stop putting you down the way she does.'

'It doesn't bother me – I'm used to it.'

'That's not the point! You're a grown woman and a very talented one at that, and it's time she gave you the respect you deserve.'

'I'm just glad that we haven't had to see much of each other since I grew up. You should have seen the ghastly clothes she dressed me in when I was little – all frills and bows. I hated them!' Ginny shuddered at the memory. 'I was being used as an accessory, like those horrendous film stars who carry little dogs about in their bags. If I'd been a boy I really do believe that she would have forced me into velvet suits, like little Lord Fauntleroy. I do so envy the sort of childhood you had, being brought up in Linn Hall.'

'It was fantastic. Cam and I had a great time, roaming the estate, damming the water at the top of the hill, and pretending to be Indians stalking the gardener. It was the gardener before Duncan – Jinty's dad, old Norman Cockburn – and he was a decent sort. He trained Duncan up fresh from school so that the estate would have a gardener when he finally gave up work.'

'Just the way Duncan's training Jimmy now.'

'You're doing most of the training.'

'It's a real pleasure – he's a natural gardener, that boy. He absorbs knowledge like a blotter. If you had the money, I'd suggest sending him on courses during the winter months, but since you don't, I'm happy to teach him what I've learned.'

'So you're planning on staying here through the winter?'

'I'd like to, if that's OK with you and your parents.'

'It's very OK,' Lewis said as they arrived in the stable yard.

As soon as the news of Alison's and Ewan's engagement was out, Naomi had arranged a vestry meeting with the two of them.

'I know it's short notice,' she said when the ring had been admired and the three of them got down to business, 'but I would love to see you two marrying in the church on the day before Harvest Thanksgiving, because Ewan's a farmer and you, Alison, will be a farmer's wife – and . . .' she added with a warm smile, 'the mother of a future farmer, according to Jamie. It's the perfect time for the marriage, especially as most of the produce on show will be coming from the Tarbethill Farm allotments. We could have the church decorated for both occasions. It's legally possible for you to marry on that date under the law, but it would mean a bit of a rush for you and your families. What do you think?'

'I'd marry Alison tomorrow if I could,' Ewan said at once. 'I just wish I'd had the sense to propose a lot sooner than this.'

'Ewan,' the minister told him, 'we all wish that!'

'And given the fact that you kept me waiting for so long –' Alison took her fiancé's hand in hers – 'I say the sooner we marry, the better.'

'You're suddenly looking fantastic – what's the secret?' Marcy asked as Helen dumped a wire basket filled with shopping on the counter.

'Never ask an agony aunt to reveal secrets.'

'It's nothing to do with being an agony aunt, so reveal it at once.'

'Dr Finlay's typist is getting back to work, which means that he doesn't need me any more – which means that I'm free to get on with the serial – just when I'm finally beginning to get to grips with it.'

'Is that all? You're positively glowing like a teenager in love. You're not expec—'

Helen giggled, then ordered, 'Wash your mouth out, Marcy Copleton! We're most certainly not adding to the family. I'm just pleased to have some of the work pressure taken off.'

'You'll miss the money.'

'He paid me well, and I've got enough tucked away to do for a while – now that,' Helen said, '*is* a secret.'

'Well, I think it's good news because we all thought you were taking on too much work. Thirty-seven pounds and fifty-six pence, please. It's none of my business,' Marcy said as her friend handed over two twenty-pound notes, 'but that's about twice what you usually pay. Expecting visitors?'

'No, just celebrating getting more time to myself. I'm planning a special family dinner tonight, and the wine's for me and Duncan to enjoy when the kids are in bed. He deserves a treat for being so understanding about all the extra work I've been doing.'

'Well, good for Duncan,' Marcy was saying when a gust of laughter came from the store room at the back of the shop.

'Having Kay working here seems to be doing Sam some good,' Helen commented. 'He's been really cheerful recently, in spite of having to wear that heavy cast.'

'Yes, he has. Helen,' Marcy said on impulse, 'could you and I have a chat some time? I think I need some advice from a friend I can trust.'

'Any time,' Helen said cheerfully as she lifted her shopping bag from the counter. 'Though not tonight. Some time next week do?'

'Fine,' Marcy agreed.

Angela Steele's estimated cost of the work she could carry out on the ground floor of Linn Hall arrived a few days after she and Meredith had met at Linn Hall. The Ralston-Kerrs – parents and son – studied it that night when Lewis had finished work.

The letter carried some stipulations. 'I am fully aware,' Angela had written in a strong, flowing hand below the typed figures, 'that you will have to consult experts before any work starts in order to ensure that the electrics, plumbing, draining and heating are in good condition, and that you also have to acquire funding. Once those matters are settled I will be happy, if you so wish, to go ahead with the renovation as already discussed, but only on condition that I am in sole charge of the work, and there is no interference from outsiders, or any talk of television documentaries.'

'I think it's very reasonable,' Lewis said, after careful perusal. 'The costing *and* the stipulations.'

'So do we,' Hector said, and Fliss nodded.

'I'll start putting out feelers regarding loans, then. And I'll reply to this, agreeing with her requests. Ginny's mother will soon depart for Spain and her television work, which I would call a relief to us all. We'll need to start checking the electrical work and so on in the meantime – and invite Andrew Forsyth here to discuss the next stage in the house renovations.'

Jenny's husband Andrew was a trained architect employed by a Kirkcudbright company, and he had been of great assistance to the family when they first began the task of renovating Linn Hall.

'Good idea,' Hector said, and his wife nodded agreement.

'There's something else I wanted to ask you about.' Lewis folded Angela's letter and tucked it back into its envelope. 'How would you feel about Rowena Chloe coming here to live with us?'

'You mean all the time instead of just holidays?' Hector asked.

'That's right.'

'What would Molly say – and her parents?'

'Molly seems to be settled in Portugal now, and Rowena Chloe only sees her on occasional visits back here. She's not shown any desire to take the kid to live with her.'

'Which is a blessing,' Fliss said quickly, 'because if she did that we'd never see her.'

'I know, and I reckon that if she's not going to be with her mother most of the time, then she should be with me. The Ewings are good to her, and they look after her well, but they're both working; if this were her main home she'd see the three of us all day and every day. She could spend time with her other grandparents the way she spends time with us at the moment.'

'What brought this on?' his father wanted to know.

'She's starting school next year, and when she was born I set my heart on her going to Prior's Ford Primary. I thought then,' Lewis said with a sudden touch of bitterness in his voice, 'that Molly and I would be married, and our daughter living here, by the time she reached her fifth birthday. I was watching Lynn with the kids when she brought them to the estate a few weeks ago, and she's so good with them. They all adore her, and what's more important, they trust her. That's the sort of teacher I want for Rowena Chloe.'

'Molly and her parents might not agree with your plans, Lewis.'

'I know that, Dad, but I've got rights, and I'm going to do my darnedest to have her here, with us. Even if it doesn't work out I want her to know when she's older that her daddy wanted her to be with him and did all he could to make it happen. But first I need your agreement.'

'You have it,' Hector said at once, and Fliss nodded.

'I just hope that Lewis's plans for Rowena Chloe don't fall through,' she said that night when she and Hector was going to bed. 'It would break his heart.'

'I think he's got a good chance of success. After all, he *is* her father.'

'Yes,' she agreed, while deciding to have a word with Jinty when she could. According to Molly, Lewis was her daughter's father, but Molly Ewing, both Jinty and Fliss felt, could not entirely be trusted to tell the truth.

Twenty-Seven

With the wedding looming on the horizon, Jess McNair and Gracie Fisher were in a mutual whirl of excitement and activity, meeting each other at least once a day and talking on the phone between times. If it hadn't been for Jess's duties at the farm and Gracie's in the pub, they would have been inseparable.

'Are we going to be able to redecorate Ewan's bedroom before Alison moves to the farm?' Jess agonized. 'And then there's wee Jamie – he can have the room that used to be Victor's, but that'll need redecorating too. Bert was never one to spend money on the house, and when we had the dairy herd the bedrooms were just somewhere to sleep between dusk and dawn.'

She and Gracie were sitting in the farm kitchen. 'Let's go and have a look,' Gracie suggested. Then, when they went upstairs, she said, 'I see what you mean, Jess. The two rooms are spotless, but very what-d'you-call-it – mannish. We can move Jamie's bed over from the pub, and once his toys are here, and the nice wee desk me and Joe gave him for his homework when he started school, it'll make a big difference. And we've just got time to put some fresh paint on the walls of both rooms and buy new rugs for the floors and curtains for the windows.'

'Ewan's room needs a nice dressing table and a second wardrobe as well.'

'Joe and I could buy sets of bedding as our wedding gift,' Gracie offered.

At the same time a deep voice shouted, 'Are you there, Mum?' from the kitchen.

'Up here, Victor,' she called back.

'Hello, Gracie – what're the two of you doing up here?' he asked when he appeared.

'We can't expect Alison to sleep in this room when she and Ewan are married. It's not comfy enough,' his mother fretted. 'And we've got just under four weeks to do something about it!'

'So ask Jeanette to help you.'

'Your Jeanette?' Jess echoed, flustered.

'She's the only Jeanette I know.'

'But – d'you think she'd be willing to help us?'

'Mum, she saw to all the furnishing and decorating in our house, and she loves dressmaking. She's got her own sewing machine, and I reckon she could run up new curtains for you in a weekend. D'you want me to bring her here tonight so that you can talk about what needs doing before the wedding?'

'That would be great,' Gracie said at once. 'Alison could come as well, if I can get Joe to agree to look after Jamie.'

'Right – seven o'clock do you both? See you then,' Victor said and headed back down the stairs.

'We could fairly do with the extra help. What's worrying you, Jess?' Gracie asked when her friend continued to look doubtful.

'Jeanette's a town girl with no interest in farming – that's why Victor moved to the town and began working for her father when they began to talk of marrying. They've been married for the best part of a year, and they live in Clover Place, but she's hardly ever visited here. I've always thought of her as bein' too stuck-up for the likes of us.'

'The important thing right now is that the lassie's got a sewing machine and knows how to make curtains. She could be a blessing to us, and this wedding's giving you and her the chance to get to know each other,' Gracie said. 'Did Victor say he'd bring her here at seven? Joe can be left with Jamie whether he likes it or not, and with Alison and me here as well you'll not be on your own with Jeanette. We'll be sure to get here a bit earlier than her, to make things easier for you.'

By the time Victor and his wife arrived at the farm Gracie, Alison and Jess were all waiting.

'Where's Ewan, Mum?'

'In the milking shed.'

'Alison, you don't mind if I drag him off for a drink, do you?'

'I'd agree if I were you, Alison,' said Jeanette. 'Best to get them both out of the way so that we can get down to business.' She was small, scarcely reaching her husband's broad shoulder, with short, straight brown hair that fitted her head like a shining cap. She was inclined to plumpness, and sharp dark eyes dominated her round face.

'No, Jeanette's right – you two are best out of the way.'

'Go on now,' Jeanette told her husband briskly, 'but don't you overdo the drinking.'

★   ★   ★

Victor found his brother standing in the middle of the old, empty milking shed. 'That's all the women got together now to talk weddings to their hearts' content, so you and me are off to the Cuckoo.'

'Sounds like a good idea. Naomi Hennessey's heard of a man who might be interested in renting this place out.' Ewan indicated the large, empty area. 'He's from Poland, she says, and he's a glass-blower.'

'What does a glass-blower do?'

'According to Naomi they make ornaments – vases and bottles and such – by melting the glass down then blowing through a long pipe to turn it into the shapes they need. He wants to work in the country, but near to the sort of shops that sell ornaments. What d'you think?'

'If this place suits him, I'd say go ahead and rent it. No sense in leaving a big space like this doing nothing, is there?'

'What if I manage to get a new dairy herd together and we need the shed?'

'That's not going to happen for a while yet, and when it does, we'll work something out. Concentrate on the present, Ewan, an' leave the future to look out for itself. You're about to take on a wife, and a kid too, so right now you have to think about the money that rentin' this place could bring in. You've landed lucky, to my mind,' Victor added. 'You're not just gettin' a wife – you're gettin' a damned good business manager into the bargain. I know that Jeanette's been good for me, and I reckon Alison's goin' to be good for you and Tarbethill.'

'I was just thinkin' about how Dad would feel if he knew that a foreign glass-blower had taken over his milkin' shed . . .'

'It's *your* milkin' shed now.' Victor clapped a hand on his brother's shoulder. 'And it's your farm, and it seems to me that he'd be grateful one of us is keepin' Tarbethill together and lookin' after Mum. Come on now – I'll buy the first pint.'

In the farmhouse, Jess was already seeing an entirely new side to the stranger that her firstborn had married.

'So,' Jeanette said as soon as Victor had left them, 'let's get down to business because we've not got much time, have we?'

She opened the shopping bag she had brought with her and spread a generous handful of magazines on home decorating and furnishing across the table.

'Before we start making plans I thought you'd like to have a look at these – they've got some good sensible advice on colour schemes. When it comes to curtains for the two bedrooms, the sooner we all agree on colour and materials the sooner we can get the material and I can start making them. And you'll probably want the rooms freshly painted as well – I reckon that the four of us, with Victor and Ewan roped in, can manage to get everything done in time for the big day. But first,' she added, beaming at the other three women, 'let's go upstairs and have a good look at exactly what we're going to have to tackle in the next few weeks.'

'It's getting so that I'm running this place on my own,' Joe complained to his regulars that evening. 'Even when Gracie's here, instead of at the farm making plans with Jess, all she seems to be able to talk about is this wedding.'

Bill Harper nodded. 'It's what women like to talk about best, all their lives. They start when they're little girls playin' with their dolls, it gets worse as they go through school, and then it's like a feeding frenzy when they reach the stage where they're old enough to start eyeing up potential husbands. Finally comes the engagement and all the weddin' planning – and the spending.'

'He's right,' Bill Harper chimed in. Bill's daughter Tricia had married Doug's son Derek the year before, and the young couple now lived in Jasmine Row, formerly the village alms-houses. 'And then the cycle begins all over again once they're old enough to be mothers of the brides.'

'Or grooms,' Doug said with a nod. 'There's nothing the average woman likes more than a wedding, whether it's hers or someone else's. Evenin', Duncan, fancy a game of darts?'

'Why not? And a pint to go along with it.'

'So how's your problem?' Bill enquired as Doug went over to the dart board and Joe began to serve someone else, leaving the two of them alone.

'What problem?'

'The one you were tellin' me about a wee while back.'

'Och, that!' Duncan's voice was dismissive, his gaze wandering. Bill eyed him closely. 'You took my advice, didn't ye?'

'I don't know what ye're talking about!'

'Aye, ye do, and ye did take it – I can tell just be lookin' at ye. Ye're lookin' happier than usual, and Margie was just sayin' the other day that your Helen's lookin' fair pleased with herself.'

'Don't be daft!'

'You owe me a pint.' Bill grinned as Doug called to them both to get a move on, and the McNair brothers arrived.

'I was thinking,' Sam Brennan said, 'of asking Kay if she'd like to stay on in the shop once I'm back to normal.'

'Why would you do that? We've always managed fine on our own, and you've never thought of bringing in more staff before.'

Marcy's voice was sharp, and he raised his eyebrows before saying, 'I thought you liked her.'

'I do, but the plan was that she would move on once you were back to your usual self. What's happened to make you change your mind?'

'She's a very efficient worker and good with people. We're not getting any younger, and this could be our chance to take on a reliable assistant. It's going to have to happen one day, isn't it?'

'I haven't even begun to look that far ahead, and I'm surprised that you have. You've only ruptured an Achilles tendon, for goodness' sake – you're not going senile or suffering from heart trouble!'

'You don't have to snap my head off! It's just a suggestion. When we *do* decide that we need assistance we might have a problem finding the right person. I just thought that since Kay's eminently suitable and already working in the shop, this could be the time for you and me to start thinking ahead.'

'Kay's a backpacker, Sam; she's enjoying being here at the moment, but she'll soon be bored and eager to move on.'

'Not necessarily. She's told us herself that she loves working here, and she likes Prior's Ford. I'm sure you'd enjoy a bit more freedom than you have just now – time to meet up with your friends, or go shopping, or just have a half-day off now and again. Even if Kay does want to move on, is it such a bad idea to let her know that we'd be pleased to see her back when she's ready to settle down?'

'Sam, if there's one thing you hate, it's spending money unnecessarily, and that's what you'll be doing if you offer Kay McGregor a full-time, permanent job now. It would be unfair if she accepted and then you changed your mind once she was settled.'

'I don't know why you're getting so upset, Marcy – I'm thinking of your interests as well as mine.'

'Let's leave it until you get that cast off,' Marcy suggested. 'Kay's happy to stay on as long as she's needed, and that'll give us both time to think it over. We can discuss it then and make a definite decision.'

Sam shrugged. 'If you insist. I just can't understand why you're so against the idea.'

'I'm not against it; I just feel that this isn't the time to speak to Kay.'

The phone rang in the Campbell house that evening. 'It's for you, Mum,' Gemma shouted.

'Coming!' Helen, helping the younger children with their homework, went into the hall and picked up the receiver. 'Hello?'

'Helen, it's Marcy. I asked you the other day if we could have a chat – would tomorrow suit you?'

'Er – yes. How about here, at two o'clock. Can you get away from the shop for an hour?'

'I should be able to,' Marcy said, and then, with a short laugh, added 'after all, it's easier to get away from work at the moment, with Kay there to take my place.'

Twenty-Eight

'I'm actually here to talk to Lucinda Keen,' Marcy said, and Helen's eyebrows rose.

'Is it something serious?'

'Potentially. And very, very private.'

'Both Lucinda and I are good at keeping secrets. I don't have many secrets of my own,' Helen said thoughtfully. 'My life's more of an open book that doesn't make for exciting reading; most of the secrets in my head belong to other people. And they're completely safe, so go ahead.'

'Sam's decided that we should ask Kay if she'd be willing to go on working for us permanently.'

'That sounds reasonable. She's a nice girl,' Helen said. 'Efficient, friendly, with a great sense of humour. And you two could do with a bit more help in the shop. Kay being there would give you the chance to get some time off, individually as well as together. Sam's a man who doesn't suffer fools gladly, but I've noticed that he feels comfortable with Kay. He gets on well with her, which should be a plus for you.'

'That's just the thing, Helen. I think he wants her to stay because he's falling in love with her.'

'What? Surely not!'

'I know him better than anyone else does, and I'm sure that I'm right. It didn't entirely bother me because the arrangement is that when he's free of the plaster cast, Kay will be off on her travels again. I reckoned that Sam would miss her, but he'd get over it. This sudden suggestion that she should stay on permanently has floored me. I can't let it happen, Helen.'

'But she's young enough to be his daughter,' Helen protested. 'I know that you two have had your ups and downs, but that's because neither of you suffer fools gladly. When something annoys you, or Sam, you come right out with it and clear the air. I'd say that your relationship's as solid as a rock; he loves you!'

'I know, but that's part of the problem. That's why Sam's falling for the girl – because she's so like me when I was her age.'

There was a pause before Helen said firmly, 'Now you're starting to sound like a woman with a silly obsession. Kay likes travelling and seeing different places, and meeting new people – just as you used to, until you met Sam and settled down here. Other than that, you've got nothing in common.'

Marcy heaved a sigh. 'I see that I'm going to have to tell you the whole truth, Helen. I'd hope to be able to avoid that. Kay and I have more in common than you think – she's my daughter.'

Helen's eyes widened, and her mouth opened then closed several times. Then she said, 'I think I'd better go and make a fresh pot of tea.'

'I can't believe,' Jess said to Naomi, 'that I never realized what a nice lassie my Victor's married to! Gettin' to know her is like gettin' him back into my life as well. How is it that we never were friendly with each other before this?'

'I suppose it has to do with the fact that you come from entirely different worlds – town life and farming. I imagine that Jeanette was just as shy as you were about making an attempt to bridge the gap. It took Ewan and Alison finally getting engaged to give Jeanette the chance to feel that she could be of use to you. And now you're suddenly going to have two nice, friendly daughters-in-law to spend time with. Didn't I tell you that your life was going to improve?'

'They both got on so well, too – Alison and Jeanette. When Ewan and Victor came back from the Cuckoo the other night, it all ended up like a party.'

'And you got a lot of plans made for the bedrooms, too?'

'We did!' The two of them were in the farm kitchen, and now Jess went to the big dresser and pulled some magazines from a drawer. 'Jeanette brought a bundle of them, and she and Alison settled on colour schemes for both bedrooms in no time at all. She left these for me, marked where they've decided on colours and furnishings. Look—'

She spread the magazines open on the table, flicking through the pages. 'This is the colour they've chosen for Ewan and Alison's room, and over here is the style of curtains that Alison wants, only not that colour. The two of them are going shopping together on Saturday to choose materials. Jamie's comin' here for the day because the pub's got some evening bookings and Gracie needs to concentrate on cooking. And look at this, Naomi—'

She flipped through another magazine until she found a picture of a child's room. 'What d'you think?'

Naomi studied the photograph. 'Jamie would love that, I'm sure.'

'It won't be exactly like that, of course, but Alison's going to use that colour on the walls, and Jamie's bed's being brought over from the pub, and Gracie and Joe are going to buy the bedding for both rooms as their wedding gift.'

'Can I have a look at the rooms?'

'Of course you can!' Jess led the minister upstairs. 'This is Ewan's; you can see for yourself that it would never do for Alison! And across the landing, here –' another door was opened – 'is where Jamie's going to sleep. We've decided to buy a modern wardrobe for him, and Ewan's shelving the cupboard where Victor kept his clothes, so that Jamie can use it to store his toys.'

'Are you going to paper any of the walls?'

'No, they'll be painted. It's quicker, and Alison says there's no need for fancy patterns.'

'You'll need to get your own room done up too – it wouldn't be fair to leave you out,' Naomi suggested, and Jess beamed.

'That's just what Jeanette said! But we're going to leave my room until after the wedding, because there's not much time. Jeanette's promised to take me shopping so that we can choose everything for my room together. And she says that I should choose some nice wallpaper for myself as well.'

'When is the painting going to start?'

'Tonight. Victor's room first, then Ewan can sleep in it while his is being done. It's a blessing that we don't have to do the milkin' any more,' Jess said as the two of them went back downstairs.

'Can I help with the painting?'

'You?'

'You don't have to look so shocked!'

'It doesnae seem right, the minister paintin' walls for us.'

'Even ministers have time off, Jess. I love painting walls, and I've got my own brushes. I bought them two years ago when I decided that the manse needed freshening up, but I've never got around to starting the job. It's strange,' Naomi went on as the two of them returned to the kitchen, 'how cleaning someone else's house or weeding someone else's garden or painting someone else's walls is always more interesting than doing our own. I'll come round this evening, brush in hand, if that's all right.' Then, as Jess still looked doubtful, 'How about doing a deal? I get to help Ewan and Victor and whoever else has volunteered to paint the bedroom walls, and in return, next year the McNair family will help Ethan and me to freshen up the manse.'

In Helen's living room, she and Marcy were on their third cup of tea, and Marcy had almost finished explaining how she had discovered the daughter she had managed, years ago, to forget about.

As she listened, Helen was also thinking about Greg, Lachlan, Gemma and Irene. 'I can't believe that you could agree to give birth to someone else's child, and then walk away and get on with your life as though it had never happened,' she said when Marcy had finished. 'I couldn't have done that, not with any of my four. I'd have found it easier to kill myself, to be honest, And I couldn't have a child to a man I didn't love.'

Even Marcy looked quite shocked at the idea. 'I didn't actually *sleep* with him,' she protested. 'There are other ways, you know.'

'I suppose there are. But how could you just walk away and leave your own tiny baby behind?'

'That was the hard part. We're different, you and me. I'm guessing that you came from a proper family, Helen, and that you were loved as a child.'

Helen nodded. 'I was, but as a child, you take love for granted.'

'And when you don't get it, you take that for granted too. I remember deciding when I was still in primary school that I wasn't ever going to have children of my own. I meant it, even at that young age, and I never changed my mind, even when I was pregnant. But when she was born I realized that it wasn't that easy. It wasn't easy at all. I would have given anything to keep her, but that meant taking away the child that I had promised to the Metcalfs – and I couldn't do it to them, not after they had been so good to me. In any case, how could I have looked after her? I had nothing, other than the money they were going to pay me for giving them a child.'

'What makes you think that Sam's falling for Kay? Because he senses a link between you?'

'Partly this.' Marcy took the photograph of herself and the Metcalfs from her bag and handed it over. Helen took it and said almost at once, 'You're right – Kay does look like you did at her age. And the Metcalfs look like a really nice couple.' She handed the photograph back.

'They were the salt of the earth; the only people who genuinely cared about me and liked me for who I was – until I came to Prior's Ford. The other reason why I think Sam's falling for the young me rather than Kay herself is that the first time she came into the shop when it was empty, and started talking to us, he was surprised to find out that she was one of the young people who come to work every summer at Linn Hall. He was convinced that she lived here because he felt that he already knew her. He just couldn't recall her name.'

There was a long silence before Helen said slowly, 'Marcy, I have never, in all the time I've been writing the agony aunt page, read anything like your story. I'm used to people dealing with difficult children, or difficult partners – even difficult in-laws. I don't know what to suggest to you.'

'I know exactly what you mean; that's why I wanted to talk to someone, and I knew that you would probably understand more than the others since you deal with other people's problems. It seems to me that I should either tell Sam the truth, which I don't think I can, or tell Kay that she has to go.'

'But that would make her feel as though it's her fault for having sought you out.'

'I know. I can't do that to her – in her shoes, I would probably have done the same thing. It's certainly not her fault.'

'Look at it from this angle,' Helen said after a further moment's thought. 'As the situation stands, she's planning to leave once Sam gets back on his feet, so to speak. That's going to happen in another few weeks, isn't it? Why not just leave things as they are until then. Sam's already agreed to do that, hasn't he?'

'Yes, let's do that.' Marcy glanced at the clock. 'I'd better get back – I said I wouldn't be long. Thanks, Helen, you've been wonderful; you've no idea how relieved I am to have someone to share this with.'

'What is it they say? Oh yes, a trouble shared is a trouble halved,' Helen said.

'Very true.' On her way out of the room, Marcy nodded towards a book lying on top of a small cupboard. 'I see you've become hooked on Lilias Drew's novels.'

Helen picked the book up and slid it into a drawer. 'It's not mine – a neighbour insisted on lending it to me, but I've decided that I'm not going to read any novels until I compete the serial in case I pick up other writers' ideas without realizing it.'

'Probably wise,' Marcy said, nodding. 'I remember how upset you were when they said that that episode was too spicy. You must have been affected by something you read.'

When her visitor had gone, Helen returned to the living room and took the book out of the drawer, chastising herself for having forgotten to put it out of sight before Marcy's arrival. Malcolm Finlay had given it to her that morning when he dropped in another academic article.

She opened it and, for the umpteenth time, read the inscription, written in his now-familiar hand: '*To Helen Campbell, a most extraordinary woman, with my everlasting gratitude, Lilias Drew. Best wishes for your own writing.*'

She had never had a book signed by the author before and couldn't believe that she actually had one now. But sadly, she would never be able to show it to anyone.

She took it upstairs and hid it at the back of the drawer where she kept her neatly-folded blouses, to be read once her serial was complete and safely in the hands of the magazine editor.

For years, when typing out academic articles and papers, she had only seen the words, never the meaning, and when she started on the Lilias Drew manuscripts it didn't occur to her at first that she was taking in not only every word, but every action and every emotion. And considering that he was a rather shy middle-aged man, Malcolm Finlay had an incredible way of creating word-pictures.

She had been genuinely startled when told that her serial work was becoming too sexy for the magazine, but it wasn't until the day Marcy and Jenny teased her about it that she realized she was going to have to start drawing a clear line between Malcolm's fiction writing and her own.

But Dr Finlay had certainly helped to reignite the passion she and Duncan had known years ago, and for that, she was grateful to him.

'Hi, Ginny, it's me. Are you free to talk?' Fergus asked.

'Yes, I am.' Ginny settled herself down on a bench by the pond. 'I'm just doing some tidying up in the rose garden.' She held the mobile out at arm's length for a minute, and then put it back to her ear. 'Did you hear the water splashing into the pond?'

'Uh-huh, sounds good. How are you fixed for a day out next Wednesday?'

'That should be all right. We're winding down for winter so I've got more free time than usual.'

'Good. I'm looking forward to it,' he said. 'Can I collect you early, say about ten? I want to take you to see a small estate not far from where you are, but we'll probably spend quite a lot of time there.'

'It sounds interesting.'

'I hope it will be. See you on Wednesday, then. I'm looking forward to it,' he said.

Twenty-Nine

'So — did you buy a whole lot of art that you don't even understand?' a well-known American accent enquired as soon as Clarissa answered her phone.

'Good afternoon, Amy.'

'It's mornin' here. Did you?'

'I didn't buy any of the pieces in the art exhibition, but I did understand what they were all about, and I agree with Alastair that the exhibition was well worth seeing.'

'So why not buy any, then?'

'For one thing, my house is already full of Alastair's paintings, and for another, other people were buying them. Most of the young woman's work was sold by the time the exhibition ended.'

'I hope Alastair got a hefty bonus for settin' it all up.'

'He did, and a lot of praise. I was very proud of him.'

'So you should be – tell him that I am too. How did the rest of your visit to Glasgow go – was the double room in the hotel nice?'

'It was, and we both enjoyed our stay. His parents were in town for the exhibition too, and we all had a really good time. His mother and I went on a shopping spree, and I bought a beautiful costume, the sort of thing I'd never have thought of buying for myself in my old life.'

'Good for you! Wear it at Christmas so that I can see it.'

'You're coming over for Christmas? That's lovely!'

'No, you're comin' *here* for Christmas, if I have anythin' to do with it. You, Alastair and Stella. I hope that Stella and Alastair can get time off because you're invited for New Year's too. Me an' Patsy have set our hearts on it. You recall me tellin' you about my cousin Patsy? I couldn't visit Scotland this year because I was seein' her through gettin' her new hip.'

'Of course I remember – how is she?'

'Back playin' golf most days, an' I'm back home. I had enough of bein' a golf widow when my Gordon was alive, so when Patsy reached that stage I knew that she didn't need me any more. Anyway, while I was with her she heard all about you an' Alastair an' Stella, an' it was her idea that we should all meet up so that you three can try an American Christmas. What d'you think?'

'It sounds lovely – I'll let Alastair and Stella know right away, and I hope that they can both arrange the time off.'

'Tell 'em that me an' Patsy won't take no for an answer.'

'Where are we going to stay – with you?'

'Patsy said make it Florida, where she lives.'

'Well, there should be plenty of hotels in Florida.'

'What have hotels got to do with anythin'?' Amy said scornfully. 'We'll be stayin' with Patsy.'

'Has she got room?'

'Has Patsy got room? She's got twenty bedrooms an' a guest house in the grounds. She's got a swimmin' pool an' a sauna an' a gym an' goodness knows what else. I spent three months with her this year an' I still haven't seen everythin' she's got.'

Clarissa was confused. 'But when she had her hip operation you went to look after her – if she lives in a mansion, hasn't she got any staff?'

'Of course she's got staff! She's got wall-to-wall staff, not countin' the private nurses, but none of them are family, Clarissa. A woman needs family when she's poorly, even if she *is* a millionaire.' There was a pause, and then Amy said, 'Hello – are you still there, or have we been cut off?'

'Yes, I'm still here. It's just that – the way you spoke about your cousin earlier this year I thought that she was a widow living on her own.'

'That's right; she's a millionaire widow without any family except me. I told you she'd been married three times, didn't I? Widowed three times too; the first was well off, the second very rich, the third a multimillionaire. Patsy certainly wasn't a slouch when it came to pickin' a husband,' Amy said. 'If she marries again I reckon it'll have to be to a billionaire. I'll call next week, to give you time to get Alastair and Stella set up for Christmas. I tell you, Clarissa – we're all goin' to have a great time! When they came up with that sayin', "the hostess with the mostest", they were surely talkin' about my cousin Patsy.'

'Dad, can I have a word?'

'Of course you can.' Joe Fisher had been taking a quick break from his work to read the paper in the kitchen; now he laid it down to give his daughter his full attention.

'It's about the wedding.' Alison sat down opposite, and Joe noticed that she was twisting her sapphire engagement ring nervously around her finger.

'I hope you're not going to tell me that Ewan's taken cold

feet, or that your mother's come up with some idea that's going to cost me a lot of money?'

To his relief, she laughed. 'No to both guesses. Ewan can't wait for our wedding day and neither can I. And Mum hasn't thought of anything you need to worry about. Everything's going to plan. The farm rooms are all ready now, and I'm going to walk across the village green to the church from here with you and Mum and Jamie. All the clothes are ready, and Bill Harper's going to lend his vintage car so that Ewan and Victor and Jess can ride in style from the farm, and then Ewan and I can use it to go to the village hall for the reception. It's all going to be perfect, and I love the idea of having a village wedding!' She smiled at him, her brown eyes sparkling.

'But?'

The smile vanished. 'I have a huge favour to ask you, Dad.'

'Go on.'

'This is my second wedding . . .'

'I know that,' Joe said. 'I gave you away that day, if you remember.'

'Yes, you did. And I know that you're planning to give me away again, but I wondered if, as a special favour, I could be given away by someone else.'

'Didn't I do it right the last time?'

'You were perfect, Dad.'

'The speech – I let you down with my speech.'

'No, you didn't. In fact, that's something I'd forgotten,' she said. 'I'd still want you to do a speech at the reception.'

'So I'm not going to be passed over entirely. But who's going to give you away if I don't do it?'

'Someone who's worked very hard to bring me and Ewan together,' Alison said. 'Ewan and I were talking about the wedding last night, and we decided that with your blessing, we'd both love him to be part of the ceremony. It's Jamie.'

The door opened. 'Joe,' Gracie said, 'I could do with a helping hand.'

'Coming.' Joe got to his feet. 'Of course you've got my blessing – and Jamie can help me with the speech as well. Why didn't you say all this earlier, instead of taking up all my time off from the bar?'

★   ★   ★

Ginny was quite pleased to know that Fergus Matheson was taking her out for the day on Wednesday because Lewis had been withdrawn and irritable throughout the first half of the week and she was sorely in need of a change of scene.

'What's happening around here?' she had asked Jinty. 'Just as Duncan began to mellow, Lewis has become grumpy. It's almost as though they've decided to change places.'

'I can't speak for Duncan other than to say that it's nice to get a smile out of him and long may it last. My mother used to say when I was in a mood that if I wasn't careful the wind would change and my face would stay that way – perhaps the wind took a sudden change just as Duncan had a funny turn. As to Lewis – did you know that he's decided to try to get custody of Rowena Chloe so that she can come and live here instead of just visiting?'

'I didn't hear a thing about it!'

'That surprises me – he's usually keen to get your opinion on everything. He's told his parents, and Mrs F told me. They're all for it. He's got a good chance if you ask me, now that Molly's living abroad with her boyfriend. Lewis has always wanted Rowena Chloe to go to the local primary school, same as he did, and as he says, if she came to Prior's Ford then he and his parents are all here all the time, so she'd never be without family around all day every day. And she'd spend time with the Ewings just as she spends time with us.'

'No wonder he's not himself. He has a lot to think about.'

Jinty nodded. 'He's got an appointment tomorrow with a solicitor, to find out what sort of a chance he has. Mrs F's in a right state of nerves about it – her worry is how Lewis is going to take it if he loses.'

'I know what you mean. He adores that little girl – who wouldn't?' Ginny said as they heard a car draw up outside the kitchen door.

'Anyway, it's the Ralston-Kerrs' business, not ours,' Jinty said briskly. 'Off you go and enjoy your day – you've earned it.'

Fergus was getting out of the car when Ginny emerged from the kitchen. 'Hi, you all set to go? You look great,' he went on when she nodded.

'I thought this outfit would be all right.' She was wearing

the clothes she had recently bought on a shopping trip – chocolate brown cord trousers, and a cream blouse beneath a yellow pullover. Her brown anorak was draped over her arm.

'It's perfect.' He opened the passenger door for her.

'I didn't know exactly what your plans are for the day.'

'Oh, a bit of this and a bit of that,' Fergus said as he skilfully turned the car and headed round the house and down the drive, where Lewis was pruning the shrubbery near to the gates. Fergus tooted the horn as they approached and Lewis turned and gave a brief, unsmiling wave as they went by.

When the car paused at the gates to allow a van to pass, Ginny glanced into the wing mirror and saw that he was standing there, pruning shears in one hand, watching them leave.

'First of all,' Fergus said when they had left Prior's Ford behind, 'I thought we'd enjoy a pleasant drive through some of the great countryside this area has. You've not had the opportunity to take a really good look round this part of Dumfries and Galloway, have you?'

'No, I haven't.'

'Then this is your chance to just sit back and enjoy. There's a really terrific hotel I've eaten in a few times, and I thought we'd have lunch there.'

The drive, as he had said, covered some magnificent countryside, and the lunch, when they finally arrived at the hotel, an old manor-house overlooking the Solway Firth, part of the border between Scotland and England, was superb.

'Have you heard from Meredith since she and Angela last met at Linn Hall?' Fergus asked as they enjoyed their meal.

'No, she's been very quiet – I'm glad to say. I felt so sorry for Mr and Mrs Ralston-Kerr, being caught like that between two strong-minded women – if you don't mind me calling your friend Angela Steele strong-minded.'

'Of course not – she *is* very strong-minded. As is your mother.'

'To be honest, I'd describe my mother as being self-centred. She had no right to interfere in what was really a business discussion between the owners of Linn Hall and someone who may be able to help them to restore the place. It's just a pity that it was my mother who thought of Miss Steele – she seemed to see that as giving her the right to interfere.'

'When does she leave for Spain?'

'In a few weeks, and she'll be away for at least six months, which is a relief.'

'Then look forward to enjoying the next six months,' Fergus advised. 'Shall we finish off with coffee?'

They had only driven for some twenty minutes after leaving the hotel when he slowed the car and indicated before turning into another driveway, shorter than the one at Linn Hall and sadly neglected. It ended in front of a two-storey house that was clearly unoccupied. Fergus stopped the car and hurried to open the passenger door.

'What are we doing here?' Ginny wanted to know as she got out.

'This,' Fergus said with a grin, 'is where you, poor girl, are being expected to earn your lunch.' Then as she stared at him, totally bewildered, 'No need to panic, I just want you to have a good look around the place and give me your thoughts on what could be done with it.' He opened the boot. 'I've brought wellingtons and overalls for both of us so that we can scramble around without ruining our clothes.'

'Who owns this place?'

'I do, as from last week.' He shook out a pair of overalls. 'I think these should fit you – and this pair of wellingtons too. There's a bench by the door that we can use.'

'So you're going to live here?' Ginny asked as, overalls on, they sat on the bench to pull the boots on.

'I'm not really sure – I might do the place up and sell it on. It was originally an impulse buy. I came to have a look because I like this area; the house is in good condition, but the previous owners were elderly and, as you'll see for yourself, the gardens have been sorely neglected. They cover three acres – not much compared to Linn Hall, but it's all nooks and crannies, and I'm sure that a lot could be achieved by the right gardener. That's why I want your honest advice.'

'I'd be happy to give it.'

'Come on . . .' He got to his feet and reached out a hand to help her up. 'The overalls are a bit big for you, but better than being too small. What about the boots?'

They too were slightly large, but completely usable. 'Lead on,' Ginny said. 'I can't wait to see what sort of potential this place has!'

Thirty

'What's your professional advice?' Fergus asked two hours later. 'Are those gardens worth renovating?'

'Definitely! Fergus, this place is beautiful; the soil's good, and there's so much that could be done with it. There are some healthy shrubs and trees that just need a bit of tender loving care, and I love the little unexpected statues we kept coming across. There's an interesting mix between wild areas and cultivated areas, not to mention the little dell that would make such a good secret garden. Someone's loved this place, and then had to leave it – and it's been waiting ever since to be wakened with a kiss, like the princess in a fairy-tale!'

'You've got a brilliant imagination – try to remember what you've just said. It will sound perfect in the series.'

'What series?'

'Haven't I mentioned that yet? Ironically, it was Meredith's idea for a televised Linn Hall makeover that gave me the idea,' he went on as they stripped the overalls off and changed back into their shoes. 'It seems to me that this little estate would be the ideal venue for a televised garden makeover – a series starting with spring, then going through the seasons – summer, autumn, winter and ending with the following spring. Because this place is made up of a series of different areas, viewers – including those with small gardens – could be shown how small areas can change with each season and still be a pleasure to enjoy. What d'you think?'

'I think it's a great idea.'

'I hoped that you might. Now all I have to do is sell the idea of a garden restoration series to a producer.' He glanced at his watch. 'We've got time to have a look round the house if you're interested, before we head back to Prior's Ford. There's electric light inside, and water. It'll be cold, but it'll do to wash our hands.'

'I'd love to see it.'

'We'll stop for dinner on the way back,' Fergus said as he brought the keys from his pocket.

The house, too, was a delight. It was quite small, with three rooms and the kitchen on the ground floor and three bedrooms, one en suite, and a large bathroom upstairs. The rooms were all generous, and as the house itself overlooked the Solway Firth, with part of the garden running down to the water's edge, the drive and the main door gave access to the rear of the property rather than to the front.

'So you think that viewers would like my idea of using this place as the subject of a garden restoration series?' Fergus asked when they had returned downstairs and were sitting on the upholstered window seat in the living room, looking out on the water.

'I think they'd love it.'

'It's going to be a tough struggle to get the go-ahead – it always is – so I'll need to have plenty of ammunition. For instance, I'll need to be able to say that I've already got someone who knows about gardening and is available and willing to present the series. Someone with the flair and imagination that you have,' he said, looking right into her eyes.

'Me? You want me to advise you?'

'And to go before the cameras. You'd be perfect, Ginny.'

'I couldn't possibly do it!'

'Of course you could.'

'No,' she insisted, 'no I *couldn't*! I'm not like my mother – or my father. They both look terrific on film, but I don't even take a good photograph. You can try a test if you must, but you'll see what I mean right away. I can advise you if you want me to, but that's all.' She knew that she was gabbling on, out of sheer panic, but it was difficult to stop.

'Let me show you something,' Fergus said calmly, producing his video cam. 'Have a look at this.'

They sat heads together, watching as Ginny, in her normal gardening clothes, showed off the Linn Hall estate – the lawns, kitchen garden, rose garden, lake; by the time it got to the grotto and exotic plants at the top of the hill, her hair was damp with rain but her enthusiasm was as strong as ever.

At last he switched it off. 'Do you still think that you couldn't manage to do a television series?'

'It's really not the right thing for me.'

'But having seen that, you have to admit that basically you *could* do it. You're a natural, Ginny.'

'I forgot that that little camera was on, at the time. Television cameras are entirely different – I'd freeze, and start stammering, or not know what to say!'

'You'll still forget that the cameras are running; people do, every time, because they're concentrating on their subject. It's not as if you're going to be in a studio – you'd be in that garden –' he pointed out of the window – 'doing what comes naturally to you: talking about how to improve it. You'd be planting, pruning, concentrating. What you said earlier, about the garden being like a fairy-tale princess waiting to be kissed back to life – viewers would love it!'

'No, I'm sorry, I couldn't,' she said emphatically.

'Not even to show your mother that you may not be a glamorous actress like her, but you're talented enough to star in a television series?'

'That prospect,' said Ginny, horrified at the thought of challenging her mother, 'just makes me even more determined not to do it. If you want me to give you some advice on this garden, I will. But that's as far as it goes.'

Fergus glanced at his watch. 'We'll talk about it another time; for now, we'd better be on our way if we want to enjoy a leisurely dinner. You're still OK about us having dinner before I take you back to Linn Hall, aren't you?'

'Yes of course – as long as we don't have any more discussion about you-know-what.'

'Fair enough.' He stood up. 'There's still a lot to be done before I can even start to plan a series like that in any case. But I like the idea, so I'm going to speak to a few people.'

'Including a professional presenter,' Ginny said firmly as she followed him out of the house.

★   ★   ★

'Did you enjoy your day out yesterday?' Jinty wanted to know when Ginny came into the kitchen for her morning break.

'Yes, it was all right.'

'Where did you go?'

'To the Solway Firth, to see a house that Fergus has bought.'

Lewis, who had been making a fuss of Muffin, looked up. 'He's moving to this area?'

'I don't know – he doesn't know. He might have it done up and then sell on. It's a lovely house, with a fantastic garden – all nooks and crannies, and it runs right down to the water's edge. But it's been neglected for a while. He wanted me to have a look at it.'

'What were your first impressions?' he wanted to know.

'There's a lot of potential in it.'

'And he wants you to take on the job?'

'He didn't say that.' It wasn't exactly a lie; he wanted someone capable of doing the work on film, and Ginny wasn't the right person for such a task.

Alison Greenlees and Ewan McNair were married in Prior's Ford Church at the end of October, on the day before the Harvest Thanksgiving service.

Work had already started on the Thanksgiving decorations; the church was massed with autumn flowers, and two small bales of straw were placed on either side of the altar, as were two huge urns filled with great branches of glowing crimson rose-hips from the roadside hedges.

The church was packed, as it always was at local weddings; Ewan, Victor and Jess had been driven from the farm in Bill Harper's vintage car, Gilbert MacBain was playing background music on the organ, and now everyone was awaiting the arrival of the bride.

Ewan, in a state of nerves, had just asked Victor for the fourth time if he still had the ring, and when assured that it was present and correct, had insisted, for the fourth time, on being shown it. Victor had then informed him, in a low, pleasant voice, that if he asked one more time he was going to find himself rammed head first into one of the bales.

Ewan was now facing the altar, but with fists clenched and

eyes tight shut, when he felt a light touch on his arm and Naomi's voice said, 'Ewan, are you all right?'

He opened his eyes. 'Naomi?'

'Yes, it's me. I'm wearing my wedding finery in your honour – or should I say, it's wearing me,' said Naomi, who was usually garbed for Sunday services in a black suit and a black top with her clerical collar showing. 'But don't let it frighten you.'

Today she was resplendent in a floor-length black cassock and clerical collar worn below her university gown and hood, and the outfit was finished off with a white preaching scarf, reaching to the ground and embroidered near each end with the burning bush, the symbol of the Church of Scotland. But the warm smile on the round brown face was quite definitely Naomi's.

'I wondered if you were all right,' she said, 'because your eyes were closed and your face all screwed up. Are you in serious pain, or is it just normal wedding nerves?'

'He's drivin' me mad,' Victor hissed. 'I hope Alison gets here soon.'

'So do I,' Naomi said. 'It's a lovely day, and this outfit's not only heavy, but very warm as well.'

'I was trying to remember my full name for when I have to say it. I keep forgetting it!'

'Don't worry, you only have to repeat it after me – Ewan John McNair.'

'Oh yes, of course,' Ewan said thankfully as the soothing organ music gave way to the opening bars of 'Here Comes the Bride'.

'Good – here we go!' Naomi stepped back and looked down towards the church door. 'Turn round and look, Ewan,' she suggested. 'That should calm you down.'

He did as she said, and his mouth fell open as he saw the woman he was about to marry come slowly down the aisle towards him, hand in hand with Jamie.

Alison wore a long, pale-green silk gown that followed the outline of her slender body without being too tight. The neckline was low and draped in soft folds, and cap sleeves left her slim arms bare. Tiny multicoloured silk flowers were scattered through her fair hair, and she carried a small bouquet of freesias in her free hand.

Six-year-old Jamie wore a grey suit – jacket, waistcoat and trousers, with a grey patterned cravat tucked into the neck of his white shirt. Mother and son both shone with happiness as they walked down the aisle towards the altar.

When they reached it, Alison bent and whispered to her son, then kissed him and handed him her bouquet. As he carried it carefully to the empty seat beside his grandparents and Jeanette, Alison took Ewan's hand and they exchanged a smile before turning to face Naomi.

She beamed back at them, and then began, 'Today, it is my very great pleasure to officiate at the marriage of two very special people who have finally found each other . . .'

Thirty-One

'Where's Sam?'

'Gone for his daily exercise walk,' Marcy said. Sam had been released from his plaster cast the week before and was on a course of exercises to strengthen his leg.

'So we're free to talk?' Kay cast a glance round the empty shop.

'For the moment.'

'Did you know that he's asked me to stay on in Prior's Ford?'

'He's offered you a permanent job?'

'So you didn't know.'

'He talked about it a few weeks ago, but I thought I'd persuaded him to say nothing to you until he'd got completely over the accident. I assumed that he would speak to me before he made the offer to you, but apparently not. What did you say?'

'I asked for time to consider it – because I wanted to know what you thought.'

Marcy bit her lip. 'I can't tell him the truth. I probably should, but I just don't know how he would take it.'

'There's a slight complication, Marcy.'

'I know – he's getting too fond of you.'

Kay blinked at her in surprise. 'You knew?'

'I know Sam,' Marcy said wryly. 'He's like a book that you can't understand at first, but once you get used to it, it suddenly becomes easy to read.'

'That's an interesting thought, but it wasn't actually what I was going to say. I was going to say that I'm beginning to get fond of him, even though I haven't known him for as long as you have.'

'Really?' Marcy was astonished. 'You're falling for Sam?'

'A little, but even although he's quite a bit older than me, it could so easily become a lot.' Kay gave a sudden grin. 'I must be more like my mother than either of us first thought.'

'It's certainly something that I never expected to happen. What are we going to do about it?'

'Not "we" – me. I'm moving on, Marcy. I find your Sam attractive, but I've got no desire to fall for my mother's partner,' Kay said, wrinkling her nose. 'I need to make my own life, but I don't want to lose contact with you now that I've found you. Can we keep in touch – emails, letters, phone calls? And maybe a visit, once enough time's passed?'

'I want that too,' Marcy said as the bell rang to indicate that someone had just come into the shop.

'I would have loved to come to the village to say goodbye properly to everyone, darling,' Meredith said, 'and to you as well, of course. And I had been *so* looking forward to that day's shopping in Edinburgh to let me buy you some proper clothes, but this sudden invitation has made it all quite impossible. You do understand, don't you?'

'Of course, Mother,' Ginny said into the phone.

'Perhaps next year. And you'll tell them all how sorry I am to miss saying goodbye in person?'

'Yes, Mother.'

'And please pass on a word of advice to those charming Ralston-Kerrs from me . . . I think that they should try to find another interior designer to restore their lovely home. I've been having second thoughts about Angela Steele – she's not the reliable woman that I thought she was. Not at all! You will tell them that, won't you, Genevieve?'

'Of course, Mother.'

A muffled voice was heard in the background, and then Meredith chirruped, 'Must go – the taxi's here. Lots of kisses!'

'You too, Mother,' Ginny said, but Meredith had already hung up.

'What was all that about?' Lewis asked. The two of them were sitting in his van in the Linn Hall stable yard, having just returned from a trip to a garden centre for some winter plants. 'Are we going to have a goodbye visit from your mother now that the play's over?'

'Sadly, no.'

'Good. I mean,' he said hurriedly, then after a pause, 'to be truthful, I mean – good.'

'She *had* planned a farewell visit, but now someone who was in the play with her has invited her to spend a couple of weeks in France with them before she goes on to Spain. She's in the taxi right now on her way to Edinburgh Airport.'

Lewis grinned at her. 'Your mother's gain is our loss. Anything else?'

'Only that she wants me to say goodbye to all in Prior's Ford on her behalf.' She started to get out of the van, but he put a hand on her arm to stop her.

'Ginny, I haven't told you before, but I'm hoping to get Molly and her parents to agree to let Rowena Chloe move here, to Linn Hall, since Molly seems to be settled in Portugal. She'd visit her grandparents regularly, and her mother too, but this would be her main home. I've spoken to a lawyer, and he seems to think that I've got a fair claim. Am I doing the right thing?'

'It's not any business of mine, Lewis.'

'I value your opinion.'

'Then yes, I think you're doing the right thing.'

'Good.'

'There's something *I* haven't told *you*, Lewis.' She hadn't meant to say it, but the words were out before she could stop them. 'That house Fergus Matheson bought by the Solway Firth – he's hoping to do a television series on the garden restoration, if he can get the go-ahead.'

'And he wants you to be involved.'

'How did you know?'

'Because you're so good at that sort of thing. Who else would he ask?'

'I've told him that I wouldn't do it if it meant me actually having to appear on camera, but if he wants me in an advisory capacity, I'd really like to be involved. It's a fascinating garden; not nearly as large as Linn Hall, but really interesting. I thought I should tell you, just in case. The grounds here are more or less finished now, and Jimmy's very reliable; you don't really need me, do you?'

'I suppose not, and I wouldn't want you to miss out on something you really want to do,' he said, opening the driver's door. 'Better start that unloading before it gets dark.'

Helen's fingers sped over the computer keys. 'So near, and yet so far,' she muttered through gritted teeth as she worked.

The first four episodes of the magazine serial had been revised and accepted and now she had reached the fifth and last episode, the final stretch. It was also proving to be the hardest, and although the length was similar to the others, this one seemed to her to be longer, harder, and taking for ever.

'I hate goodbyes,' Kay said. The three of them were standing outside the village store, Kay's rucksack on the ground at her feet, waiting for her taxi.

'You should have let me drive you to the train station,' Sam said gruffly, but she shook her head.

'You've been kindness itself to me, both of you. I'd rather say cheerio here in the village, where it all started. But now that we've met, I fully intend to come back for visits, if that's all right.'

'Of course it is,' Marcy said warmly. 'Any time.'

'If you're ever looking for a job, there's one here, in the shop,' Sam told the girl as the taxi turned into Kilmartin Crescent.

'Thanks, Sam – and thanks so much for the bonus, it's going to come in handy.' As the taxi drew to a stop before them, Kay hugged Sam, then threw her arms round Marcy, whispering into her ear, 'I'm so glad we found each other!'

'Keep in touch,' Marcy whispered in return as the taxi driver stowed the rucksack into the taxi's boot and Sam opened the passenger door for Kay. She put one foot into the vehicle, and then turned swiftly to blow a kiss before taking her seat beside the driver.

As the vehicle began to move, the passenger window opened and Kay waved to them until the taxi was out of sight.

'That was odd,' Sam said.

'What was?'

'When she turned back to face us – when she was halfway into the car there – she did it just the way you sometimes turn back when you're on your way somewhere and then remember something and turn back to say it.'

'Perhaps she picked up one of my eccentric ways over the past two months. I didn't know you'd given her a bonus.'

'Didn't I say? I thought she deserved it.'

'She did. She was a really good worker.'

'D'you think she'll keep in touch, or was it just one of those things that young people say and don't mean?' he asked.

'Oh, I think that she meant it. Let's get inside; there's definitely a hint of winter in the air now. I'll put the kettle on.' Marcy slipped her hand into his, and together they went back into the shop, Sam still limping slightly.

Ginny was perched on top of the grotto, dressed warmly against the October day in a thick polo-necked cable-knit sweater and fleece-lined anorak, boots and heavy woollen trousers. It was early afternoon, and below her, the Linn Hall estate was settling into a winter slumber. Beyond the estate a slight mist had started to blur the village roofs. Winter was beginning to signal its imminent arrival and for some reason, it was making her feel lonely and depressed. Even the grotto wasn't lifting her spirits.

'Hey!' she heard Lewis call from over the brow of the hill. 'Anyone there?'

'Yes, and I'll be down in a while,' she shouted, hoping that he would go away. Instead, she heard him come along the wooden walkway built to protect the special plants from the public, and a few moments later he was standing below her.

'What are you doing up there on a day like this? You'll catch a chill!'

'I'm fine – I'll be down in a while,' she said grumpily. Then the ivy covering the grotto started to rustle and a moment later his woollen-hatted head appeared over the edge of the roof.

'I come bearing a message.' He settled down beside her. 'You left your mobile in the kitchen –' he handed it to her – 'which isn't like you at all. If it hadn't rung it would probably be in Muffin's stomach by now. It's all right; I cleaned it up with a wet wipe after I had eased it from his mouth. I hope you don't mind, but I answered it.'

'Who was it?'

'Fergus Matheson. I told him that you must be outside somewhere, and he wants you to call him back.'

'OK.' She pushed the phone into her anorak pocket.

'If you're not going to get in touch with him now, I might as well tell you what he had to say. He's had an interested response to his idea about a documentary on that neglected garden of his – early days yet, he says, but he needs to start putting some plans together. Schedules or something. And he's set his heart on you presenting it.'

'I've already told him – I can advise, but I'm not going before a camera.'

'He told me that he videoed you when you showed him round this place and you're very photogenic.'

'So he says, but I'm not doing it – OK?'

There was a pause, and then Lewis said, 'That puts me in a bit of a spot.'

'It's got nothing to do with you, Lewis.'

'It has, actually. I told him that you would do it.'

'What?'

'I think it's a really good move for you, Ginny. This place is more or less up and running, and as you said, now that we can afford to have a bright kid like Jimmy McDonald on the payroll, we should be able to keep it going. You'll get bored soon and want to move on to some new challenge – and what would be better than Matheson's offer? It would mean that you're still working in Dumfries and Galloway, and I hope that you'll still be staying here, with us – with me. And perhaps with Rowena Chloe if we're lucky enough to get her here to live. She adores you, Ginny, and she'll need you. You're one of the family.'

'So I am – I'd forgotten about that – the kid sister!'

'Which one of us came up with that stupid phrase?'

'I think it was you.'

'I must have been a fool. You're much more to me than that, Ginny.' Suddenly, his voice and gaze were serious. 'You've been more than that for a long time, but I made such a mess of things with Molly that I didn't want to do the same with you. It was the decision to try to give Rowena Chloe a proper family life that made me realize just how much we both need you here. You'd be the perfect mother for her.'

'She already has a mother.'

'Molly's not a patch on you. Nobody else is, or could ever be. I should have said this to you ages ago, I know,' he hurried on. 'I should have said: Ginny Whitelaw, I'm crazy about you and will you please marry me and never leave me or Linn Hall. I'm saying it now, so what do you think?'

Ginny drew a deep breath. Suddenly, she felt quite dizzy, as though, had he not been holding both her hands tightly, she might have tumbled off the roof. 'I think – yes, yes and yes again,' she said, and then, at last, she knew what it was like to be kissed by the only man she had ever loved, or would ever want to love.

'And,' Lewis said breathlessly five minutes later, 'I want you to take that job with Matheson if it actually happens. Agree to be the presenter.'

'I don't want to even more now. I want to stay here with you!'

'Not on top of the grotto, I hope, because it's getting pretty cold up here.' Lewis took off his woollen cap and pulled it over her head, then kissed her nose. 'I want you to take the job for two reasons, my darling. The first because it would really annoy my future mother-in-law to know that the daughter she keeps putting down is going to be a television presenter in her own right . . .'

'That's a very good point!'

'I'm glad you agree, Mrs Ralston-Kerr-to-be.'

'And the second reason?'

'At the risk of sounding, mercenary, my love – your earnings could help to pay for the ground-floor restoration,' he said, and he kissed her again.

Down in the village at that moment, Helen typed the words 'and he kissed her again'. Then she sat back and wondered if it was too soppy an ending to the serial.

'Leave it as it is,' she decided aloud.

After all, everyone likes a happy ending.